DEAD
DON'T LIE

L. R. Nicolello has had an obsession with all things suspense since she was old enough to pick out her own books. She decided to combine that passion with her love of action flicks and strong female protagonists in *Dead Don't Lie*, her debut romantic suspense novel. She, her amazing partner in crime and their ninety-pound "dog child" reside in Texas, where she is working on her next novel, *Dead No More*. Visit her at www.LRNicolello.com or follow @LRNicolello on Twitter.

DEAD
DON'T LIE

L. R. NICOLELLO

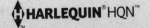
HARLEQUIN® HQN™

Recycling programs
for this product may
not exist in your area.

ISBN-13: 978-0-373-78500-1

Dead Don't Lie

Copyright © 2014 by L. R. Nicolello

Printed in U.S.A.

www.Harlequin.com

To the incredible women in my life—you know who you are—your sass, beauty and courage in the face of adversity is not only stunning, but truly inspiring. I am a better woman because you're in my world.

"Never, never, never give up."
—Winston Churchill

PROLOGUE

Fifteen years ago

WITH MUSIC PUMPING and strobe lights flashing, the air felt electric. Alive. The catwalk called to her, its thin, reflective surface beckoning as it sparkled and glistened—a million flecks of diamonds waiting. For her. Without wavering, without hesitation, eighteen-year-old Evelyn Maslin answered its hypnotic call.

She put her forefinger into her mouth, puckered her lips around it and pulled. A bit of fire-engine red lipstick rimmed her finger. A stagehand racing by her slid to a halt. The double take he gave the red on her finger almost snapped his head clear off his shoulders. He held out a tissue, his expression slightly awestruck.

She accepted his offering, bit back the smirk dancing on her lips and wiped the lipstick from her finger. As she returned the used tissue to the stagehand, she shrugged nonchalantly. *What?*

His face flushed. He ducked his head and rushed off.

Laughing, Evelyn held out her fingers and flipped them over to check for any remnant of lip stain. With an eagle eye, she investigated her outfit in the full-length mirror, turning to the left, then the right. Good. Everything appeared normal and in place. God forbid she'd have a wardrobe malfunction on her first sashay down the catwalk.

She wasn't a prude. How could she have been? Changing in front of virtual strangers was part of her daily job description. Still…the sheer thought of her breasts popping out of her flimsy, Greek goddesslike chiffon dress mortified her.

The music's tempo changed, morphing into the next number. Taking another deep breath, commanding the butterflies to at least fly in formation, as they refused to leave, Evelyn waited for the signal. At the stage manager's tight nod, Evelyn stepped out onto the stage.

For a second, the glaring lights left her bedazzled, and the electrified atmosphere sucked the air from her lungs. As she adjusted, she felt all eyes on her. The blood in her ears pumped in time with the tempo of the song blasting over the speakers. Her heart thumped against her chest, it, too, keeping pace with the deep bass as she placed one bejeweled foot in front of the other.

Breathe. Just breathe.

She kept her eyes glued in front of her and focused on each calculated step. One wrong placement and her balancing act in the five-inch stilettos would end with a face-plant.

The end of the runway arrived without incident. She bit back the giggle bubbling in her throat, which definitely didn't fit the sex-goddess persona she was channeling. Gracefully, she pulled her hands to her waist and popped her left hip as she and her little sister, Olivia, had practiced a million times growing up. She wished Olivia could see her now. Evelyn's heart raced as the spotlights captured her in their mesmerizing glow. She tossed her long hair ever so gently, then paused.

All of five seconds had passed.

Stomach quivering, Evelyn turned to strut back down the catwalk, her mind tumbling over itself.

HER FIVE-INCH HEELS might have been exquisite, but they were hell to walk in. Evelyn's sandals dangled from her fingertips as she and her roommate, Anastasia Kulik, ambled down the Naviglio Grande canal. The two friends took their time as they walked the quiet Milan streets, over the cobblestones and past the closed storefronts.

"Oh, my gosh, Evelyn. Did you see the way Raphael looked at you tonight? Seriously! It's like the gods of luck follow you everywhere. I'd do anything to have Raphael stare at me that way." Anastasia smiled suggestively. Mischief sparkled in her chocolate-colored eyes. She shook her head, pushed the blond curls off her face and clucked her tongue like her Russian babushka. "And you act as though you didn't even notice."

Evelyn grinned at her companion. "The only thing I concentrated on tonight was not falling flat on my face." Heart still racing from the show, she swung her shoes by their thin black straps. Her smile grew wider.

She was in *Milan*.

When she'd gotten *the call* and heard that she'd defied the odds and been chosen from the hundreds of girls vying for this contract, Evelyn had burst into tears. Then she'd done a happy dance with her sister before throwing herself on the sofa and giggling like the teenager she was. The only thing that would make this experience more amazing? Having her little sister here with her. But hell would freeze over before her mother allowed that to happen. Evelyn was still shocked that her parents had allowed *her* to come to a foreign country, by herself, before college. But they'd said yes, so she'd packed her bags.

And now, Evelyn was living her dream.

She glanced down the deserted street. During the day, it bustled with locals and tourists alike. But during the late-night hours, after the crowds cleared, quietness settled over the tranquil canal water, and the occasional patio light glistened off the water's glassy surface.

She couldn't wait to call her sister, to tell her everything about this place and this magical night. She checked her watch and sighed. It was just after three in Phoenix. Olivia would be getting out of school, heading for practice. With the national cheerleading competition fast approaching, Olivia's time in the gym had quadrupled. It had been a week since they'd last chatted as a family. *Tomorrow.* Tomorrow, she'd call Olivia and tell her everything.

Anastasia stopped in the darkened street outside the now-familiar red door of their apartment and said teasingly, "Whatever. I bet you didn't have to concentrate on anything."

She hitched her oversize bag up her thin hip and dug through its endless bottom, searching for the keys to their tiny two-bedroom apartment. "You were perfect tonight. I saw it. We all saw it. The crowd collectively held their breath when you stepped onto the runway."

"Come on…"

"I wouldn't be surprised if tomorrow they swept you into a photo shoot for the cover of *Vogue Italia*." Anastasia continued to rummage through her purse. With a small sound of victory, she finally held up the keys.

Evelyn followed her roommate into their apartment and flipped on the light. She dropped her bag onto the antique table in the foyer and glanced at the answering machine. No messages. Just as well. She was exhausted. All she wanted was her warm, soft bed. And maybe some hot mint tea. Maybe.

"I have to admit, I'm jealous." Anastasia reappeared from her closet-sized room. She'd shed the black leggings and massive sweatshirt. A short red skirt hugged her curves and a low-cut sheer tank played peek-a-boo in the dim light with her red sequined bra. Fastening a large silver hoop through one ear, she looked at Evelyn in the mirror. "And I've never been jealous of anyone. Ever."

"You have nothing to be jealous of." Evelyn opened her bag, grabbed an elastic and pulled her hair back into a sloppy bun that slanted to one side. "I'm not Raphael's type."

Anastasia swung around. Hope, and the tiniest bit of suspicion, flashed in her eyes as she fastened the second hoop. "Really?"

"Really." Moving to their petite kitchen, Evelyn spoke over her shoulder. "I've heard from a very reliable source that blonde, brown-eyed beauties are more to his liking."

Tea could wait. She opened the refrigerator door and took a bottle of water from the top shelf. The rest of the shelves sat bare. Tomorrow she'd have to go to the market.

"Us blue-eyed girls?" Evelyn pointed to herself,

feigning complete and utter disappointment. "We don't stand a chance."

"That's the best news I've heard all week." Anastasia bounced on her toes, then rushed over and kissed Evelyn on the cheek. She stole the water from Evelyn's hand, twisted the top and tilted her head back to take a sip. Holding the bottle out to her roommate, she smirked. "Because guess who's going to be at Silver-Tongue Club tonight?"

Evelyn took the bottle back and suppressed a smile. "Raphael?"

"Yes." Glittering dots danced in time to Anastasia's animated movements as the red sequins made a soft rattling noise. "And guess who else is going tonight?"

"You?"

"Us." She clapped her hands, as thrilled as a child on Christmas morning.

Evelyn's grin vanished as she slid toward the kitchen doorway, inching away from her wild, party-crazed roommate and toward the sanctuary of her small room.

"You." She leveled the bottle at Anastasia and moved three steps closer to her escape. "There is no *us* in this equation tonight."

Anastasia's lower lip jutted out, making her appear even more like a Russian goddess. She followed Evelyn down the miniature hallway. "Please?"

Evelyn laughed and walked into her room. "No."

"Fine." Anastasia pouted. "But I'm not taking no for an answer next time."

"Deal." Evelyn smiled at her new friend. It was hard to believe they'd only met six weeks ago. She'd gotten lucky with the roommate her agency paired her with—not all the girls could say the same. She placed her hands on Anastasia's bare shoulders and steered her to the front door. "Now, go have fun. But be safe, okay?"

Anastasia reached for her bag on the floor and slung it over her shoulder as she pulled open the door. She looked back at Evelyn and grinned. "Don't wait up for me."

With Anastasia gone, silence blanketed the apartment. Evelyn grabbed her bag off the table and padded to her room. While she loved the lights and the runway, she was a bookworm at heart and had her eye on the latest biography her folks had sent. Evelyn hooked her foot around the bedroom door, tugged it shut and turned the lock with the other. A thin overnight package marked Fragile sat on her desk. She glanced at the return address and smiled.

It was from her family.

She opened the package. A DVD fell from the box. Evelyn squatted in front of the TV, slid the silver disc into the machine and pressed Play.

Black-and-white snow fuzzed the screen at first and then faded to a dark, unfocused image. She sat on her bed. Slowly, the picture corrected itself and the color returned. Frozen, she gawked at the small screen, not comprehending what it showed. Horror crept into her stomach as her eyes and brain connected the images to reality.

Her mother and sister sat huddled, ankles and wrists bound. Sweat and blood marred their beautiful faces. Olivia hid hers in her mother's side. Tears streamed down her mother's cheeks, and pain radiated from her as she stared straight ahead, unmoving.

Why was she not comforting Olivia? Why was her

mother crying? What was happening? Where was her father?

A tiny movement at the bottom left corner of the screen caught her attention. It was her father, blood-ied and beaten. Arms and feet shackled, pulled tight behind him in an awkward, bowed position. Evelyn squeezed her eyes tight, trying to dislodge the foreign image of her father.

He murmured. Evelyn opened her eyes. She strained to hear, but couldn't make out what he said. In a trance-like state, and without glancing away from the screen, she reached for the remote and pressed the volume but-ton. Her father spoke again and bucked against his re-straints.

"It's going to be okay." Slurred words fell from swol-len lips. His mangled face was almost unrecognizable. "It's going to be okay. I swear. It's going to be okay."

Evelyn's throat tightened. Her mother's chest rose and fell with each rapid breath. Soft sobs broke from her bleeding mouth.

"No, it won't. He took my baby...."

Evelyn's eyes snapped back to Olivia. A deep red slash spread from ear to ear. Evelyn's stomach heaved, threatening to empty itself as the shadow of a person stepped into the edge of the screen.

"What do you want with us? We haven't done any-thing to you." Her father's panicked voice broke as the figure kicked him in the face.

Evelyn's hand flew to her mouth. She swallowed a scream. Her mother whimpered softly. Her father moaned, writhing in agony. Then her mom's blue eyes grew wide as their captor—careful to stay to the pe-rimeter of the video—walked toward her.

"Please," her father screamed. "Please. I'll do whatever you want. Don't hurt her. Please. I swear. Tell me what you want."

The figure ignored him and raised his arm. Evelyn saw the gun at the same time her father did. Her mother shut her eyes and bowed her head.

Bullets ripped into her broken body.

"No!" Evelyn's father cried out.

The shadowed figure took three quick, long strides toward her weeping father. He knelt at his side and yanked hard on her father's hair, exposing his neck.

"Why?"

Without answering, the shadow pulled a knife. Her father's neck ripped open.

Evelyn turned and vomited onto the floor. When the convulsions stopped, she wiped the back of her hand shakily across her mouth. She lunged for her desk and rummaged through the mess.

"Where is it?" She cursed aloud, frantic for the lifeline to her family. Her father insisted that she have a calling card at all times.

Her dad. She whimpered.

"Daddy..."

Grabbing her black wallet from her bag, Evelyn tore through its contents. Her fingers landed on the worn calling card. She snatched up her phone, breath coming in shallow gulps. She punched her father's cell phone number into the lit keypad, its soft green illuminated lights taunting her.

She commanded herself to calm down. She didn't know anything yet. The DVD could've been a prank. *It could be...has to be.*

She concentrated on the shrill ringing of the phone.

It felt distant, foreign. For the first time since she'd signed her modeling contract and boarded the flight from Phoenix to Europe, she truly felt the distance from her family.

She felt completely alone.

"Hello?" a rough, gravelly stranger's voice answered.

"Who is this?" Evelyn's voice cracked, emotion and confusion clouding her senses.

"Detective Nikols with the Phoenix P.D. Who is this?"

"My family…" Her words sounded hollow.

"Evelyn?" The voice on the other end of the line softened. "Evelyn Maslin?"

"Yes," she whispered. She wrestled the next sentence out of her mouth, determined to voice it. "This is Evelyn Maslin. My family? Tell me what happened to my family."

The pause on the other end of the line lengthened, making her heart threaten to stop even before the detective pulled in his breath to speak, even before the words fell from his mouth.

"Ms. Maslin, we've been trying to track you down. I'm so sorry to have to tell you like this…"

Evelyn's vision narrowed, and her stomach sank. She slid down the cool wall and dropped to the floor. The detective's voice faded as her perfect, larger-than-life world shattered into a million painful pieces.

CHAPTER ONE ·

Present day

EYES FOCUSED ON the mark one hundred yards in front of her, Evelyn pulled the trigger. Anticipating the buck of cold metal in her hand, her body absorbed the kickback as three short bursts echoed in her ears. Her lips twitched into a tight smile. She couldn't have been more accurate if she'd been at point-blank range.

Evelyn holstered her piece, pushed her protective glasses up and smirked at the man standing next to her. Detective Ryan O'Neil pressed the green button to their right, refusing to meet her gleeful stare, and watched as the tethered paper target danced its way down the shooting lane closer and closer into view.

Her partner sighed ruefully. "Two to the chest, one to the head. Not bad, little Miss Evelyn Davis, not bad."

Evelyn flinched slightly. Most of the time, she wasn't bothered by the new name she'd adopted fifteen years ago. But every so often, hearing "Davis" instead of "Maslin" still shocked her a bit. It seemed like today was going to be one of those days.

Ryan pulled the target sheet from the hanger and waved it in Evelyn's face. He grinned, the dimples in his cheeks deepening. Standing at six foot one and a solid 190 pounds of pure muscle, Ryan had the eye of every passing woman. His easygoing smile and casual mannerisms perfectly balanced out her sometimes cool, detached approach to their work. They were the perfect pair, and in looks, they could easily pass as siblings.

The paper fluttered from Ryan's fingers to the shell-covered, dirty concrete floor. He ran his hand through his thick mass of dark curls, sapphire eyes twinkling as he said, "But can you do that with your *left* hand?"

They both knew she wouldn't, or couldn't, refuse his challenge.

"That's 'Detective' to you, sir. And you know I can."

She'd needed the release of the gun range after closing the Langdon case. Seeing those broken and battered little girls had taken its toll on her—physically and emotionally. It had been a long time since she'd needed to go that deep into the psyche of a monster, but someone had to do it—no one else on the force had seen past Adam Langdon's stellar résumé, perfect face and solid alibi.

Evelyn had.

Going on nothing more than a hunch, she'd followed Langdon after work one day. After being detained and released due to lack of evidence the bastard had gotten cocky, not bothering to cover his tracks. He'd led Evelyn straight to his lair—off the grid and hidden—where, unbeknownst to her at the time, his newest victim lay bound and gagged. That sixth sense she'd grown to trust had pushed at her, demanding attention. So she'd done the only thing she could: called for backup and went in alone. Though he was bigger, she was running on righteous anger and quickly got the drop on him. By the time Ryan and the backup arrived, Langdon was in cuffs and the kidnapped little boy sat huddled in Evelyn's lap, crying softly. Old VCR tapes lined the closest shelves, some dating back fifteen years, of his previous victims.

She'd craved Wild West justice for Langdon. Instead, they'd shipped him to Clallam Bay Corrections Center just southeast of Neah Bay. She wanted him out of Washington State altogether, but knew he wouldn't last long at CBCC. That gave her some sense of justice served. Even the cruelest killers wouldn't accept some things—and a murdering child molester was one of them. But he wouldn't be able to touch another child. He likely wouldn't be able to do much of anything soon. Her lips tugged up as the dark, primal thought passed through her mind.

"Okay." Ryan's voice pulled her back to the present. "Let's see you prove it."

He pulled out a worn leather wallet, grabbed a crumbled twenty and slapped it onto the counter in front of them. He stuffed his wallet back in his pocket, then clipped another paper target to the hanger. "Right now."

"I hate to take your money, O'Neil. But if you insist…." Evelyn shook her head. All thoughts of Langdon vanished.

She was in her element, and Ryan was toast.

She turned, pushed her protective eyepiece back into place and picked up her department-issued 9mm. She flicked off the Glock's safety and raised her left hand. Focusing her breath, she concentrated on the flimsy target swaying from its ride down the shooting range. With each controlled breath, she slowed her heartbeat. She locked onto the bull's-eye. Her mind morphed the thin target into the still-nameless face that tormented her dreamless nights: her family's killer.

Without hesitation, her pointer finger squeezed the trigger…and blew a hole through the target's middle.

"And that, O'Neil—" she holstered her piece, pivoted and grinned at her partner's blank face "—is how it's done in the big leagues."

"Impressive." He sank against the wooden stall, hand rubbing the stubble on his chin as he studied Evelyn's obliterated target.

Evelyn picked up and tossed the empty shell casings into the trash. Ryan crossed his arms across his barrel of a chest and kicked a few casings her way. "So, Kate and the kids want you to come over for dinner tonight."

Evelyn stopped short and glanced up. Ryan smiled.

She didn't want to disappoint the kids, but what she really needed was a bottle of Malbec and a bubble bath. She shook her head. "Ryan, that smile of yours isn't going to help you."

"My killer smile may not have worked on you. But I have one better."

Evelyn groaned and leaned back on her heels.

"Kate said she won't take no for an answer. Be there at six o'clock, Davis."

There was no arguing with Kate O'Neil. Evelyn knew it. Ryan knew it. Hell, even Kate knew it. Evelyn sighed. She'd clearly lost this battle.

"I guess I'll see you at six, then." She threw a shell casing at Ryan's head, but he ducked without so much as a blink. "But I'm bringing a date."

"Oh, yeah?" Ryan's eyebrows arched together. "Who's the lucky man?"

She fluttered her lashes. "His name is Mr. Malbec. Ever heard of him?"

Ryan's deep laugh bounced off the wooden walls of their shooting stall. "Nice one, Davis, real nice."

Evelyn picked up her gear and made her way toward the exit. She pushed open the door, turned and winked at her partner. "Thought you'd like that."

"Six o'clock, Davis. And don't be late," Ryan shouted after her.

EVELYN STEPPED OUT of Starbucks, nursing her double-short, no-foam, soy latte as she crossed the cobblestoned street and walked to her favorite spot in Seattle—Pike Place Market. Heading straight to the end of the market, past the infamous fish-throwing stand, she turned right. She let the heavenly scent of lavender lead her, its invisible tether reeling her in. The soft aroma invaded her senses and melted the stress of the preceding weeks. She filled her lungs with the delicate fragrance. Tonight, after dinner at Kate and Ryan's, she'd sit in a hot lavender bath and let the rest of the stress seep out of her pores.

Arriving at the stall she sought, she smiled at Josie's familiar face. Pixie-like with her petite figure and a voice to match it, the vendor's eyes crinkled as she grinned at Evelyn.

"How are you this evening, Detective?"

Evelyn shook her head, still smiling. "Just Evelyn tonight. I'm officially off the clock and desperately need some lavender oil and bath salts."

She swung her small black bag to her front and riffled through its contents. Where was her wallet? She carried the smallest purse possible, yet always managed to misplace things. Would wonders never cease? Finally locating the item she was searching for, Evelyn looked up. Josie's head was down as she leaned over the counter that overflowed with lavender and stretched to reach the bath salts.

"Are you ever truly off the clock, Evelyn?" the tiny woman asked as she pawed though her lavender products. She put the oil and salt into a tiny opaque bag and held it out to Evelyn. "Somehow, I doubt it."

"Well, this—" Evelyn exchanged money for the bag and held it up, the soft scent floating up to her nose "—helps with my half-hearted attempt. Thank you."

"You're most welcome." Josie winked and turned to help the tall man who had strolled up to her small boxy stall.

Evelyn left. She walked back through the marketplace, soaking up the late afternoon activity. She didn't have to be anywhere for an hour or so and had every intention of enjoying her downtime. God knew she needed the break, and this was the perfect place for her to get it.

She loved Pike Place Market. The hustle and bustle was strangely refreshing, and she came here as often as possible. People never seemed to have a care in the world as they purposely, yet leisurely, went from stall to stall searching for that perfect treasure. It was a place to enjoy, a place to discover. And nowhere else could she fade into the background so quickly and easily.

HE FOLLOWED BEHIND EVELYN, twirling a lavender sprig. Just far enough away that she wouldn't notice him in the sea of people, but close enough to smell the lavender trail wafting behind her. He seethed as she ambled from one marketplace stall to the next. He'd wanted to move in, destroy her as she'd laughed and bantered with that vendor woman. He'd even stepped closer, his hands twitching in anticipation. But no, it wasn't time.

Not yet.

So he'd bide his time, and watch, then make her feel pain she'd never known before. Then. Only then would he take her.

His step lightened, the mental picture of her bleeding out at his feet pulsing through him. He stopped behind the column, held his breath and waited for her to finish at the wood-carver's stall. She laughed. Anger burned in his eyes. *How the hell can she be cheerful? She doesn't deserve it. Not with what she'd done, and what she'd taken from him.* He crushed the lavender sprig in his hand and threw it to the ground. She didn't deserve happiness, but that would soon change.

He'd see to that.

CHAPTER TWO

KATE THREW THE wide glass door open. Evelyn smiled and held out the bright assortment of lilies, roses and baby's breath that she'd picked up at Pike Place Market.

"For you."

Kate's face lit up. "Thanks, sweets. They're beautiful. How do you manage to find these? I swear, I never have the same luck when I venture down there."

She put the flowers down on the foyer table, turned and pulled Evelyn into a massive bear hug. As they stood at the same height of five foot ten, it was easy for Kate to do. The affectionate contact surprised Evelyn every time she found herself in her friend's tight embrace. She had accepted Kate's need to hug her. But it wasn't always like that. After her family's death, Evelyn had kept everyone at arm's length—literally.

"I knew you wouldn't say no." Releasing her hold, Kate stepped back. Her curly red hair fell to one side as she tilted her head slightly. She clucked her tongue. "Wow, Ev. You look awful."

Evelyn laughed and tucked a strand of hair behind her ear. "Thanks."

She was forever amazed at her friend's bluntness. It was the trait that had initially drawn Evelyn to her. The moment Ryan introduced them, a tight bond had formed between them. Knowing where she stood with Kate had been a welcome place for Evelyn. And eight years later, she still appreciated Kate's candor and friendship. Looking at the green-eyed beauty, one would never guess that she was a cutthroat, shoot-from-the-hip, take-no-shit assistant district attorney.

"Just saying how it is," Kate teased as she closed the door behind them.

Kate moved across the foyer, entered the dining room and flipped the light switch. Evelyn followed behind her. The clear, blown-glass chandelier twinkled to life. The room had plush cream carpets and pale blue walls. The table settings were laid out on the pub-style table.

For six.

Evelyn, plus the O'Neil clan, made five.

"Why are there six plates on that table?"

She pushed down the frustration bubbling inside her. If she had known Kate planned to pull this tonight, she would have declined—and nothing would have stopped her. Damn Kate, always trying to set me up.

"Are there?" Kate smiled innocently.

"Tonight, of all nights? You know how much the Langdon case took out of me. And how much I hate you trying to set me up." Evelyn fought to keep her voice level.

Kate giggled.

"Why are you laughing?"

"Ryan owes me ten bucks." Kate reached for the sixth place setting and gathered it into a neat pile. "Do you honestly think I would have made this a blind date? Tonight? Not in a million years. I haven't seen either of you in weeks, and I want you all to myself. Besides, Ry thought it would be funny to see how long it took you to notice the number of place settings. I told him less than two minutes. He said ten. We bet, and I won."

Evelyn should have known better. Heat kissed her cheeks. Apparently she needed this evening with her friends more than she realized.

Kate balanced the plate setting on one hand and reached for the flowers. She stopped, tilted her head. "Hear that?"

Little feet clapped down the hardwood floors, tiny giggles bouncing off the hallway walls. Evelyn grinned. She dropped to her knees and waited for the assault to commence.

Right on cue, Ava, Kate and Ryan's six-year-old daughter, charged around the corner, long blond hair swinging wildly, and flung herself into Evelyn's open arms.

"You're here! You're here!"

Ava tightened her grip around Evelyn and squeezed. Her little face pressed into the soft curve of Evelyn's neck. She returned the child's hug and quietly sighed. Kate knew her too well. This was exactly where Evelyn needed to be tonight.

Here with this family...her adopted family.

Ava pushed back from Evelyn's embrace and, despite her lisp, babbled a mile a minute. Evelyn and Kate exchanged an amused look—the child was an attorney in the making. Evelyn turned her attention back to the chatty child as Kate headed toward the kitchen.

"Ry, can you grab me a vase?"

A baby's contagious laugh pulled Evelyn's lips into a smile, and she shifted Ava to one side to lock eyes with the little love of her life.

Liam O'Neil. At sixteen months, he was still a sweet

baby to her, but he'd started to tear around the house as soon as he learned to walk, and his constant nonsense babble was heartwarming to hear. Liam hesitantly toddled toward her, his eyes sparkling with determination and untold mischief. *Oh, dear.* He took after Ryan with his playful demeanor, jet-black curls and matching dimples.

Liam was going to be one solid heartbreaker when he grew up.

His feet got ahead of his small body as he glanced up at Evelyn and he face-planted. Hard. His chin connected with the floor with a hard crack. Ava's jabber halted. Her eyes grew wide as she stared at her brother's crumpled figure.

He lay there for a minute, hugging the floor, his tiny body a statue. A whimper escaped his lips as he slowly lifted his face toward Evelyn. His chin quivered and tears collected in his eyes.

Evelyn set Ava down and, in two steps, scooped him into her arms to cuddle him close to her.

"Look at you, little man. You're okay, sweetheart." She lightly kissed the red, angry knot on his chin. He whimpered again, fat tears threatening to roll down his cheeks.

"You're okay. See? All better."

Evelyn pushed the curls away from his eyes. Liam tentatively smiled up at her. She kissed the tip of his nose and felt his body relax. She looked into his eyes, the stress of the Langdon case gone. She didn't know how or why, but the tiny man in her arms pushed back the darkness in her world.

Seeing that her brother wasn't broken, Ava once again launched into chatter about the red-haired boy who sat behind her in class, always pulling her hair. Why did he do that anyway? When no one answered, she embarked onto her next story.

"Kate, can I get a bag of frozen peas?" Evelyn grabbed Ava's hand, cradled Liam to her chest and headed toward the kitchen.

RYAN AND EVELYN'S phones beeped at the same time. In tandem, they reached for them. Their delightfully calm and refreshing evening crashed and burned.

Ryan skimmed the text and set down his frosted mug of Guinness. "Son of a bitch."

"Ryan," Kate chastised between clenched teeth, casting a quick glance at Ava.

A look of chagrin crossed his face. Kate had a mouth that made the trashiest sailor blush, but demanded clean language around the children. It was one of the many contradictory things about her partner's wife, and Evelyn knew he loved every single one of them.

Ava giggled at her parents' exchange, nothing lost on her brilliant young mind, and went back to her favorite meal: cedar plank salmon. Which still boggled Evelyn's mind—what six-year-old loved salmon? But after one nibble off Evelyn's plate when Ava was five, the little munchkin was sold. Liam stuffed mashed potatoes into his mouth without the use of his fork, which now lay on the floor. Kate had given up that fight not even five minutes into dinner, as he insisted on using the utensil as a drumstick against the wood. Fearing for her lovely table, she'd left the fork on the floor when it went flying after her son's last particularly creative drumming session.

Evelyn scanned the message and silently agreed with

Ryan's choice words. She pushed back from the table and ruffled Liam's curls as she popped another piece of asparagus into her mouth.

"Gotta go, babe." Ryan stood, leaned over to his wife and kissed her.

Ava scrambled down from her chair and threw herself at Evelyn. "Don't go, Ev. You haven't seen my new book yet."

"I see how I rate." Ryan chuckled, then shrugged on his North Face jacket.

Evelyn hugged Ava tightly. "Next time, sweets. That's a promise. Okay?"

After letting her go, Evelyn leaned down to hug Liam, who was reaching up from his high chair. She laughed as he dug his chubby face into her neck and gave her a slobbery, openmouthed, potato-covered baby kiss.

God, she loved this family, these kids. No one could replace her own family. Ever. She ached for them daily, the pain still as fresh as it was fifteen years ago. But the O'Neil clan came a close second.

The gaping wound in her soul healed a bit with every minute spent with them. She didn't know if she'd ever be whole again—some days, she doubted it completely. But this family made her feel like she had a fighting chance, and she'd do anything for them.

Ryan stood by the door. "Let's go, Evelyn. The captain will piss himself if we don't get there soon."

"Ryan." A groan of exasperation escaped Kate's lips.

He shrugged, a sheepish smile crossing his face. It morphed into a smirk as he took a giant step forward and wrapped Kate in a tight embrace, noisily kissing her. Ava squealed in protest. Twisting out of her husband's arms, Kate blushed and rolled her eyes at Evelyn.

"But he will. Truly. Piss himself," Ryan said straight-faced. He laughed as he dodged Kate's playful swat.

No need to remind Evelyn of that. Captain Kessler's temper was legendary. Hot lava bubbled just beneath the surface of his even, cool disposition, just waiting for the right moment to erupt. It didn't do so often, but when his temper flared, it was hot and violent.

She tried her best to stay on the easygoing side of his demeanor, but something told her that tonight they just might see him explode. Nothing in the message she'd received alluded to that, yet her instincts screamed that something was amiss. Something big. And ugly.

Evelyn blew out a long breath. *So much for time off.* She kissed Kate on the cheek. "Thanks for the dinner. Who knows, maybe one of these days you can teach me how to cook."

Kate smiled. "That'd be nice."

"You? Cook?" Ryan snorted, pushed open the front door and stepped out. "Not possible."

Smiling, Evelyn shrugged into her black lightweight North Face jacket, then followed Ryan into the foggy Seattle evening.

CHAPTER THREE

IT HAD BEEN fifteen years. Still…she didn't think she'd ever stop missing the constant sun and warmth of Phoenix. Shivering in the wind, she zipped her jacket, hunched her shoulders against the bone-chilling drizzle that fell from the sky and headed toward the station's metal double doors. Admittedly, this misty Pacific Northwest weather suited her—the Evelyn of today. The Evelyn who'd once soaked up the golden sun in Phoenix and traipsed through Milan without a worry in the world had gone into hiding a long time ago. Her chest tightened. She wasn't sure she'd ever see her again, or if she even existed anymore.

The station's small foyer sat vacant except for the young officer perched behind the front desk. He lifted his head. "Detectives."

"Sampson." Evelyn nodded. "What's going on tonight?"

His brows pinched together. "Sorry, Detective. Haven't heard a thing."

She frowned. "Okay. Thanks."

A sick sense of dread twisted her stomach. She and Ryan rode to the third floor in silence. This was their night off. Being called in, especially after working the Langdon case nonstop, only meant one thing: trouble.

A soft chime announced their arrival. Captain Kessler sat on the desk closest to them—Evelyn's desk—his face stormy.

"It's about time," he said. He pushed his tall, lanky frame off the corner of her desk and glared at them. *Has he been waiting for us?* Evelyn cast a quizzical look toward Ryan. He shrugged.

"Come on." Kessler marched down the hall to his office door.

They passed through the bull pen to follow him. It was small, cramped almost. A dozen or so ancient metal desks butted up against one another. Each pair of detectives faced their partner. Ryan's desk proudly featured his family's framed smiling faces. Evelyn's was mostly empty. No personal knickknacks, save the oversize black coffee mug she'd picked up at the market and one photo of Evelyn with Kate and the kids.

Normally bustling with loud—sometimes bordering on obnoxious—activity, the open space was vacant, quiet. She glanced at the assignment board. The detectives were all out. All of them.

Evelyn started to shake off her jacket.

"Don't even bother, Davis," Kessler called to her.

She shrugged back into the empty sleeve. Her brows lifted in surprise at the captain's agitated jitteriness. With a lift of his broad shoulders, Ryan turned and headed toward Kessler's office. Evelyn followed.

"I'm sending you over to Mercer Island."

Evelyn and Ryan exchanged guarded looks. *Not good. Not good at all.*

"That's Sanderson's precinct." Ryan leaned against the door frame, weary of the coming storm.

Despite her best attempts, anytime Evelyn and Sanderson were in the same vicinity, sparks flew—and not the good kind. Sanderson had made his disdain for her obvious on several occasions. Ever since he'd screwed up the close on the one—and *only*—case they'd been forced to work on together, his dislike had boiled over to sheer black hatred. Evelyn groaned inwardly.

She'd put up with a lot of bullshit being a woman on the force. But his chauvinistic, Neanderthal behavior was the worst. He was cocky, quick to leap to broad conclusions and straight-up sexist. There wasn't a woman in the entire SPD who could stand to work with him. And to think she'd just been about to spend a relaxing evening with Kate and the kids.

"Yes." Kessler gave Ryan a hard look. "Is that a problem, O'Neil?"

Ryan raised his hands. "Nope. Not for us, sir."

"The chief…"

"Excuse me, sir." Evelyn threw a shielded glance at Ryan. "The chief?"

Chief Diaz had been responsible for bringing her to the Seattle Police Department. He, Captain Kessler and Ryan were the only officers privy to her complete, sealed file. Though she knew the chief had watched over her—and her career—like a concerned older brother, once her move had been completed, she'd set out to prove herself, *by* herself. And prove herself she did. Her promotions, as the youngest woman to make detective, had been of her own merit. Still, she wasn't deaf to the murmurs that the chief favored her.

Having him involved tonight spelled disaster. She took a deep breath and shifted her weight. Kessler's blue eyes were dark with concern.

She didn't need any more trouble from Sanderson. Her working relationship with him had gone from bad to worse when she had made detective before him. He'd protested just loud enough and made a not-so-subtle hint about her connection with the chief. It was a load of shit. But still...try as she might to ignore his egotistical arrogance and remain calm and professional, he always found a way under her skin.

Since her promotion, she and Ryan had been kept away from Sanderson. But apparently their luck had just run out. *Great.*

Kessler glared at her from hooded eyes and motioned for her to sit, which she did. He ran his forefinger over the top of his thumb, picked at his cuticle. Evelyn frowned. She'd picked up that tell during the first month reporting to him. What was making him so anxious?

"Given your background and your closing rate, the chief believes you'll be an asset to the case."

She leaned back into the uncomfortable chair, its faux leather groaning.

"And the case is?" She crossed her arms, cautiously intrigued.

Kessler hesitated. His face was ashen, the calm in his eyes dissipating.

"Captain?" Ryan broke the silence in the fishbowl room.

Kessler cleared his throat and, without blinking, answered. "It appears to be a family annihilator case. But something is off...."

She froze as the term *family annihilator* tumbled from Kessler's lips. A low whistle came from Ryan as he rubbed his hand over the black scruff on his jaw.

She balanced on the edge of an emotional cliff, and she knew it. Out of the corner of her eye, she saw Ryan take a step toward her. She gave a tight shake of her head. He stopped, lifted a brow.

Evelyn straightened. She'd opened up to Ryan years ago, after an interrogation that had shaken both of them. She trusted him, and he'd sworn to always keep an eye out for her—no matter how independent and strong she thought she was.

But she didn't need Ryan, or anyone for that matter, to keep her from tumbling over the cliff's edge. She could manage it herself, for crying out loud. She reined in the suffocating emotions. She was seasoned at corralling her galloping heart—she'd spent years perfecting the task.

With the help of her therapist, she recognized that emotions didn't make her weak, but strong. She wasn't a statistic, but a survivor. Everything she'd walked through made her the woman—and most importantly, the detective—she was.

Kessler picked up a thin case file off his desk and leaned toward her.

Swallowing hard, Evelyn took it from him. She knew her partner had noticed her brief hesitation and seen the emotions dance behind her eyes. To most people, she was unreadable. But Ryan wasn't most people. He read her like an open book. He'd noticed. If Kessler did, he didn't say anything. Her lips tightened into a hard line as she flipped the file open.

"Appears?" she said to no one in particular as she studied the photos.

"Yes. It's the second such case in the past two weeks—in the same precinct, with similar family units. Those photos—" Kessler motioned to the brightly colored crime scene images "—are from the first."

She flipped through the photos. The wife's body lay at the feet of what appeared to be her husband. The back of his head was missing. Evelyn swallowed the bile that rose in her throat. With each sweep of her eyes she cataloged the grisly images of the husband and wife. She continued skimming through the photos, then stopped. A young child lay on her back, a deep, crimson gash across her throat. Evelyn's hand trembled. Her throat tightened, rage and grief warring within her.

"Have either of the husbands recently lost their jobs?"

"No. They're both successful in their respective industries," the captain replied.

Evelyn tapped the photos on the table.

Something wasn't right.

Men who took their family's lives fell into one of two categories: angry at their partners and seeking revenge, or hopeless and despondent and believing their family was better off dead. It was usually a reaction to a loss of some kind—a job, a wife. They were typically mid-thirties to middle-age, socially isolated and had been depressed or frustrated for a long time. For many family annihilators, the act of murder was a way to reestablish control.

At first glance, neither of these men fit that profile.

So what triggered this violence?

"Family annihilator cases are extremely rare, especially with family units like this," she said without looking up.

"I agree."

"Do we have any leads?" Ryan sat next to Evelyn, peering over her shoulder at the photos.

"Why bring us on now? Why not with the first case?"

Evelyn passed the glossy five-by-sevens to Ryan and glanced over at him uneasily. She hadn't wanted to hand the photos over, concerned about how they might affect him. They made the perfect pair: he was lighthearted, she was serious; he played by the book, she pushed the boundaries. While she held people—and the emotions they garnered—at a distance, Ryan was all in. Had always been all in. It was one of the many qualities that she loved in her partner; he felt deeper than any man she'd ever met. And she couldn't even imagine what those pictures would do to him if they'd hit *her* so hard.

Ryan began to flip through the photos, then stopped. He looked up, his face hard. "Tell me this isn't happening. Tell me this isn't fucking happening. Here. On our stomping ground."

He held the same photo of the young child with her throat slit that she'd stopped at. The child looked to be about Ava's age. His hand shook. A muscle in his jaw jumped. They'd seen some twisted things while working homicide. The seasoned—burned-out was more like it—detectives told them it'd get easier. That seeing the capacity of the sickos out there was par for the course. They encouraged both her and Ryan to disengage. Total bullshit. So yeah, she could only imagine that the photo made him see red.

"The Langdon case was a priority," Kessler said. "We needed your full efforts to close that one down. At the time, we thought it was a one-off. But with this fresh crime scene…"

Evelyn's mind scrambled to categorize the information they'd been given. Her gaze swept to the captain. She did a double take. The corners of his mouth were

turned down in a tight grimace as he clenched and unclenched his fists.

Evelyn leaned forward and gripped the armrest.
"Does the chief think serial?"

Ryan's head snapped up.

"I didn't say that." Kessler's jaw twitched. No police
officer in his right mind voluntarily labeled someone
a serial killer until they had to. No one wanted that on
their watch.

You didn't have to. Evelyn dropped back into her
chair. She'd been right. Again. Whatever they were
about to step into would make the Langdon case appear like a walk in the park.

"We aren't officially saying or thinking anything."
Kessler scrubbed his face, then glanced between the two
detectives. "Two family annihilator cases in as many
weeks is suspicious. Chief Diaz wants you and O'Neil
to head up the investigation and report directly to Assistant Chief Pugel and himself."

The captain's secretary rapped on the door frame and
stuck her head into the office. "Sorry for interrupting,
sir, but he's here."

"Thanks. Tell him I'll be with him shortly."

Evelyn threw Ryan a guarded look. She'd never
known Kessler's assistant to interrupt him. Ever. So
who the hell was important enough to do so now?

Captain Kessler stood. The detectives mimicked his
movement. Evelyn glanced over her shoulder, following the captain's gaze. A tall handsome stranger clad in
a perfectly tailored black suit leaned against her desk,
animatedly speaking into his cell. She couldn't place
him. But damn, he was beautiful. The stranger caught
her staring, smiled and tipped his head in her direction.

Evelyn's heart jumped. *What the hell?* She swung her attention back to Kessler, momentarily uncomfortable with her reaction. *Where did that come from?*

"CSI is already on scene, but nothing was moved," Kessler said. "Get over there, and get fresh eyes on it. Now."

CHAPTER FOUR

IT DIDN'T SURPRISE Ryan that they'd been put on this case. Some might question the decision, given his partner's background—if they even knew, which most didn't. But the chief made the right call. Evelyn's instincts were primal. In one breath, she could transport herself into the mind of the predator, see what he saw and think how he thought. If a psychopathic serial killer had unleashed fear onto the streets of Seattle, there was no one better than Evelyn Davis to bring him down. Ryan floored the gas.

Watching Evelyn work had freaked Ryan out the first year of their partnership. Kate had chuckled at him when he'd mentioned it. She'd told him to chill out and bring his new partner by so *she* could meet *her* new friend.

One case under their belt together, and he was sold. How could he not be? She'd empathized with the grieving widow, whom the rest of the squad felt was a victim, all while asking the right questions to pull out the truth: that the woman had, in fact, murdered her husband.

He'd rolled with Evelyn's instincts from that day forward, letting her take the lead. She still mesmerized him. She caught things before anyone else did, connected dots that had barely surfaced and her closing rate of 80 percent compared to the rest of SPD's 50 percent continued to push her into the spotlight—which made her squirm, and him laugh. It was quite possibly the only tell that made her human, instead of a demigod.

So while he wasn't surprised that Chief Diaz asked for them, he wondered what the hell his partner was thinking. How well had she compartmentalized the information they'd been briefed on?

Ryan knew what she'd kept guarded from everyone, what her background held. He'd made it a priority to get beneath her carefully constructed barriers when they became partners. He needed to know the woman who held his life in her hands. Fiercely private, she'd kept everyone at arm's length. A year after she'd met Kate, and only when certain of her safety, she'd finally let her guard down. But only around him and Kate, and only so much.

After Ava was born, she'd let him and Kate in—truly in—and what Evelyn entrusted them with horrified them. She'd gone from partner to family that night.

A normal person would've become a statistic. But Evelyn wasn't normal. Instead of losing herself to the grief, she focused on bringing justice to victims' families. He'd once asked Evelyn why she'd become a cop. She'd quietly told him she wanted to give closure to families—the one thing she'd never gotten, and the one constant that drove everything she did.

He doubted she'd ever fully let them in, and that was okay. She had trusted him—trusted them—with her darkest moment. In turn, he trusted her with his life.

A question gnawed at him, despite his best attempt to eject it from his mind. He took a hard left, tires squealing. Would this case hit too close?

She'd shifted into herself as she absorbed the case

file details. He'd seen it before. When she didn't want to deal with some unseen emotion or issue, a hardness descended. Her sapphire-colored eyes darkened, her lips set into a firm line and her already impeccable posture straightened even more. Fascinating as it was to see someone change like that, he didn't like it. He hated to see her prepare for some invisible battle, shielding herself from some unseen attack, leaving him—and anyone else, for that matter—helpless to defend her.

"You okay?" He glanced at her.

"You know I am."

"Do I?"

CHAPTER FIVE

RYAN'S LINE OF questioning was spot-on. Evelyn couldn't fault him for that. She would've been asking the same thing if the roles were reversed. But they weren't. She gritted her teeth, irritation ripping through her. For being caught off-guard, for allowing the emotions to seep back in where they didn't belong, for being vulnerable.

"Yes." She forced the word past compressed lips.

He nodded, the movement brisk. "Okay, then."

"Okay, then."

They pulled into the snaking driveway. Ryan whistled. The majestic colonial rose from the evergreen carpet that blanketed the ground. Perfect landscaping drew their gazes to the grand structure of the main house. Evelyn couldn't help but imagine the family enjoying a rare, million-dollar summer evening, watching the sun dance with the edge of the lake. She shuddered. They'd never do that again.

Figures rushed back and forth, their dark silhouettes a stark contrast to the bright lights shining through the windows. A vibrant red door, etched glass panels on either side, stood slightly ajar.

Evelyn knew what awaited them. Her stomach dropped.

"You know, Kate and I toyed with the idea of moving to Mercer." Ryan's voice interrupted her thoughts. He put the car into Park and sighed. "Now…it's lost its charm."

Evelyn ignored him and got out of the car. "Shall we get this over with?"

They signed the front door log, then stepped into the mammoth foyer. Two curving stairwells mirrored each other, ascending toward the second-floor landing. A rather large and, by the looks of everything around them, expensive crystal chandelier hung suspended over their heads. Two officers huddled by a black grand piano in hushed conversation.

Evelyn walked past them without a word and entered the family room. Careful not to interfere with the CSI unit or touch anything, her eyes took in every awful detail.

In front of the large marble fireplace lay two blonde girls in their pajamas. Bound and gagged. One with a bullet hole through her forehead, and the other with her throat slashed. Evelyn walked over and looked into their faces, sadness washing over her. Even in death, they appeared sweet…innocent.

She took in the scene at her feet. Something was off. What was it? She bent down again and leaned in. "What in the world?"

The younger child's wrists were cinched tight behind her back, causing an involuntary arch in her body. She hadn't had any way to defend herself as the knife ripped into her neck. Strangely, the older one's hands had been bound in front. They huddled together. The younger one slumped into her sister's chest, her head resting at an odd angle against her big sister's shoulder. The older girl couldn't have been more than fourteen.

Olivia's age.

Evelyn banished the thought and focused on the girls in front of her. In her mind's eye, she could see the older sister scooting closer, reaching her arms around her dying sister and cradling her. Blood from the gaping slit in the little girl's throat soaked the front of her sister's yellow pajamas and formed a dark crimson puddle around them. Evelyn frowned. That blood looked darker than the splatter on the fireplace, almost as if the blood on her chest—her sister's blood—had dried before she'd been shot.

Evelyn jerked back. Her stomach rolled. "Ry—"

She looked up and into the scowling face of her nemesis, Detective Josh Sanderson. *Shit*. She'd walked right by him on purpose and assessed the scene on her own with fresh eyes. Hadn't that been Kessler's direct order?

Wrong move.

She stood and tipped her head in recognition. "Sanderson."

The short athletic man's face twisted into a snarl. She swallowed a sigh. *Were they really going to go around this mountain again?* Once, in a drunken stupor, the narcissistic, arrogant man in front of her said that had they met at a local bar, and he didn't know anything about Diaz's golden girl, he'd have loved to see what was beneath the jeans and black North Face jacket that hugged her curves just right, positive that it would only be better than his wildest imagination.

She'd wanted to clock him. Ryan had done it instead.

"I'd say it was nice to see you, but it isn't. This is my case. What are *you* doing here?" Sanderson asked in an icy tone.

She ignored his glare and locked eyes with him. Apparently being polite wasn't in the cards tonight. Fine. She doubted he knew that they now led this investigation. If he did, he wouldn't have been so pleasant—if she could call this pleasant.

"Chief Diaz sent us over. What have you got, Sanderson?" Evelyn asked.

Ryan walked up, crossed his arms. Evelyn bit back a smirk. Ryan would surely win any pissing match with Sanderson, and the other detective knew it.

Sanderson glanced between the two detectives and shoved back his cheap blue suit jacket, looping his thumbs through his belt as he jerked his head toward the elegant family room. "Family annihilator."

"Shit," Ryan muttered under his breath.

She normally dealt with Sanderson's kind in a perfectly PC way, took all the egotistical bullshit in stride. And judging by the way Sanderson glared up at her now, she'd have to do it again—take his bullshit. She took a deep breath—no use egging him on any more than her sheer existence on planet Earth already did.

"And how did you come to that conclusion, Detective Sanderson?"

She'd meant it as a polite question, trying to be cordial. Sanderson's face reddened. The vein in his neck bulged.

"Listen, Davis. It's a theory." Although anger had pushed color to his face, icicles dripped from his tongue. "Just because you have the chief wrapped around your little finger doesn't mean you can come in here and make accusations."

She seethed, but managed to ignore the underhanded, out-of-line remark—she'd deal with that later—and tilted her chin down to look into his shadowy eyes.

"Yes, actually, I *can*. I'm the senior officer here and we—" she pointed to Ryan and then herself "—have the lead on this case. Not to mention that this little 'theory' of yours, the one you so flippantly expressed, is one you *cannot* substantiate until further into the investigation. If ever."

Sanderson took a menacing step toward her.

Evelyn's pulse jumped angrily as she also took a step forward. Before she could respond, Ryan stepped between the two detectives and shoved an open hand onto Sanderson's chest.

"How about you stop right there, Sanderson," Ryan said in a gruff, don't-mess-with-me-you-little-shithead voice. "You can call the chief and confirm what Detective Davis just said."

Sanderson tried to take another step toward Evelyn. Ryan's face hardened. "Make the damn phone call."

Sanderson shot a look past Ryan's shoulder. "This isn't over, Davis."

Turning on his heel, he stormed into the kitchen, punching numbers into his phone as he went.

Ryan grabbed Evelyn's wrist and towed her outside, where he released her.

"Okay, look, I know you were trying your best to be nice—" he rubbed his hands over his face "—but are you out of your mind?"

"Ryan—"

"Stop. Anything that puts Sanderson on edge weakens this team. You know that. I know that. So what the hell's going on? Are you—"

"I'm fine."

Evelyn wasn't sure she could explain her actions. They were just as foreign to her as they were to Ryan.

Her cool, steel-like outer shell, which had served her well the past fifteen years, had just cracked, ever so slightly. And that scared the hell out of her. At the sound of Sanderson uttering those two horrid little words, she'd wanted to rip off his face and weep at the same time. If he had pushed it much further, she didn't know how she would have responded.

Ryan paced in front of her, hands clasped behind the back of his neck. He halted, stared at the floor, then glanced back at her. "No, Ev. You're not."

She went to argue, but snapped her mouth closed as he put up his hand.

"Maybe you're too close for this one."

"What? Why?" She felt her cheeks flush. "Because tragedy struck my family? Is that it?"

"Maybe."

He'd said it so softly as he sagged against the porch railing, watching her, that she almost missed it. *Almost.*

Rebellious tears gathered in her eyes. She couldn't believe he'd thrown her family's murder into her face like that and questioned her ability to do her job. He knew the job meant everything to her, kept her sane. She'd never jeopardize her position. How could he not trust her to handle herself and put her work first? Her heart stumbled and her shoulders sagged. How could he think she wasn't okay?

But was she really fine? She'd already harnessed the ghosts of her past—and their occupying emotions—twice. In less than two hours. She grimaced. Okay, so maybe he was right. Still…she wasn't ready to give in to that emotional tailspin. Not now.

"Don't use that against me, Ryan. I'm a damn good cop, and you know it."

He jerked back as if she'd struck him. "Evelyn. I'm your partner. I'm looking out for you. That's what partners do. I'm concerned."

She glanced up at him, heat rushing to her cheeks again. She shouldn't have pushed Sanderson so far. She hung her head. "You're right."

"Sanderson's an asshole. But I've never seen you react like that. The chief put you on this case for a reason, and it wasn't because of your pretty face. You know these types of cases better than anyone on the force, and your instincts are right on target."

She walked toward the open door. She peered through the grand foyer at the room that held the family and shuddered, a chill racing down her spine. "Just because it looks like a family annihilator, Ry, doesn't mean it is. If the media even gets a whiff of that theory, they'll run with it."

"I know," Ryan said.

"There won't be anything sacred left for this family. Everyone will believe this man, this father and husband, killed his family—even if we've proved otherwise."

Her throat closed around unspoken emotion. She knew all too well what the media could do. Her father's name and dignity had been shredded once the media sharks had sunk their teeth into the "family annihilator" tag. The grisly video Evelyn had received from the killer came too late to clear her father's name in the eyes of the public. She'd had to flee Phoenix, its warmth, its sun, its beauty—the media had seen to that. She shook her head and vanquished the dark, haunting memories that rose from the depths of her soul.

She faced her partner and stuck her hands deep in her pockets. "The first look doesn't always mean everything. The dead don't lie. We just have to see what they're trying to show us."

"You're right. They don't. So whatever ghosts keep surfacing, push back. Lock them down." He took two steps to stand beside her and studied the house. "We've got a job to do. That family needs us. They need *you*."

She nodded. She wouldn't allow the horrors of her past to hijack her present. She was stronger than that. She had endured more than most people had in a lifetime and made it out the other side. Ryan was right: whatever dark shadows clawed at her needed to be caged. Permanently.

Taking a deep breath, she stepped into the grand foyer. "Okay, gentlemen. Show's over."

The officers chuckled.

Evelyn moved back into the family room and knelt beside the sisters, once more swallowing the rage and grief that gripped her throat as she stared into the faces of two innocent lives taken far too soon. "Ry—come over here. This is what I wanted to show you earlier."

Ryan hurried over and squatted next to her. "Talk to me."

"Notice anything different between these blood-stains?" She pointed to one area, then the next.

Ryan studied the blood splattered from the gunshot wound and that from the knife. He turned, horror in his eyes.

"Holy shit." He sat back on his heels and motioned to the oldest. "Her sister bled out in her arms, and then she was shot."

Evelyn nodded. Her heart twisted. *What type of monster are we dealing with?*

"I'm going to grab the coroner to get the time of death for both girls." Ryan rose and walked out of the room.

The older girl's face was frozen in panic and anguish. Evelyn knew that helpless feeling. Her sadness morphed into a fierce rage that simmered beneath her skin. No one should have to die like that.

She stood, pulled out a thin notebook and pen and scribbled a few notes. Snapping the book closed, she shoved it into her pocket and went over to the woman, their mother. Broken and riddled with a dozen or more knife wounds, she lay at her husband's feet. Defensive bruising covered both arms and blood congealed above her split lip. She'd put up one hell of a fight. Evelyn knelt beside the body. "Good for you, ma'am."

From her crouched position, she checked the man sitting in the recliner. From this angle, he looked to be asleep. She moved an inch to the left and saw the back of his head splattered against the artwork just behind him. She straightened. This wasn't a family annihilator case. She knew it. But still…she needed to conduct a thorough examination of every inch of this family's life.

"Fin?"

The officer to her right jumped. His young face lit up as his eyebrows scrunched together.

"I need you to verify if either parent had a lover on the side. Pull their phone records and check for large cash deposits or withdrawals. If either one of them had a secret life that would provoke all this—" she gestured around her "—I want to know about it."

The officer nodded as he scribbled down notes.

If they were going to see this case for what it truly was, Evelyn needed to investigate all possible triggers. It was a long shot, but she knew finding out that a spouse had a lover was such a spark, and she wanted to rule it out. Hopefully, once they were done, they'd clear the man staring up at her with lifeless eyes.

Then they could focus on catching the sick, twisted bastard who had done this.

Sanderson rejoined them, face flushed. Evelyn could only imagine the tongue-lashing the chief had given him. Would he ever learn it wasn't a pissing match?

"We need as many eyes on this as possible," she said. "This makes two similar cases, and no one wants a third. If it's not a family annihilator case and, in fact, the same guy, we want to catch him. And fast. So what do you see?"

He studied the room.

"It's like he just sat, sucked the gun and blew his head off." Sanderson walked over to her as he shoved his hands in his pockets. "It feels too easy, almost staged."

"I agree."

Sanderson eyebrows arched in disbelief.

"What else?"

He circled the husband, stepping around the wife.

"It's strange that it doesn't look like he put up a fight. At least…" He faltered, glanced at the two young girls and cleared his throat. "At least at first glance, but I don't know."

"The autopsy will confirm that tomorrow." Ryan joined them again. He tipped his head toward Evelyn once, the muscle in his jaw jumping.

Her mind flashed back to the DVD of her own family's brutal murder as she viewed the tragedy in front of her. In vibrant color, she saw her father begging the murderer for mercy, Olivia's neck slashed, the defensive wounds on her mother. She had been a tigress until the end....

"Ev—" Ryan whispered.

Her eyes focused again on the vicious scene in front of her. Sanderson was right in his assessment. There didn't appear to have been a struggle. But the autopsy would reveal what lay hidden beneath.

"Are you finished here?" she asked the CSI officer, motioning to the girls.

He nodded.

She crouched beside the girls and studied their bodies more closely. Gently, she reached out, put a gloved finger to the first girl's eyelids and closed them over lifeless, terrified blue eyes. She shifted her weight and repeated the gesture to her sister's eyes.

"I'll find the bastard who did this. I promise." She stood.

Ryan spoke quietly behind her. "We'll get this guy, Ev. But I need you all here. We need you all here to nail him."

"I know. I'm sorry about earlier." Evelyn's shoulders slumped. "It hit a nerve. It won't happen again."

"Yes, it will."

Who was she kidding? Clearly not Ryan. She hated that he was right. It would happen again. And continue to happen until she found the one thing that continued to elude her: closure. The same darkness that drove her at work, always fluttering in the back of her mind, haunted every second of every day. She had to stay one step ahead of it, or it would consume her.

He sighed. "It's what makes you so good at the job. That drive for justice. You just won't stop. You're a bulldog—a gorgeous bulldog—but a bulldog nonetheless when it comes to finding justice. You don't take that lightly. It's what makes you...well, you."

She shook her head, not sure how to respond. "You're right. I let my guard down, and all my emotions came flooding out. I'll get it under control. I promise."

Their phones buzzed simultaneously. A message from Captain Kessler illuminated the small screen.

Need you in my office. ASAP.

Evelyn set her jaw stubbornly. Had that bastard Sanderson really had the balls to submit a complaint against her? She looked up at Ryan. "I need to be on this case."

"I get it, kiddo, I do."

Evelyn zipped up her jacket, hunched her shoulders against the cold rain and followed Ryan out to the car.

Did he really?

CHAPTER SIX

SPECIAL AGENT MARCUS MORETTI didn't move from beside the captain's desk, just watched as the two detectives stepped out of the elevator. If he hadn't all but perfected his poker face during his years at the Bureau, he'd be a lost cause.

Evelyn Davis wasn't just beautiful—she was a knockout of epic proportions.

The rumors of her past life as a supermodel paled in comparison to the goddess staring back at him. He locked eyes with her sapphire gaze and his stomach tightened. He swallowed hard.

Focus, Moretti.

He saw Kessler motion them forward. Evelyn tossed her coat over the back of her chair and said something to her partner that Marcus couldn't make out. Her partner smiled a tight, wary smile and followed her to Kessler's office. *Shit. Nothing like starting out on the defensive.*

Marcus pulled his gaze away from Evelyn's lips and studied the two detectives as they approached. He'd requested both their files before accepting this case. Ryan O'Neil's jacket had all the typical information. Evelyn Davis's, on the other hand was surprisingly thin, especially for someone with her reputation. She was the reason he'd said yes to this assignment. With her experience and skill set, he definitely wanted her on his team. But he couldn't help but wonder if maybe, just maybe, something was off, and he had to get to the bottom of it first. He needed to find out what, exactly, was missing from her file.

Evelyn walked into the office, her expression cautious yet questioning, reminding him of a black panther coiled to spring. He tried to read whatever he saw swirling just behind her guarded gaze, but he got nothing. He'd hate to play against her in poker. He got the feeling she would wipe the floor with his ass.

He smiled at her. She didn't return the gesture. *Well, okay, then.*

"Captain?"

Kessler motioned toward him. "Detectives, this is Special Agent Marcus Moretti. The mayor called in a personal favor to have him consult on this case. Special Agent Moretti, these are my lead detectives on the cases in question, Ryan O'Neil and Evelyn Davis."

Marcus moved from his spot and extended his hand. Ryan leaned forward first, shook Marcus's hand, then moved aside for his partner. Marcus looked between Ryan and Evelyn as he stepped closer to her. *There's always an alpha in a partnership, so which of you is it?* She reached for his hand and nodded. He locked eyes with her again. Her soft but firm grasp surprised him. He let go and crossed his arms over his chest, resuming his seat on the edge of Kessler's desk.

The captain cleared his throat. "The mayor requested the chief bring the FBI in to consult on this case. Last night's murder was the second in just as many weeks. We need all the help we can get to shut this down, and fast."

"Great. We'll get set up down the hall." With that, she turned and walked out, followed by her partner.

Marcus's eyebrows arched in surprise. He'd expected her to push back, not usher him into the middle of their investigation.

Kessler stood. He motioned to the door. "After you, Agent Moretti."

Marcus followed behind the two detectives and couldn't help but notice the way Detective Davis's titanium-colored suit hugged her in all the right spots. Not boxy, like so many of his counterparts, but sharp, professional and feminine. The Bureau office gossip hadn't been wrong. The woman walking into the conference room was smoking hot.

Factoring in his time as a Navy SEAL—when his life, and the lives of his team, depended on reading people—and his stint with the Behavioral Science Unit at the Bureau before being tapped for the black-site task team, Marcus could read her body language like a well-used playbook.

The guarded glances his way and the tiny muscle in her jaw tweaking. Oh, yeah. She was more than slightly pissed at his presence. He got that. Most Feds and local law enforcement had a standing feud. Each thought the others were incompetent, and unable to work a case as efficiently as they could.

He, however, didn't subscribe to that line of thinking. Did she?

Marcus pulled out a chair, settled back and addressed the officers. "You know, contrary to popular belief, Detective Davis, agents at the FBI aren't idiots."

Her eyebrows shot up. A smiled played on her lips, and her eyes sparkled with silent laughter. She sat.

"I don't think FBI agents are idiots, *Special* Agent Moretti."

"No?"

"Nope. As a matter of fact, one of my closest friends is FBI." She picked up a file and tapped its edges against the long conference table. "However, I do know that some federal agents don't like to play nice with the local police. They tend to hold their cards close to their chest while citing the oh-so-familiar, yet still completely infuriating, need-to-know line. And if we want to catch this guy before he kills again, we can't have that. We're on the same team, in here and out in the field. End of story."

Marcus smiled. "I couldn't agree more."

Tilting his chair back, he laced his fingers together and hooked them behind his head. He watched her for a moment, intrigued. Then he leaned forward again. A sharp thud bounced off the walls as the front two legs of his chair reconnected with the floor. "Your close friend is FBI? How'd you two meet?"

There was that guarded look again.

"It's a long story, and a personal one at that." She stared at him, expressionless. "My apologies if this comes off as rude, but I have no intention of sharing it with you."

He chuckled. "Fair enough."

She motioned to the case file in front of him, changing the subject. "So what do you have so far?"

This one's all business. He normally liked that. It was his own mode of operation. But he was trying to build rapport with her. *So much for that idea.* He sighed, then picked up the files. "This is what my teams have pulled."

He slid the matching files across the table. Evelyn and Ryan reached for theirs simultaneously. Marcus took note of how in sync the pair was. Was there something going on outside of the station? He made a mental note to check.

"We have info on the two families—the Garlands and the Middletons. They both lived on Mercer Island on waterfront properties. Both are families of four. Both have two daughters—"

"What are their names?" Evelyn interrupted.

"Pardon?"

"Their names? The children. What are their names?" Marcus could have sworn the piercing blue of her eyes deepened as she stared at him. "These are not just victims, Agent Moretti. Just a few days ago, they were full of life, hope, dreams."

"I understand—"

"I don't think you do. It's easier to distance yourself. But it's tragic when a person whose story just got cut short is objectified to nothing more than the title of 'victim.'"

"Ev..." Ryan murmured in a soft warning.

She ignored him.

"Their names, Agent. You know, Cynthia Garland, age fourteen. Christina Garland, age twelve. Cynthia was caught up in the latest wave of team whoever." Evelyn waved her hands in the air. "Christina loved all things Disney."

She stared straight into Marcus's face and locked eyes with him. Marcus knew she meant it as a challenge, but strangely, he didn't feel it. He only felt drawn to her. His pulse quickened. Definitely not what he was expecting.

"Ashley Middleton, age six. Samantha Middleton, age four. Ashley loved horses and recently won her first blue ribbon at a show. Samantha wanted to be an astronaut and, according to the neighbors, liked to walk around with a flight helmet on."

"Ev." Ryan coughed into his fist.

She stopped short, blinked at Ryan, then glanced down, seeming flustered.

Marcus waited. Watched her closely to see how long it would take her to collect herself. She raised her head less than three seconds later. *Impressive.*

Marcus smiled, put down the file in his hand and calmly picked up where she'd left off. Maybe, just maybe, he'd found the last member of his special task-force team.

"Both husbands worked in high-profile jobs. Scott Garland was the lead engineer of Boeing, and James Middleton was the founding and managing partner of Middleton and Houghes, the largest law firm in Seattle. Neither were home a lot, but they weren't absent fathers by any stretch of the imagination. Both Meagan Garland and Kimberley Middleton were your typical stay-at-home mothers, but also socially engaged and involved in multiple charitable organizations, as well as being active in their children's lives." He leaned back in his chair. "All these individuals are victims of brutal acts of violence. I'm also painfully aware, Detective Davis, that they're all someone's family members, that people loved them and are grieving their untimely and unjust deaths."

He watched her face fall. *What the hell?* Quickly, he mentally skimmed the information he knew about her and remembered reading that she'd lost her family. *Shit.*

He should've known this type of case would hit a tender spot. He'd have questioned her humanity if it didn't.

"We aren't heartless animals," he said in a softer tone. "My deepest apologies if it came across that way."

Ryan's eyes widened and a small smile tugged at the corner of his mouth. The captain's face remained unreadable as he glanced between his star detective and Marcus.

Her next move would determine everything, including whether or not he'd continue to evaluate her for his task-force team. He needed strong team members, individual thinkers willing to toe the line when needed, but confident enough in their own ability to step off that line if justice required it. It wasn't easy, and only a very special person could handle both.

He hoped Evelyn was such a person.

Color kissed the top of her cheeks, making her look all that much more appealing. He'd never met someone like the woman sitting across from him. In the ten minutes that he'd known her, she'd questioned him, put him in his place, treated him as her—

He went rigid. He'd never met a woman who was his equal and acted like it. Sure, there had been plenty with the potential, but none that had stepped up to him like she had.

And he had to admit, he liked that.

Tilting her head slightly, she smiled at him. His stomach tightened again. Apparently oblivious to his inner battle between intellect and libido, she took a deep breath. "My apologies for assuming the worst. You're right. The only animal is the one who is still on the loose."

Marcus breathed a sigh of relief. Impressive. He'd

definitely found his last team member—if she'd only say yes. He caught her eye, nodded, then looked down at the case file in his hands. "Right, then. Shall we nail this asshole?"

CHAPTER SEVEN

SHE'D BEEN RIGHT. After digging through the lives and histories—and more importantly, the autopsy reports—of both families and coming up empty, they now, without any doubt, had ruled out the family annihilator label, though it didn't make this case any simpler. If anything, it made it harder.

The whirling of the ceiling fan stirred the warm, calm air in the bull pen. Evelyn sipped her Starbucks latte and reached for the coroner's reports. Ryan cradled his phone between his ear and shoulder and scowled at something said on the other end. His pen tapped the edge of his desk in rhythmic bursts. Evelyn tuned out her partner and riffled through the reports again, determined to find something—anything—that would give them a break in these cases.

Their killer had taken his time with the Garland family. She shuddered. There were no defensive wounds on the father, because he *couldn't* defend himself. He'd been injected with a paralyzing agent. Evelyn's stomach clenched. Even if he'd wanted to fight to protect his family, he'd been powerless to do so. Unable to move, he'd watched as the madman slashed his youngest daughter's throat, then shot his oldest. Aside from the horrific, psychological last moments as her sister bled out in her arms, the oldest had died a quick death.

But what he'd done to the mother, she couldn't go over that again. Not without her rebellious mind flashing on colored photos of her own mother. Evelyn shook her head to clear the vivid images, scanned through the statement again until she landed on the detailed report of the father. He'd been tortured in ways that would make even the toughest SEAL's skin crawl before having the back of his head off blown off.

She put the report down and rolled her shoulders in small circles. The mayor was breathing down their necks for any forward movement, and despite the detailed and graphic autopsy report, they had nothing to offer.

She sighed and closed her eyes. It had been a long day of canvassing the neighborhoods, researching, looking for connections between the two families and interviewing the next of kin, which had been beyond brutal. If Evelyn had to console one more grieving family member without being able to assure them of anything, she might scream.

Her eyes burned, the hours of reading taking their toll. She and Ryan both needed a reprieve, just a brief one, to recharge and regroup. But they wouldn't get it. Not with the predator still at large and nothing to show for their hours and hours of tedious, eye-crossing work. She rubbed her eyes, then reached for her lukewarm coffee and took a sip. Silently whining wasn't going to fix anything.

Her mind drifted toward the handsome Fed. He'd been called away to a closed-door meeting with the mayor down at city hall. Which was fine with her. Evelyn didn't want to have to rub shoulders with any politician right now, nor did she want to be within five feet of the Fed. His absence was a much-needed relief—every time she was near him, her skin tingled and her heart kicked into overdrive.

She set the mug down, glancing at the report and waiting for the black letters to refocus in front of her.

Ryan slammed down the phone. "This is total bullshit."

Evelyn looked over at her partner. He ran his hand over his chin stubble and pawed through the papers on his desk.

"We've got nothing. No one heard anything. No one saw anything. We've got no fingerprints, no fibers. Nothing." He picked up his cup and threw it across the room. It shattered into a hundred tiny pieces and dark liquid stained the floor where it pooled. "It's like this guy's a ghost."

"He isn't a ghost. We'll get him."

"Yeah? When? When he takes out another family?"

"Ry…" The words caught in her throat. Kessler made his way toward them, fatigue and frustration pulling at the edge of his eyes.

"Captain, everything is under control," she said.

"Actually, Davis, it's not. Both of you, go home." He held up his hand to stop their protests.

Their mouths snapped shut.

"It's not a punishment. It will all be here tomorrow. I need you fresh. Well, as fresh as can be. You've been running hard without so much as a break. The chief and I have noticed. Now, go home." He put his hand on Ryan's shoulder and gave a quick squeeze. "Ryan, tuck your kids into bed and enjoy a night with your wife."

Evelyn stared, dumbfounded at the rare show of emotion from the captain.

"Davis..." He looked at her for a moment, then shrugged. "Do whatever you do and be back in the morning."

Ryan stifled a laugh at the awkward exchange. Evelyn threw him a quick glare, but bit her lip to keep her own laugh from escaping.

"I want you out of here in five minutes. Don't make me tell you again. Get some sleep. I need you here before the sun gets up." Kessler turned and headed back to his office.

Ryan sighed. "He's right—"

"Of course I'm right," Kessler called over his shoulder. "That's why I have this office and you don't, O'Neil."

EVELYN ENTERED THROUGH the front door and went straight to the kitchen. She'd stripped the house to its studs and remodeled it entirely after moving in. Her home was her sanctuary, the kitchen one of her favorite spots.

She pulled out a large glass goblet, reached for the Malbec and glanced at her answering machine. No blinking lights. She sighed. No surprise there. Aside from Kate, Ryan and the kids, her circle of friends was quite small.

The job was her life. Her life, the job...and not many men understood that. She'd tried, had gone on a few dates, but finally gave up after the last man told her that being with a cop wasn't such a turn-on after all.

After she poured the wine, she leaned against the cool granite counter and looked out the window over her kitchen sink. She had a clear view of sweet old Craig Meyer puttering in his kitchen next door. She smiled and took a sip of wine. *Maybe he was baking tonight.* Occasionally, he'd bring her some pumpkin muffins, which she adored. It was the only time she ever saw him. He mostly kept to himself, but hopefully he'd bring some baked goods over soon.

Glass in hand, she reached for the bag of lavender she'd bought before the murders and headed toward the stairs, desperate to relax. She couldn't wait to slip into the hot water and let the strain of the past week seep from her cells. She hadn't realized just how much this case had leached from her until now. Every muscle screamed at her. Her legs felt like lead as she slowly climbed the steps. *Lavender heaven, here I come.*

But she didn't make it to her watery bliss. Instead, the small office directly across from her master suite called to her. She stepped into the room, moved to the desk and sank into the black leather office chair.

Grisly case photos, case files, newspaper clippings and handwritten notes—some colored with age— peppered the wall. Large eight-by-ten, colored photos of her family adorned it as well, a constant reminder of her loss. Sadness rolled over her, its familiar chill lingering as she settled into the chair. She took a sip of wine and swallowed back tears. Stepping into this room always tore at the scabs around her heart, opening the wound deep within her soul. She knew it, yet couldn't break the hold it had over her.

The same drive to bring closure to the families she encountered on an almost daily basis also drove her to this room time and time again to bring closure to her own loss.

Tremors had torn through her the night she'd brought Kate and Ryan up here for the first time. The thought of losing the people closest to her had made her stomach roll. She'd half expected them to drag her straight to the closest psych ward. Who obsessed about their family's murder but a crazy person? Instead, Kate walked up to her, wrapped Evelyn in her arms and whispered, *I get it*. Ryan had solemnly paced in front of the wall and started reading. When he'd turned to look at Evelyn, his face was soft. She'd sagged against the table and nodded, a small quiver of a smile on her lips.

And that was that. They were family.

The three of them didn't talk about it often. They didn't need to. It was Evelyn's battle, which they'd respected. She'd been forever grateful for their silent strength. Kate would occasionally ask her how it was going. The two women didn't need to clarify what *it* was—they knew.

As Evelyn sipped her Malbec and studied all the information that hadn't changed in fifteen years, her cell chirped. Setting the glass down on the desk, she grabbed her phone. A message from Kate illuminated the small screen.

I know what you're doing, E. Go to bed. You can't cover my hot husband's back if you're falling asleep. Love you. K

Evelyn laughed. Her friend knew her too well. She hugged herself as she turned back to the wall. The vise around her heart tightened. Would she ever crack this case? Ever bring closure to the always-present questions surrounding her family's death? Would she ever be able to move on to the next season of life, and all the promise it held: A husband, a family? Or would she be like her adorable, but completely isolated neighbor—alone, tethered to this wall for the rest of eternity?

She pushed herself up from the desk and looked again at the wall as a wave of fatigue washed over her. Sighing, she put down the now-empty goblet. Kate was right. Evelyn needed sleep—desperately. She pulled her shirt over her head, crossed the hardwood floor to her room and wrestled out of her jeans. With zero regard for her nightly routine, she crawled under the extra-heavy down cover and closed her eyes.

Within two heartbeats, Evelyn was asleep.

It seemed like only minutes later that shrill sounds jostled her from a dreamless sleep. For a moment, she lay there in the dark, fully awake, staring at the ceiling fan swirling on its axis. Another scream from her phone jerked her upright. Reaching for the obnoxious device, she cast a peek at the red digits of the alarm clock sitting on her nightstand: 4:00 a.m. *Shit.* This couldn't be good.

"Davis," she said, already rolling out of bed and reaching for her jeans.

"We have another one," Kessler's voice barked through the phone. "I need you down here. Now."

CHAPTER EIGHT

EVELYN'S STOMACH CHURNED. This marked the third case mimicking a family annihilator in as many weeks. One was uncommon, two completely unheard of. Now a third one. *Crap.* If the chief wasn't thinking serial killer before, he certainly was now.

She drove through the black wrought-iron gates of their latest victims' home. Her MINI Cooper's tires crunched. She pulled up next to Ryan's FJ Cruiser, threw her car into Park and took a deep breath. She got out of her vehicle and faced the house. Even darkness couldn't hide its beauty. It wasn't quite grandiose, but it was close. She sighed, then hunched her shoulders against the cold wind and marched toward the curving marble steps that lead to the ornate glass doors. Ryan met her on the top stair.

"You look like hell," she said.

"Right back at'cha, babe."

He handed her a steaming cup of coffee. "Compliments of Kate."

"I love your wife." She inhaled the strong aroma, grateful for her friend.

"Not more than I do." He smirked and jerked his thumb toward the door. "Our babysitter is inside."

"Oh, yeah?" Evelyn raised her eyebrows and looked toward the house. Her heart raced a little at the thought

of seeing Agent Moretti. *Where did that come from?*
"When did he arrive?"

"About ten minutes ago."

"Great. Who's heading up the CSI team?" She didn't
want to think about the handsome Fed any more than
she had to.

"Jake Campbell."

Perfect. He knew his stuff. She raised her cup, sipped
the molten liquid and stepped into the house.

They found Jake and Marcus in the oversize living room to the left of the grand foyer. A white marble
mantel framed the walk-in fireplace that took up half
the far wall. Two purple wingback chairs flanked it. A
matching set mirrored them. Above the mantel sat a
large portrait. The family's faces smiled at them. Twin
frames sat to the right, showcasing the children.

"Jake?"

As Ryan and Evelyn approached, the CSI officer rose
from his place in front of one of the chairs. He barely
looked old enough to drive, and still had the acne to
prove it, but he was one hell of an investigator. If Evelyn had her choice, she'd handpick him to be her CSI
lead every time.

"Hey, guys," Jake said.

"Agent," Evelyn said and nodded in Marcus's direction. *How was it possible for him to look so good even
just after 4:00 a.m.?*

"Evelyn." Marcus smiled, pulling heat from every
cell within her.

"What have we got?" she asked, turning her attention to Jake.

Jake shook his head. "Whoever did this is certifi-
ably nuts."

"You won't get any argument there," Ryan agreed.

Jake motioned for them to circle the chair. Evelyn looked at the man's head, or what was left of it, and her stomach heaved. *Should've grabbed a scone before chugging that coffee.* She swallowed hard. Just like the last male victim, his head had been blown off. And just like the last scene, the wife lay at her husband's feet.

Jake knelt, and they followed suit. With the tip of his pen, he pointed to a crimson stain seeping through the woman's green silk pajama top. "See here. She was shot in the heart, then stabbed repeatedly. Twenty-seven times."

"Holy shit," Ryan said. "You sure?"

"See the lack of blood spray?" Jake pivoted on his toes and pointed to the wall. "If her heart was still beating while the unsub inflicted these wounds, there'd be more blood splatter."

Ryan turned away from the woman's mutilated body. "That's truly disgusting."

Evelyn whistled. "That's a whole lot of rage."

"He's escalating his pace." Marcus looked up, concern in his face.

She rose. "And we've still got nothing."

Evelyn scanned the room. Something was missing. Rather, not something, but someone.

"Where are the children?"

Jake shook his head, eyes downcast. "They're upstairs. Both smothered in their beds."

Evelyn glanced at Ryan, who'd lifted his eyes to meet hers. Their guy was accelerating his pace and switching modes of killing with each new crime scene. That didn't fit the typical serial, unless he was taunting them with the switch-up. Was something pushing him? Was he ramping up to something? Or was he just enjoying the power and needed more to get off? If so, he was more sadistic than she'd originally thought—and that was saying a lot.

EVELYN HAD PUT a rush on the autopsy, but hadn't expected the results so soon. It wasn't the best scenario in the world to be called to after lunch, but death didn't care about convenience. The doc had called. So here they were, headed to the icebox. She hoped Marcus could keep his lunch down. The man hadn't left their side since this morning.

The autopsy room's two glass doors vanished into the recesses of the wall. The cool air slammed into Evelyn as the morgue's distinct smell rode on its chilly gust. Despite years of visiting this place, it still made her insides crawl. Every time she stepped over the threshold, her own loss pounded against the back of her throat. She couldn't prevent her mind from rushing back to the first time she'd been in a morgue. The smell of the chemicals. The bone-chilling cold. The sound of the slab being pulled open, and her father's lifeless body being displayed for her to identify. She shuddered. The sooner they could get this over with, the better.

With his back to them, Dr. Chapman placed a heart onto the scale and stepped away. Green numbers jumped around until landing on a final weight. He scribbled something onto a legal pad sitting on the metal table.

"Hey, Doc," Ryan said.

Chapman turned and smiled grimly at them. He used the back of his hand to push his goggles up his wide nose. Wisps of unruly white hair stuck out from beneath his cap. He reminded Evelyn of Santa Claus—only creepy.

Marcus stepped forward and extended his hand toward Chapman. "Special Agent Marcus Moretti."

Chapman looked at him and scowled, raising hands encased in bloodied gloves. Marcus dropped his hand and quickly stepped back.

"Yes, I'm well aware of who you are, Agent."

Evelyn resisted the urge to laugh. There wasn't enough money in the world to convince her to shake hands with Chapman when he was elbow-deep in an autopsy. Ryan pressed his lips together, no doubt swallowing his own laughter.

"Anything useful?" Evelyn walked along the line of covered bodies, scanned the toe tags and stopped in front of a foot marked "Jason Howard."

Chapman sighed. "I wish I could help you bag this guy, Detective Davis. Truly, I do, but he was very thorough."

"I don't think *thorough* is quite how I'd put it. Psychotic, yes—thorough, no."

"Easy, tiger," Ryan whispered into her ear.

Marcus chuckled, a deep dimple appearing in his cheek. Evelyn flushed.

Apparently she'd pulled the feisty card this morning, yet Ryan was as calm as a Seattle summer day.

Chapman let out a long breath. "I agree with your assessment, Detective. The guy is a psychopath. Anyone who would do such atrocious things to innocent children is a monster in my book. But that doesn't change my findings. He was meticulous. This guy left nothing—no traces, no hair follicles, no blood, no fingerprints—at the scenes, or on any of the victims, for that matter.

My guess is this isn't his first rodeo. But, as you always say, Detective Davis, the dead don't lie."

She nodded. Marcus tilted his head, a question flashing across his face. She ignored it and focused on the doctor's report.

Chapman turned his attention back to the organ on the scale. "I'm confident you'll find this guy—just let them tell you their story."

CHAPTER NINE

THE NEXT MORNING Ryan blew into the bull pen like a volcano ready to explode. His jacket flapped around his shoulder harness as he stormed toward her. Evelyn's eyebrows shot up. She could count on one hand how many times she'd seen him this spun up. Whatever had set him off must've been good…or really bad. From her seat, she held up the cup of coffee she'd poured for him and waited.

He grabbed the mug and shoved the *Seattle Times* under her nose. "Have you seen this horseshit?"

"No, I can't say that I have."

He marched around her desk and dropped into his chair. Thumping down his mug, caramel liquid splashing over the sides, he ripped open the paper and started reading.

"'Dear Editor—you'd be wise to advise the ever-glorious Seattle police force that I will kill one of your precious Seattle families every week until she figures it out. Think fast, sweetheart.'" Ryan slammed down the paper. His eyes grew dark. "Why would they print this shit? And who the hell is *she?*"

"Evelyn is." Marcus walked up, coffee and doughnut in hand, and sat on the corner of her desk. What was with him sitting on people's desks? Didn't his mother teach him manners? But she couldn't ignore how exceptionally sexy he looked in his tailored tan pants, crisp white shirt, leather shoulder harness and red tie. And those curls. Good god, those curls. She shook her head at the rogue thought.

Get it together.

"What?" Evelyn pushed back her chair, creating distance between her and the handsome man invading her personal space. She hadn't meant to be sharp, but the lack of sleep and the heavy weight of this case chipped away at her normally poised, self-controlled demeanor. Its eerie similarity—however vague it might be—to her own family's murder unsettled her. Add the fact that the fifteenth anniversary of her family's death was just a few weeks away, and it was no wonder that she was a bit impatient with Marcus.

But now she was noticing how sexy he looked? *Good grief.*

She glanced up at him. He smiled and her heart took off.

"You can't possibly know that he's referring to me."

His shoulders raised in a slight shrug. "True. I don't. But I'd bet my pension on it."

"Okay, I'll bite," Ryan said. "Talk, Mr. Special Agent Man."

She shifted in her chair, lips curled in a tiny smile. She enjoyed the play between the two men, and Ryan was in rare form today.

Marcus swallowed a chunk of blueberry doughnut before answering. "It's Marcus. No need for formality. We're a team now, right?"

Now *that* she hadn't expected from the Fed. Trying to take over—yes. Putting them all on equal ground—no. She reached for her coffee.

Ryan nodded. "Fair enough. Marcus it is. Start talking."

"It's deductive reasoning, really. Anyone with half a brain and access to a computer can do a search and find the names of the SPD detectives."

Evelyn snapped her fingers. She smiled at Marcus, picking up on his train of thought, and cut in. "Then all they'd have to do is call in an anonymous tip and ask to speak to the lead detective."

"Exactly," Marcus agreed. "The poor shmuck on the other end of the line—no offense—"

"None taken." Ryan shrugged, the fire in his eyes tapering.

"—gives Evelyn's name out, and bam. The bastard knows who the lead detective is."

"Holy shit." Ryan rubbed the back of his neck. "It can't be that easy."

Marcus smirked. "It is. I called in to check my theory myself."

A laugh erupted from Evelyn before she could swallow it. "You didn't."

"I did." Marcus winked and got up from the edge of her desk. He walked to the old desk they'd dug up for him and sat.

"But why?" He looked at Evelyn pointedly. "Why go through all that trouble to single you out?"

Evelyn shuddered. The thought of this psychopath zeroing in on her made her blood run cold. "I have no idea."

LATER THAT AFTERNOON, Evelyn left the station, having volunteered to do the Starbucks run. The moment she disappeared down the stairs, Ryan turned to Marcus. "Why are you really here?"

He looked at Ryan, deliberating how to respond. Someone didn't ask that type of question unless they already knew the answer. It annoyed Marcus, but he got it. He'd done the same thing many times over. So why was Ryan asking? Marcus watched him closely. Unless Ryan was trying to vet him to see how up-front and honest he'd be—which again, Marcus understood perfectly.

"Why do you ask? It should be obvious. The mayor called, the Bureau answered."

"Bullshit." Ryan's eyes flashed. "Evelyn's not the only one with friends in the Bureau. I reached out to my buddy, looked into you, just like you did us. Rumor has it you don't usually consult with local, lowly law enforcement. You head up a special task-force team. One that would benefit from an individual with skills like Evelyn's."

Marcus didn't say anything. He couldn't. Not without lying to this officer's face, which he wouldn't do. He already respected the detective too much. But he couldn't show his cards yet. He wasn't ready.

Evelyn's reputation was nearing legendary status. The Seattle field office had seen to that. Before he'd come along, she'd been approached three times to join the FBI. She'd shot them down each time, which puzzled him. Why would such a promising detective, with her off-the-chart closing rates and primal instincts, scoff at the chance to work with the Bureau? There was more room for her to excel and move up. Plus she'd have bigger cases, larger fish to fry. Most people jumped at that. Yet she'd rejected the offers. Why? From his experience, there was only one reason for someone to turn down such a prestigious offer: something was buried in their past that they didn't want uncovered.

So when the call had come in to join forces with the Seattle PD, he'd grabbed the opportunity to work with her. He could kill two birds with one stone: unravel the mystery that was Evelyn Davis and bring her onto his team, and help the SPD bag the serial killer stalking their city. Win for him, win for them.

Ryan threw him a hard look. "She won't accept whatever offer you have up your sleeve. This is her house. *We* are her family."

"First, I don't think of law enforcement as lowly. I happen to respect what you do. Second, I don't expect Evelyn to accept an offer at this stage in the game. She's turned down my predecessor three times. I'm here to help with this case."

Which was true. Well, okay, partially. Yes, he wanted to help the SPD capture the bastard. But he'd been commissioned to put together a task-force team to track and infiltrate terrorists that the rest of the alphabet agencies didn't even know existed, and he wanted Evelyn on it. He'd hoped that working closely with her on this case would give him better insight into how to convince her to join his team.

Ryan studied Marcus. He sighed and rubbed the back of his neck before smiling, all steeliness in his eyes gone. "I don't believe that pile of shit you're trying to pass off as filet mignon for one second. I think you're trying to poach my partner, but I can't help admiring you."

Marcus sat back, stunned.

"I know, I know. Here I am, busting your balls one minute, then saying I admire you the next. But I do.

I've never see someone go toe-to-toe with Evelyn so calmly and diffuse her without crushing her spirit. It's impressive. You're a good man."

Marcus smiled. "Thanks."

"And, I appreciate the Bureau's deep pockets." Ryan smirked.

EVELYN HAD BEEN phoning neighbors for hours and had come up with nothing. Likewise for Marcus, who was calling local boat rental companies, and Ryan, who was digging through phone records.

She tapped her pencil against the thin sheet of paper and stared at the words until they blurred together. She didn't need to see them to know what they said. Before sharing her thoughts with Ryan and Marcus, she'd worked and reworked her loose profile until her eyes crossed. Their unknown subject, or unsub, was most likely a white male in his late thirties, early forties. He'd be very well-educated and, at first glance, easygoing and approachable.

But Evelyn knew differently.

He most likely had extensive combat training and was volatile and dangerous—extremely dangerous. Given the rage he'd vented at the last scene, she surmised it would only take one wrong look to set him off on a rampage. She shuddered. *God help the person in his line of site when he exploded next.*

Because he would. It was just a matter of time.

Evelyn nursed her cold cup of Starbucks coffee, trying to prolong the goodness while simultaneously studying the profile and the man sitting across the room. His five o'clock shadow graced a strong, olive-toned jawline. Thick, dark eyebrows pinched together as he examined the crime scene photos. Tossing the photos down, Marcus pinched his Roman nose and closed his eyes. He tilted his head back, letting out a long breath as he ran his hands through his curly brown hair.

She hated to admit it—and it actually surprised the hell out of her—but he mesmerized her. Had from the moment she'd laid eyes on him, when he casually stood next to Kessler as if he belonged there, with them. He opened his eyes, looked up and caught her in his steady gaze. Her stomach clenched in response. She got lost in the richness of his chocolate-colored eyes. *Yep, totally mesmerizing.*

The shrill ringing of Ryan's cell phone ripped her back to reality. He answered the call. She could feel her cheeks burning, so she grabbed her mug and headed for the break room.

Now that her beloved Starbucks coffee was gone, Evelyn cradled the steaming mug of second-rate coffee and walked to her desk, careful to keep her eyes *off* Marcus. She threw herself into her chair, then took a sip of the steaming liquid and grimaced.

Ryan hung up and smirked. Evelyn eyeballed him— she knew that smirk. *No way. Not in a million years.* She was way too tired.

"Kate says to come to dinner tonight. She won't take no for an answer."

"Ryan, I—"

"She's already told the kids."

Evelyn groaned and threw a pencil at him. Ryan dodged the flying object and laughed. "You're playing the kid card now? Of all times? Really?"

She shook her head, unable to keep her grin from spreading. She loved those kids and, cliché or not, would take a bullet for them. Kate knew that and didn't think twice about using them to get her best friend over anytime she wanted, nor did she apologize for her blatant manipulation.

Ryan grinned. Deep dimples creased his cheeks and his blue eyes playfully twinkled. "What can I say? Kate wants to see you, Evelyn. Tonight. Seven o'clock."

"Fine. But tell that wife of yours she's shockingly bold."

"Fair enough." He turned in his chair and nodded to Marcus. "You, too, Moretti. Care to join us?"

Evelyn's mouth dropped open. She stared at Ryan.

One of Marcus's eyebrows shot up, but he shrugged. "Sure. Why not?"

"Great. Kate will be thrilled." Ryan turned back to Evelyn and sent her a mischievous glance.

Her heart took off at a mad gallop. She sipped her coffee, desperate to keep cool in front of the two men. She hadn't experienced this butterfly thing since high school. Peering over the mug's edge, she sent her partner a scorching look. *Don't even think about it, Ryan O'Neil.*

"Evelyn, bring Marcus with you, will you?"

"What?" She choked on her coffee. *Jackass.*

She could smell the setup and was going to kill Kate tonight. Ryan returned her glare with a knowing wink. If she wasn't so nervous at the idea, she might've laughed at the way her stomach reacted to the mere thought of being alone with Marcus. *What was she, sixteen again?*

"I'm sure he can drive himself. He's a grown man, for heaven's sake."

"True, but he doesn't know the city like you do," Ryan countered.

Marcus called from across the room, interrupting the showdown between partners. "You know, *he* is sitting right here and can hear you both."

They turned to him.

"And Evelyn's right." Marcus chuckled, shaking his head before going back to the photos in his hand. "*He* can drive himself."

Ryan grinned. "Yes, I'm sure you can. I'm not calling your superior federal-agent driving ability into question here. Even on your worst day, we all know you could outmaneuver any of us with your eyes closed and one hand tied behind you back. No doubt."

Evelyn laughed at her partner's spirited antics. Once again, Ryan managed to lighten a very, very dark day. She grew still. He was treating Marcus like one of them. Which meant—she glanced between the two men— Ryan had vetted Marcus and decided he was one of them. She stole another look at Marcus. Her stomach fluttered and her palms got clammy. Unbelievable. Why did that excite her?

Ryan put his hand over his heart, threw Marcus an exaggerated smile, then grew serious. "Not kidding, parking's hell on our street. The fewer cars, the better."

Ryan gave her puppy eyes that she swore he'd learned from Liam. "Evelyn…"

"Fine."

Bending forward, she ripped a piece of paper from her notebook and scrawled her address. Completely thrown by her response to Marcus, she tried to keep her hand from shaking as she handed him the paper.

"Be there by six-fifteen. That'll give us plenty of time—"

Ryan's muffled laughter interrupted her. She gritted her teeth and willed the blush creeping up her neck to stay put. Ignoring her immature partner, she locked eyes with Marcus. "Plenty of time to navigate the traffic."

Marcus took the paper from her outstretched hand, a sensual glint in his eyes. "I don't bite."

Evelyn's blood hammered in her ears as her pulse took off. *Oh, crap.*

"Somehow, I don't think that's what she's worrying about," Ryan quipped under his breath.

Evelyn ripped her eyes from Marcus and glared at Ryan. She reached for her pen and threw it. Ryan laughed and easily dodged her latest missile.

"You're incorrigible," she said playfully, refusing to meet Marcus's stare. Ryan was right. Traffic was the last thing on her mind. Which, quite frankly, surprised the hell out of her.

CHAPTER TEN

MARCUS LEANED OVER the steering wheel and studied the house numbers as he crept along 7th Avenue West. *Ah, there it is*. House number 2141. He pulled over and sat in silence. The house was a quintessential Craftsman-style nestled on one of the many tree-lined streets in Seattle. Everything about it screamed *home*. Better yet, everything about it screamed Evelyn Davis—or at least what he thought it would, after only being in her presence a week.

He slipped out of his vehicle and locked it. He turned, taking in the view in front of him. Even though the green siding was worn, the stark white of the trim around the large windows and door made it seem cheery. The wooden front porch was large, and a pot-bellied fire pit sat tucked into the far corner.

Nervous tension coiled in his stomach. He hadn't felt this way since picking up his high school prom date, Christina Starklyn. His brothers would give him such grief if they could see him now. *What the hell was his problem?* He was successful, smart and strong. Why was this woman reducing him to a prepubescent idiot? He rubbed a hand over his face, hesitated on the concrete sidewalk in front of her house.

Because Evelyn Davis is anything but ordinary. That's why.

"Get your shit together, Moretti," he said into the twilight evening.

He'd come to Seattle, already impressed by her reputation and jacket—and already knowing she was a stunner from the picture in her file. But the floor had caved under him when he'd met the *real* Evelyn Davis. She was brutally savvy and handled herself like a pro under pressure. And she was sexy as hell. He'd known he was in trouble from their first meeting. Every time she walked into the same room, his whole body came alive. He shook his head and pushed back any idea of why that might be.

He climbed the steps, then pressed the doorbell. He waited, the tension coiling.

Evelyn opened the door and smiled at him. His pulse jumped. Dark jeans hugged her mile-long legs, and a black V-neck shirt playfully peeked out from under the lightweight leather bomber jacket she wore.

Even in her casual attire, she was beautiful.

She stepped out onto the porch and pulled the door closed behind her. They stood face-to-face for a moment. He was tall and normally peered down at most women who stood this close to him, but she only had to angle her head slightly to look him in the eye. He smiled at her and stepped back. It took everything in him to keep his jaw from going slack.

Evelyn gave him an odd look as she stepped around him and pulled out her keys. He uttered a short laugh, and her brows furrowed in a silent question.

"I'll drive." He held up his keys.

A small smile formed on her lips. "All-righty, then."

He motioned for her to go in front of him, then followed her down the sidewalk, his heart hammering.

Keep your pants on. Sexy or not, she's off-limits, at least for now.

He opened the car door for her. She slid into the vehicle, glanced at him and smiled her thanks, then quickly looked away. *What are you thinking?* He circled to his side of the vehicle. The woman sitting in his car followed his movement and had gotten deep into his mind, whether she meant to or not.

He paused before entering the car. Someone was watching. He could feel it. The cold sensation that'd saved him more than once crept up his neck, whispering a silent warning. He checked around. The street was quiet, empty. Strange. He sat and pulled the door closed, then eyed her and smiled. "Shall we?"

THE CURTAIN NEXT door fluttered softly back to its rightful place. He kicked the end table and sent it flying across the room. Who was that man with Evelyn? Where did he come from? And why the hell did she look at him like that? How dare she seem happy...*be* happy? She didn't deserve it. Not when she had taken so much from him. Taken everything from him. He willed himself to breathe deeply, to calm the volcano that burned inside him incessantly. Isn't that what he'd learned just south of the border? To control his rage, channel it into something greater, something deeper. He was intelligent enough to know that you only act after you've controlled the power. So he'd wait. Then act.

And he would. He would take it all from her. Eventually. The image of her begging him to kill her flashed in his mind, pacifying him. Yes. He would take it all from her. But first, he'd enjoyed toying with her. He had more planned for her before this was all over. Watching her fret about the lack of movement in their case—*his* case—sent a thrill down his spine.

He marched to the old kitchen table, sank into the wooden chair and cradled his head. The volcano within him spewed acidic thoughts through his mind, consuming him again with a barely controllable rage. How could she be paying attention to that man? How could she look so happy when she should be paying attention to *him?* She was his. He owned her.

He took a swig of the stale, cheap beer and slammed the bottle down. He clenched his fists. The constant fury burned his throat. The old man huddled in the corner cried out, then shrank back.

"Don't make me hurt you, old man," he said, glaring.

He stood, walked to the kitchen window and peered out. He picked a knife from the knife block on the counter and ran his finger over the dull blade. He knew exactly how to draw her attention back to where it should be—on him.

CHAPTER ELEVEN

EVELYN AND KATE stood on the patio, enjoying the crisp autumn air. Both kids were down for the night. As the women sat by the roaring fireplace after dinner, Liam had fallen asleep in Evelyn's arms. Kissing him on the forehead before placing him in his crib felt like kissing an angel. She smiled. The little man was an inferno. Her shirt was still slightly damp from holding his body against hers—funny how something so trivial could be so sweet. In silence, the two friends watched the illuminated Seattle skyline. A ferry crossed Puget Sound, its lights twinkling on the inky ocean water. Kate sipped her Riesling and nudged Evelyn with her hip.

"Yes?" Evelyn lifted her glass and savored the Malbec as it rolled over her tongue and down her throat.

Kate looked over her shoulder, pierced Evelyn with her eyes. "So, what's going on with you two?"

"What? With Marcus?" Horrified at her transparency, Evelyn glanced away from Kate. Her cheeks burned. "Nothing. Why?"

"Nothing?" Kate snorted, then rolled her eyes. She tucked a strand of her fire-red hair behind her ear. "Oh, please. I see the way you look at each other."

"Stop. Nothing is going on. Besides, you and I both know there's a professional line that can't be crossed. If I even wanted to cross it. Which I'm not saying I do."

Good grief. She was rambling like a little kid caught with her hand in the candy jar. What was her problem? "I don't."

"Why?"

The familiar, deep ache rose, trying to smother Evelyn. She fingered the stem of her glass. She didn't want to speak the words that bubbled up into her throat, didn't want to validate them by giving them a voice.

"Ev, wh—"

"I'm stuck in this dark, shattered place. There's no room for anyone else. I'm broken, Kate." Tears stung her eyes as she whispered the bitter words that haunted her.

"Oh, sweets. No, you aren't."

Evelyn wiped her eyes with the back of her hand, then bit her lip to keep the tears at bay. "But I am. It's made me a great detective, but—"

"A kick-ass detective."

Even Kate's joking couldn't alleviate the sorrow seeping from Evelyn's soul.

"But I subconsciously sabotage any relationship before it even has the chance to work."

"I wouldn't call what you had with Chad or Todd a relationship."

Despite the dull ache in her chest, Evelyn managed a feeble laugh. "True."

"Okay, so what's this really about, then?"

"I'm stuck. I can't move past what happened to my family. It's like an avalanche of heartache and scorching pain every second of every day. I can't get away from it."

"Oh, Ev—"

"I know they'd want me to move on. I *want* to. I want more than this life I live now." She threw Kate a teary smile. "I want what you and Ry have, including the little munchkins."

Kate grinned, grabbed Evelyn's hand and entwined their fingers together.

Evelyn leaned her head against Kate's and breathed in her soft, warm vanilla scent.

"I can't start a family with someone, no matter how amazing that person may be, until I know what happened to my own. Until I close that case—until it's done—there will always be this ugly eclipse over my life, this constant ache in my heart." She took a deep breath to steady her emotions. "I can't get away from the pain. I do a great job of managing the emotions. I gather strength from them. But it's always there."

Kate let go of Evelyn's hand, threw an arm around her shoulder and pulled her best friend close.

"And Marcus?" Kate asked.

Evelyn's laugh was sad. "Even if he were interested—"

"You'd have to be blind and an idiot not to see that."

Evelyn shrugged. "Regardless of whether or not he is, I can't ask Marcus, or anyone for that matter, to walk this road with me. It's bumpy, messy and ridiculously emotional. I can't give myself to someone when I know I wouldn't be giving all of myself. I'm still a shadow of who I could be, and that's not fair."

"But isn't that *his* choice?" Kate asked softly.

"Maybe…" Evelyn grew quiet again.

They stood that way for a long time.

Finally Kate broke the silence. "But he's really, *really* sexy."

Evelyn rolled her eyes, balanced her empty glass on the smooth rail and refused to look at her friend. "He's off-limits, Kate."

"Oh, whatever. He's totally your type."

Evelyn chuckled. Her forehead muscles scrunched together. "My type?"

"Yes. Intelligent, tall, stubborn, sexy as hell—your type. And I think you're in deeper trouble than you think you are." Kate turned and leaned against the railing.

Evelyn glanced into the living room and watched the two men talk. Her heart fluttered as she caught Marcus sneaking a peek at her.

"Yep." Kate giggled, nudging Evelyn with her hip again. "So much trouble."

She's impossible. Evelyn turned her attention back to the living room. Ryan and Marcus yakked it up, laughing as they exchanged stories about who knew what. Marcus casually raised his eyes and caught her gaze, then lifted his Guinness toward her and smiled. Her pulse thumped against her ears in response to the simple gesture. *Maybe it was his choice.* Her heart skipped a beat at the mere possibility. *Oh, crap. She was in trouble.*

RYAN STOOD. "SHALL we join the ladies?"

Marcus rubbed the back of his neck and looked sheepish. "That obvious?"

"That obvious. Seeing you and Evelyn dance around each other all night has been hilarious to watch, but it's making me want to gag, man. I've had enough."

"It can't be a good idea," Marcus mumbled. He set his empty bottle on the coffee table and rose.

"Never is." Ryan laughed, slapping Marcus on the shoulder. "Let's go."

Marcus looked at Ryan. "Seriously, O'Neil, your thoughts?"

Ryan sighed and sat back down. He scratched his chin.

"What do I think? I've never seen her eyes light up the way they do when you walk in. Ever. She tries to hide it, but I'm her partner and I can read her. Her reaction to you speaks volumes to me. I think she deserves to be happy more than anyone I've ever known. You can't choose who makes you happy. They either do or don't." He shrugged, glanced toward Kate and smiled. "It's pretty simple in my book. So, if you continue to make her eyes light up, if you can make her happy, I'd say go for it. You're two professional, levelheaded adults who know how to handle themselves."

Marcus eyes widened. He hadn't expected Ryan to go there. But in one statement he'd all but given Marcus permission to date his partner, and that made him nervous—and excited. He cleared his throat and reached for his beer.

"That being said, Evelyn Davis is intelligent, stubborn and one of the sexiest women you'll ever meet. And I know she can take care of herself." Ryan leaned forward. "But I swear, if you hurt her, Mr. Special Agent Man, in any way, I'll personally track you down, rip off your balls and shove them down your throat."

Marcus's head snapped back at Ryan's ferocious words. He couldn't remember the last time anyone had threatened him like that. Yet somehow it impressed him.

"I'd never—"

"She'd kill me if she knew I'd said any of this, but she's not your typical woman. She wears a hard shell and takes all the male chauvinistic bullshit in stride."

Ryan chuckled, then snorted. "More than once, she's had to stop *me* from reacting to the shit. But underneath that strong facade is a soft, gentle, tender woman with an incredible life story to tell."

"Care to enlighten me?"

"No can do." Ryan shook his head and held up his hands in mock surrender. "That's her story to tell, if she ever does. But I can tell you this. You haven't even begun to scratch the surface."

Marcus smiled and looked out toward the two women. Kate said something and Evelyn laughed, her face soft. She was extraordinary. But Ryan didn't need to tell him that. Marcus had known Evelyn was incredible the moment he'd laid eyes on her, and he hadn't been able to get her out of his mind ever since.

Ryan slapped Marcus on the back and stood once more. "I say go for it, man."

He winked, then walked toward the patio. He slid the heavy glass door open, stepped out into the cool Seattle air and joined the women. Marcus swallowed. His heart thumped as Evelyn laughed at something Ryan said. *Her story, huh?* There was so much about that woman, so much that he wanted to know, to discover. He couldn't deny that something about Evelyn Davis drew him to her. He got up.

The real question now was, would she let him in?

CHAPTER TWELVE

THE AIR WAS ELECTRIC. This man sitting next to her, staring out the window, drove Evelyn crazy. Marcus was a walking puzzle, and she wasn't sure if she'd ever figure him out. Evelyn wanted to engage him in conversation, just so she could hear him talk, but couldn't find the right words. How could she ask someone she'd just met to open up, share his innermost secrets? And could she ask him to be honest, when she wouldn't—couldn't—return the favor? She silently cursed.

She knew one thing: he'd definitely gotten under her skin, made her squirm.

He turned onto her quiet street and pulled up outside her home. He parked the car, turned off the engine and twisted to face her. "Thanks for the invite tonight. That's exactly what I needed."

"It was all Kate's idea." Evelyn looked up at him and forgot to breathe. She had to clear her throat to get her words to form. "I swear she has this sixth sense, always knowing exactly what we need. She's spot-on, every time. It's actually pretty fascinating."

"Well, I appreciate you sharing your family. That little Liam's a total stud."

He unbuckled his seat belt and pushed opened the car door.

Evelyn laughed in agreement, but it quickly died

in her throat. He called them *family*. She glanced at him, gut twisting. *Did he know about her family? Had Ryan said something to him tonight? No. He wouldn't... would he?*

Marcus came around the car to open her door. Swallowing the panic and fear that seized her, she stared up at him, trying to read his eyes. Nothing but warmth. No pity. No veiled awkwardness. He held out his hand. She hesitantly reached toward him. He pulled her out of the car, then placed his palm on the small of her back as he ushered her up the sidewalk. The heat of his touch made her heart race and her stomach flutter. *Did he know?* If he knew, he didn't seem to care—maybe he'd already decided that he could handle her past and all that came with it. Her head spun.

"This isn't a good idea." She shrank away from him. Disappointment crushed her as his warm touch faded. Heat rushed to her face, and astonishment flooded her. *Why should she care if he was touching her or not?* But she did.

"What isn't?" He stopped and looked at her. A tender smile twitched on his lips.

She motioned with her hands. "This. Us. Don't get me wrong. You're great. And, yes, okay, clearly you're smoking hot. Any woman could see that."

She climbed the steps.

"You think I'm sexy?" He followed close behind her.

Evelyn glanced over her shoulder and glared at him. "I'm serious here—"

"As am I." Laughter twinkled in his eyes.

She focused her attention on her purse and fumbled for her keys. "There's a professional line that shouldn't be crossed. Even if there wasn't, my life is… complicated."

Marcus leaned against the porch railing. "I can handle complicated."

She forgot about her keys. Tears pooled in her eyes. "You haven't even begun to see complicated. My life brings complicated to a whole new level, one that you truly don't want to encounter."

"Shouldn't that be my decision?"

Startled, she just stared at him, mouth slightly open. *What?* Had Kate and Ryan said something to this man? She snapped her mouth shut and shook her head.

"Trust me, Marcus. It's better to not even start," she whispered. Grief wrapped itself around her heart and squeezed.

He moved toward her.

She stepped back, flustered by his presence, until she hit the door.

"That is…" She cleared her throat. "If there wasn't a professional line that shouldn't be crossed."

"Yes, you've already pointed that out."

Evelyn felt the warmth radiate from his body. She groped for the doorknob. "Well, because there—"

He leaned in and gently kissed her. The light, feathery touch of his lips on hers sent her heart stampeding and chills down her spine.

She froze for a moment, enjoying the sensation briefly before pulling away. "What the hell was that? Did you not just hear anything I said?"

"I did. It's my decision." He smiled at her. "And I've decided. Just getting a sample."

Her irritation flamed out just as quickly as it had flared. She couldn't help the curving of her lips. He'd decided, had he? "You're impossible. You'll be gone after this case is closed."

"I'm not going anywhere. You fascinate me. You're beautiful, strong, feisty and pretty amazing. So, complicated or not, I have every intention of getting to know you. All of you." He gently took her hand, flipped it and pressed his lips to her palm.

She stared, wide-eyed and slightly breathless, then pulled her hand from his and fumbled once again for her keys. Finally, she unlocked the door and pushed it open. Stepping over the threshold, she stopped and studied him. "You aren't one to give up, are you?"

"No."

"Good. Because we have a killer to catch. See you tomorrow." A brief smile spread across her features as she shut and locked the door.

She slumped against the door. A nervous laugh escaped lips that still tingled from the touch of his mouth on hers.

LAUGHING, MARCUS WALKED to his car and got in. He'd known from the moment he set eyes on Evelyn that she was different. He'd seen past the cool persona to the soft, gentle woman beneath. She cared for victims' families as if they were her own. He'd never seen someone so quickly and effectively empathize with a grieving loved one. She felt what they did and drew from it. It was mesmerizing to watch.

Their job was tedious and dark. He'd seen too many agents burn out, or—worse—grow cold. Clearly gripped by this case, he'd witnessed a depth of emotion the past few days from Detective Davis. And from what he could tell, it wasn't a bad thing, but a bridled strength. He'd often seen her pull from whatever it was that she felt in the moment to focus their investigation. Channeling emotions like that was a true skill. He knew from experience that it couldn't be taught: you either had it, or you didn't.

Evelyn Davis had it in spades.

The engine purred under him as he smiled into the darkness. Maybe something good would come out of this case after all.

CHAPTER THIRTEEN

FOR THE FIRST time in a very long time, Evelyn woke up and thought about something other than her family. She watched the ceiling fan as it made its dutiful turns. Her mind was on one thing: Marcus. The white sheers covering her window danced and billowed as cool autumn air blew into her room. She stretched, rolled out of bed and reached for her phone. No waiting messages, and still plenty of time before she needed to be in. The rich, smooth aroma of her morning coffee fix drifted up from the kitchen, beckoning to her. Silently thanking Kate for talking her into upgrading her old coffeepot to an automatic one, she headed out of her bedroom and, without hesitation, down the stairs to answer its call.

Steaming coffee in hand, she stood in the middle of her office and studied the wall, trying to look at it with fresh eyes. Nothing. She pulled up the desk chair, sat and tucked one leg underneath her. With one foot, she slowly swiveled the chair to the right, then to the left. She sipped the molten brew and stared at the old newspaper clippings, faded crime scene photos and multi-colored Post-it notes. Still nothing. Frustration ripped through her. Nothing had changed since the last time she sat here. She sighed. *Would it ever?*

Her phone chirped, reminding her of the time. She got up, set her mug on the desk and walked over to the photo of her sister. She kissed her fingers, then pressed them against the smiling face. "I'll figure it out, Olivia. I promise."

SHOWERED AND WITH her second cup of coffee in hand, Evelyn opened her front door and walked out into the brisk morning. Her boot crunched on something. She looked down, spied the yellow manila envelope and stepped back. Her blood froze. Her heart jumped so far up her throat she almost choked.

"Think fast, Evelyn" was scrawled across the front in red pen.

Without touching the package, she pressed herself into the cover of her door frame and scanned the street. She'd memorized her neighbors' cars and their license plates when she moved in and had committed their names and faces to memory. Nothing seemed out of place. No one was even out this early in the morning. So where had this package come from?

Her training kicked in. The galloping within her chest slowed to a mere trot.

Rummaging through her bag, she grabbed the latex gloves she always carried with her, yanked them on and squatted down. Careful to keep her line of sight open and her body shielded as best as possible, Evelyn reached for the package. Her thumb and pointer finger clamped down on one corner as she stood and retreated into her home. The envelope was light. It felt almost empty. She kicked the door shut with one foot, turned the bolt with her free hand and held the limp envelope at arm's length, as if it might bite her.

She grabbed her phone from her pocket and typed a quick text to Ryan and Marcus. *I'll be late. Be ready when I get there.* The message was cryptic, and Ryan would be pissed at her for not explaining. If she tried, both men would tell her not to open it but to come straight in. *Yeah, right.* That clearly wasn't happening. She shoved her phone into her pocket.

Ignoring her phone's angry vibrations, Evelyn walked to the kitchen. She placed the envelope on the counter, stepped back and chewed on her lip. Hands on her hips, she debated her next move. It was addressed to her, but should she open it? Probably not. She leaned against the counter, crossed her arms and glared at the package. If either Ryan or Marcus had received something like this, had opened it at home and not in the safety of the bull pen, she'd be livid. But…that still left the question: Was *she* going to open it?

Most likely. Better to apologize than ask for permission, right?

Besides, something in the pit of her stomach told her she didn't want to open this around anyone else.

She pulled a small paring knife out of a drawer and picked up the envelope. With a deep breath, she slid the point into the corner and tugged. She dumped the contents onto the counter. Christina and Cynthia Gardner's lifeless eyes gaped up at her. More detailed, colored photos of all the crime scenes from the case stared at her. Horror raced through her and chills snaked up her spine. A picture of Ashley Middleton's body made her stomach roll. And a Post-it was stuck on a photo of Sam Middleton.

Three scrawling words screamed up at her. "Tick tock, sweetheart."

She shoved the photos in the package and threw it into her purse. Keys in hand, she hit one on her speed dial, then cradled the phone between her ear and shoulder. She checked out her window to ensure the delivery person wasn't lurking around her house. No sign of anyone. She grabbed her things, locked her house and went out to her car.

Ryan answered on the second ring. "What the hell kind of text was that? And where the hell are you?"

As she got in her car, she ignored his questions and got straight to the point. "I received a little present this morning."

"A present? From who? I'm not following."

"From our serial killer. He—" She turned the key, then threw her car into Reverse.

"What the fuck, Evelyn?" Ryan yelled into the phone.

She held it away from her ear as she glanced over her shoulder and backed out of the driveway. "I'm on my way now. Maybe we'll get lucky and we can finally pull a print. Be there in a few."

HE LET THE curtain fall from his fingers and set the camera down. He'd captured the moment perfectly. It would be a nice addition. He wished he could have delivered the package himself. Seen her eyes widen in panic. Watch her nostrils flare as dread washed over her perfectly porcelain face, knowing he'd bested her. That he'd won. But no. Now wasn't the right time. He still had plans for her.

But soon. Very soon.

His fingers twitched in anticipation. The constant fury bubbled up, burning away the calm facade and blurring his vision, choking him. He blinked hard. Focused on his breathing. Channeled the anguish, the fury, to its rightful place.

Her.

He peered out the window again, watched her tail-lights disappear and laughed. He'd take from her. All of her. And at precisely the right moment...he'd make her scream.

CHAPTER FOURTEEN

EVELYN TOOK THE stairs two at a time. After she rounded the last flight, she halted. Both men flanked the door at the top stair, arms crossed, eyes stormy. What? Had the front desk called up when she arrived? She glanced between Ryan and Marcus. Oh, crap, she was toast. Without a word, she reached into her bag and handed the envelope to Marcus. She pushed past him, then marched by Ryan and plopped down in her desk chair. Slowly, she turned and looked at them.

"Evelyn, are you out of your mind? What the hell were you thinking?" Ryan asked, his voice cold as steel. "You should've called this in, left it where you found it, not brought it into your car. Are you insane?"

Dumbfounded, she sat there. *Insane?* Of course she wasn't insane. What was Ryan's problem? Good grief, this was ridiculous. She was an adult. She'd made a decision—end of discussion. Granted, it wasn't the best decision she'd made in a while. But still. She wasn't about to admit that now. Not in front of both men. And certainly not with them glaring at her.

"If I tried to pull this shit, you'd have my bal—"

"It was addressed to me," she said, instantly wishing she'd kept her mouth shut and just endured the tongue-lashing. It was a ludicrous excuse, but she couldn't think of anything else.

Marcus's eyebrows shot up and a smile tweaked his lips. Ryan stared at her as if she'd grown another head.

"It was addressed…" Ryan made a little choking sound in his throat, put his hands on her desk and leaned toward her. "Are. You. Fucking. Serious? You're seriously going to give me that bullshit? What if there was something other than photos in your little present? A bomb. Anthrax. You'd have my balls in a vise if the tables were turned and I'd pulled this shit on you."

She calmly watched her partner. "Are you finished?"

His eyes flashed, the blue turning the color of cool steel. "Oh…I'm just getting started, sweet cheeks."

Evelyn bit her lip to keep the grin from escaping. Despite the hellish nightmare this day was turning into, the fire in Ryan's eyes and that nickname slip made her want to laugh.

"Ry—"

He held up his hand. "He could've killed you. He just made this personal."

It's always personal. At least for her. She didn't doubt that both men glowering at her right now continued to keep the boundary between duty and personal drawn. It was something that had been beaten into them from day one in the academy. And it made sense, really. It protected your sanity. But she'd made a conscious decision as she'd been sworn in to never draw that line. Right or wrong, it didn't matter to her: every murder was personal.

"Okay, first, he didn't kill me, Ryan. I'm here. Alive. All is well." Evelyn lowered her voice as she eyeballed her partner, who was still leaning on his hands—in her personal space.

She put her hand on his shoulder and gently pushed him away. He stood and crossed his arms.

"And fine, yes, he made it personal. But instead of busting my balls—"

Marcus chuckled, which threw her off guard. She cast him a dirty look. He put his hand over his mouth, looking apologetic. She turned her attention back to Ryan, who was still glowering.

"The real question is, why? I don't have any connection with any of the victims. He could've sent this to any one of us."

"Yes, but he sent it to you," Marcus said. "And after he sent that little letter to the editor. We have to assume that the unsub has something, some sort of personal vendetta, against you, or he wouldn't have sent *you* the crime scene photos."

"Maybe he has issues with women in authority?" Ryan suggested, finally relaxing.

Evelyn shook her head. "No. That doesn't make sense. If that were his trigger, then his targets would be just that—women in authority. Not family units where the women are stay-at-home moms. And he would torture them, but he doesn't. He targets and tortures the husband."

Marcus's eyes grew dark with worry. "He's trying to taunt you, get your attention."

"Well, he definitely did that. But I'm not fazed." Deep down she was. This whole string of murders felt familiar. Personal. The fact that she hadn't figured out why by now ate her from the inside out. She'd survived to help bring justice to victims like these families, had she not? If not for that one reason, then why?

She pinched the bridge of her nose and shook the

dark thoughts out of her mind. She needed to get out of her head and into the psycho's to find him.

But first, she needed to diffuse the ticking bomb in front of her. Ryan was still clearly agitated. Worry shone brightly in Marcus's eyes.

"Okay. Fine. Yes. Opening that package was not the smartest move. But I did it. Now it's over. I'm sorry. Let's move on."

"No more heroic shit," Ryan said.

Marcus nodded.

"Promise." She smiled at the men, grateful to finally be out of the spotlight. It made her uncomfortable to be in the hot seat with either of them. She stood, reached over and picked up the photos Ryan had tossed on his desk by the edges. "Now. We need to get these to the lab, have them run for prints. Maybe he got sloppy and left one."

"You don't think he did, though, do you?" Marcus asked.

"Honestly, no. He's smart, patient. But it's a shot. And right now, we need anything we can get. I hate feeling that he's one step ahead of us."

Ryan got up and paced. Evelyn sighed. She thought she'd successfully put out that fire. Apparently not. Crap.

"Why not send them to the station?" The heat in Ryan's words rose as he aired the question. "Why to your home?"

He turned suddenly. She saw the look of horror flicker across his face.

She held her breath. *Don't, Ryan.* She knew his mind had locked onto the same question she'd landed on as she'd dumped the package's contents on her counter.

"Evelyn, how did he get your home address in the first place? It's not listed."

Crap.

Marcus's head snapped up. "Excuse me?"

He glanced from Ryan to Evelyn, then back to Ryan, irritation and concern flashing in his eyes.

"Yeah, that's right. Her address is *unlisted.*"

"Evelyn." Marcus spoke with such authority she had no choice but to listen. Not that she could've done anything else but sit captivated by him. "That complicates things—a lot. We have to consider that he's following you. Which means—"

She didn't want to hear Marcus say it, but she'd already suspected what he was about to say. She'd had that exact thought the moment the photos dropped onto her counter. The killer was watching her, had followed her to her home. The idea terrified her—and royally pissed her off. She hadn't let the last psychopath rule her every waking minute—at least, that's what she told herself on a regular basis—so she sure as hell wouldn't let *this* one scare her now.

"Consider?" Ryan asked in disgust. "I think that's pretty blatant here. Don't you? The psycho left her that little package. On. Her. Doorstep. We need to move her—"

"Absolutely not," Evelyn said. She'd let the two men stand around being all cavemanlike long enough. Yes, she was a woman. She had breasts and a pretty face that made men want to protect her. She got that. But she wasn't weak, scared or sitting in a corner crying because some prick had left her an early morning package.

She was a seasoned, sought-after homicide detective. One who didn't easily back down from a threat. And she wasn't going to back down from this one—she was going to meet it head-on. "I'm *not* going to let some psycho dictate my life. It's not happening. End of story."

"Then we get a protective detail on you," Ryan said.

"That's not—"

"Don't give me that shit, Evelyn. You want to be stubborn, fine. But it's necessary, and you know it." Ryan looked at Marcus for support.

From Marcus's perch on the edge of his desk, he nodded his head. "I agree with him."

"Fine." She threw up her hands, aggravated at being railroaded by both of them. "Plainclothes. The last thing I need is my quiet, sweet neighborhood up in arms because some cop cruiser's permanently parked outside my home."

She glared at Ryan. *What was with him today?* "Does that work for you, dear knight in shining armor?"

"For the time being."

"Good. Now that that's settled—"

The fire in Ryan's eyes vanished. In its place, genuine concern brimmed.

"I'm only trying to keep you safe," he said. "Kate would kill me if something happened to you."

A lump unexpectedly lodged in her throat.

Evelyn swallowed the tears and smiled at Ryan—her partner and her brother. "I know, Ry. As much as I fight you when you go all Neanderthal on me—"

"I did not."

Her eyebrows arched.

"Okay." He rubbed the back of his neck and looked down. "Maybe a little."

"A lot, but deep down, I appreciate it. Promise."

"I know you do." He laughed heartily.

And just like that, Ryan and Evelyn were once again in sync.

"Now can we please get back to business?" She pointed at the two men. "If you two are so concerned with my well-being, then stop playing caveman and let's figure out why this sicko is fixated on me."

As the three of them went back to work Evelyn glanced up at the ancient clock and shuddered. They were still playing catch-up to this guy, and they all knew it. With each second that passed, he continued to out-maneuver them, left them one step behind.

They were losing ground, and fast.

CHAPTER FIFTEEN

SEVEN HOURS OF interviewing witnesses and scrubbing call logs had resulted in nothing. Again. There were no prints, no fibers and nothing out of place at the crime scenes. There were no witnesses. All the properties were lakefront, so the unsub must've come in and out by boat. But even searching boat rentals resulted in a big fat goose egg.

The bastard was smart.

And Lady Luck was not on their side for this one.

At her insistence, the guys made an early evening run to the Starbucks down the street for a caffeine boost. She was glad they'd taken the break. But she'd secretly needed space from the two men after their caveman duet earlier. She'd told Ryan she appreciated his concern, and she did. Still, when he'd suggested they move her to a safe house, she'd wanted to smack him. But only for a brief moment. Then reason roared in, reminded her that if the tables were turned and some psycho had left crime scene photos at Ryan's house, there wouldn't have even been a discussion. She'd move them to a safe house immediately. End of story.

Quiet chatter between the other detectives flitted through the air. The captain had holed himself up in his office and was currently bent over a pile of reports. She grimaced. The mayor was pressuring them for something—anything—that would seem like forward motion, but Kessler took the brunt of it.

Evelyn picked up her phone, irritated at the lack of movement, and called down to the lab. "You got good news for me, McCarthy?"

"I wish I did, but no. I've got nothing—no prints, no fibers. The photos were printed on a home printer with normal photo paper. You could get the stuff anywhere—Target, Walmart, the local Walgreen's."

"Which narrows our suspect list down to, oh, a few million people in the Seattle area." She rubbed her throbbing forehead. Where was that caffeine?

"Sorry I couldn't be more help, Detective."

"That's okay, not your fault." She blew out a breath in frustration. "Thanks for rushing them for me."

"Anytime, Detective Davis."

She slammed down her phone, closed her eyes and tilted her head to the left, then to the right, trying to erase the strain pulling at her neck. How was this guy still ahead of them? He couldn't be that good, could he? She shook her head at the thought. No. She knew how to get into a killer's mind. She might need to traverse a few hypothetical paths before she landed on the one that led her home, but she always found a way.

The elevator's chime announced the arrival of her latte. She looked up, then silently swore. Instead of her much-needed caffeine fix, Josh Sanderson stepped out and made a beeline toward her. Great. She hadn't thought her day could get any worse. At the sight of the short arrogant man charging her way, she knew she'd been wrong.

"Detective Sanderson, what can I do for you?" The only thing she wanted to do for him was punch the down button for the elevator and escort him out of her *house*. That clearly not being an option, she went with being polite.

He sat on the edge of her desk, flipped his jacket open and stared down at her. His familiar gesture made her bristle. Funny how the same movement from Ryan or Marcus felt comfortable. Not so with Sanderson. The urge to smack him, then sanitize her desk, flooded her.

"Off."

His jaw jumped at her stern order. He obediently stood, then straightened his shoulders.

"Why are you here?"

"Had to drop something off to Jones downstairs and just thought I'd check in to see how the investigation's going."

She pursed her lips, felt a sarcastic quip bubble up within her and tried to swallow it. *Jones, her ass*.

"You came all this way to check in. There *is* this thing called a phone, Sanderson." Her voice took on a contemptuous tone.

"The investigation, Davis…"

She sighed. "It's going. Slowly. But we're doing all we can to track this guy. When something breaks, believe me, we'll let you know."

"Somehow I doubt that. I should've been the lead on this. Our guys would already—"

"Oh, give it a rest." Evelyn was too tired to deal with the whining complaints of this egotistical idiot. "The chief asked for us. Get over yourself."

A detective across the room chuckled. Sanderson's face reddened and his eyes narrowed. "I know all about your history."

"Excuse me?"

The elevator chimed again. Marcus and Ryan walked out. Ryan spotted Sanderson and cast an apprehensive glance at Evelyn. Her partner moved quickly to his desk and put down the coffees. Evelyn noticed the sudden shift in Ryan's demeanor but ignored him, casting a glance at Marcus. He stared back at her, curiosity and concern shining brightly in his face. She knew she looked like a small animal backed into a corner. Anger and panic radiated off her. *Damn you, Sanderson.* She turned back to the detective sneering down at her.

Ryan came around his desk and stepped up to Sanderson. "Is there a problem here?"

Marcus stood by Evelyn's side and leaned close. "You okay? You look coiled, ready to spring."

She nodded. The tension in her shoulders squeezed.

Sanderson ignored both men towering over him. "I think there hasn't been a breakthrough on this case because you can't see beyond your own nose. Someone with *your* background shouldn't be leading this case."

"You better stop while you're ahead." The words came out of her mouth low and menacing.

Panic and rage tightened her throat as she commanded herself to breathe. *How did he find out?* It didn't matter. She couldn't let the rest of her squad know about her family. It would undermine her ability to do her job and cast her in another light. No longer would she be Detective Evelyn Davis, the best profiler and closer the department had seen for over twenty years. She'd be Evelyn Davis, the victim. She couldn't let that happen. Suddenly she felt exposed, and for the first time in fifteen years, vulnerable.

Then she saw red.

Who did the other detectives come to when they were

stumped? Her. She was the only one whose close rate topped 80 percent. She'd caught more killers in her time on the force than the rest of the detectives combined.

She was confident in her skills. And she'd be damned if she let some arrogant ass push her around because she was a woman.

It wasn't by accident that she was being actively recruited by the FBI, most likely including the tall agent standing next to her. She glanced up at Marcus and smirked. He looked like he wanted to kill Sanderson. Despite the hellish hand life had dealt her, she prided herself on ignoring the continual bullshit thrown her way by the many arrogant, narcissistic assholes who couldn't see past her breasts. She'd made a good life and career for herself. She turned cold eyes on Sanderson— this specific asshole wasn't going to take that away simply because his fragile little ego had been bruised.

"I'd consider your next words carefully, Sanderson."

His eyes hardened. "You're too emotional on this, Davis, because of your family's murder."

Everyone stopped moving. All chatting within the bull pen ceased.

Evelyn jumped up. Her chair tumbled to the ground as she lunged. Simultaneously, Ryan grabbed Sanderson by the collar, pushed him against the wall and jammed his arm up under the smaller man's chin, cutting off his air supply. With the speed of a viper, Marcus grabbed Evelyn by the waist and hauled her back before she could get to Sanderson. He wrapped his other arm around the tops of her shoulders and pulled her into his chest.

"Easy," he whispered into her ear. "Easy, sweetheart."

She fought against his hold. Her pulse kicked into overdrive as she felt the erratic beat of his heart against her back. He tightened his grip and brought his mouth to her ear once more. "Evelyn, stop."

She quit struggling.

Sanderson pawed at Ryan's arm, his face going from white to red.

"Enough," Captain Kessler bellowed as he stormed from his office. "What the hell is going on here?"

Marcus let go of Evelyn but stayed close to her. Her fists knotted by her side. A calm mask descended over her face. Gone was the panic and anger. Composed defiance washed over her as she turned to her boss.

Ryan relaxed his hold enough for Sanderson to catch his breath, but didn't let him go.

"Get off me, O'Neil." Sanderson jerked his arm up. He coughed, then spun and nodded to the captain. "Captain Kessler, I was just expressing my concern with Detective Davis being the lead due to her—"

"Not another word, Sanderson," Kessler said.

Sanderson lurched as if he'd been slapped. His face reddened at the public reprimand. He pulled at his jacket, pushed his shoulders back and glanced around the bull pen. All eyes were on him.

"Sir—"

Kessler's voice rose. "If you have a concern with the decisions made by both the chief and the mayor, I'd suggest you go up the proper chain of command. Before you do that, I'd highly recommend you keep your opinions to yourself." He took a step toward Sanderson and eyed the detective in front of him. "Do you understand me, Detective Sanderson?"

"Yes, sir."

"Good. Now, get out of my bull pen."

Josh Sanderson stalked to the stairs. He shoved his palm against the door. It swung open and bounced against the cement wall. Without a backward glance, he stormed out.

Kessler swung toward his officers.

"I'm not sure what the hell just happened, but I expected better out of you two." He pointed at Ryan and Evelyn before turning to Marcus.

"Special Agent Moretti, my apologies for the theatrics. I assure you, this isn't the norm for my typically well-behaved, professional detectives."

"No need, sir. From what I could ascertain, Detective Sanderson was completely out of line in his questioning. Detective O'Neil was merely protecting one of his own, which is something I highly respect in a house, sir. And, quite frankly, applaud."

A surprised expression flickered on Kessler's face. He nodded. "Thank you, Agent Moretti." He turned back to the rest of the crew. "I think it's time for everyone to pack up."

Evelyn opened her mouth to argue.

Kessler shook his head, looking spent. "Go home, Evelyn. Get some rest. I want an incident report on my desk, first thing in the morning. I wouldn't put it past that slimy shit bag Sanderson to write up a complaint."

"Yes, sir." She nodded.

"Gentlemen, you, too," Kessler said, then walked back to this office and closed his door.

She'd completely lost control. *How mortifying.* Her face burned and her stomach clenched. Refusing to look at either Marcus or Ryan, Evelyn gathered her bag, turned and left without a word.

MARCUS WATCHED EVELYN storm off. The pounding in his ears subsided as his pulse stopped racing. He'd sensed something was wrong the instant he and Ryan had stepped off the elevator. But it was the sheer look of panicked pain on Evelyn's face that had sent his blood boiling and spurred him into instant protect mode. He'd never wanted to defend another human being more intensely than in that moment.

Marcus turned and eyed Ryan. "What was that about?"

Ryan's jaw tightened. "Some guys just can't see past the angelic face. They think that just because she's a woman, she's ruled by emotion, not logic. It's been something she's battled since she landed here. And despite proving them all wrong, time and time again, they still see a fragile woman—she hates that."

"I can see her point. She's a cop first. And a damn good one, at that."

"*I* know that, and the chief knows that." Ryan pointed at him. "Even *you* know that. But most guys in the force can't—or won't—see it. Normally, she shrugs it off or fires back with dark humor—especially when it comes to that prick Sanderson. Honestly, man, I've never seen her react like that before."

Marcus shook his head. "I'm not buying that. It sounded like more than the typical 'you're a woman, you must be weak' mantra. What was Sanderson talking about? That thing about her family."

Ryan shrugged and averted his eyes.

Marcus slammed his hand down on a desk. "Come on. I read her file. I know they're dead. Why do I get the feeling that there's something more you guys aren't sharing?"

Ryan blew out a breath. "Look. It's not my story to tell. It's not in her file for a reason. I vouch for her. She can hold her own with this case. It's not an accident that the mayor specifically requested us. And believe me, it didn't have anything to do with my rugged charm."

Marcus didn't like that answer, but knew he wouldn't get anything else out of Ryan. He couldn't fault him, not when he admired his sense of loyalty. The guy was a vault when it came to Evelyn. If Marcus was ever concerned about an interoffice romance between the two of them, that idea had just snuffed out. It was evident that Ryan saw Evelyn as a sister, nothing more.

Frustrated, he scrubbed his hands over his face, then looked at the stairwell door. A frown pinched his eyebrows together. Although he hated to oppose Evelyn, he'd sided with Ryan earlier on the safe house idea. If it were up to him, Evelyn would be in it. Tonight. But at this stage in the game, he was here on a consultant basis only.

"You going after her?" Marcus asked.

Ryan shook his head. He grabbed his pen and the yellow pad of paper sitting on his desk, scribbled something, then tore off the top sheet and folded it in half.

"No." He handed Marcus the slip of paper. "You are."

Marcus's eyebrows arched. "I am? You think that's a good idea?"

"Yes."

Marcus was startled by how much authority rang in Ryan's answer. There wasn't a hint of joking left in his voice. Ryan was dead serious.

"What's this?" Marcus glanced at the paper. "I know where she lives."

Ryan pushed his chair back onto two legs and smirked. "Yes, but do you know her favorite wine?"

"Ah, good man." Marcus laughed, then pocketed the note.

Ryan got up, grabbed his jacket and walked to the elevator. He hit the down button, then called over his shoulder, "You coming?"

Marcus followed Ryan into the elevator. The doors closed, enveloping the men in silence. An intense desire to go to Evelyn battled the regulations screaming in his head. More to the point, hadn't she drawn that line in the sand just the previous night? *You don't mix business with pleasure.* But was this really pleasure? He doubted it, not after that blowup with Sanderson. This visit was purely business, end of story. She and Ryan were his business now, his responsibility, until the case was over. Mentally cursing himself, he ran his hand over his five o'clock stubble. Who was he kidding? If he were going to check up on Ryan, the mental bullshit he'd just run through would pass. But he wasn't. He was going to check on Evelyn. And with her, it was pleasure the moment he'd set eyes on the stunning detective. That sweet kiss he'd shared with Evelyn last night left him wanting to see that softer side of her—the side she reserved for a limited few—more than ever. He smiled as he remembered the softness of her lips.

Business. Pleasure. Both. It didn't really matter at this point. He was going.

Ryan's phone chirped as the doors opened. He flipped his phone over and looked at the caller ID.

"It's the wife." Ryan grinned. "Hey, babe."

The two men walked out of the station together. Ryan lifted his hand in a silent goodbye and moved toward his FJ Cruiser. Marcus waved back. Digging into his pockets, he pulled out his car keys. Yes, there was something more to Evelyn Davis, and he'd every intention of finding out what that was.

Tonight.

CHAPTER SIXTEEN

EVELYN FUMED ALL the way home, driving too quickly and not caring in the least. Anger and humiliation ripped through her. How dare he bring up her family in front of everyone? She pounded the steering wheel, willing herself not to cry. *Oh, crap, too late.* With one hand on the wheel, she dragged the back of her other hand across her eyes, gritting her teeth against the tidal wave of emotion threatening to wipe her out. She'd been promised that the circumstances of her family's death would stay out of her file, which was the only way she'd agreed to come to Seattle.

So how the hell had Josh Sanderson found out?

She hadn't felt such defeat, such vulnerability, in fifteen years. Her lip trembled.

The case was eating at her. She knew it. Ryan knew it. And if Marcus hadn't known, he certainly did now.

Her stomach tightened at the thought of being in the ruggedly handsome FBI agent's arms. She briefly felt warm and protected when he'd pulled her back from Sanderson. Last night's excuse of professional lines not being crossed was pathetic. If she were honest, she'd have admitted to Kate that she felt his presence before her eyes found him, that she instantly surveyed any room she walked into, hoping for a glimpse of Marcus. When he'd kissed her last night, she knew it was pointless to argue against regulations, or whatever, any longer.

But that was before he'd witnessed her attempt to attack a fellow officer.

She cringed. No doubt he'd run from her complicated life now. She shook her head, then focused on the road in front of her, careful not to hit any of the pedestrians that paid no heed to the walk signals at the crosswalks on the busy street.

Evelyn wanted to be home. Needed to slip into a hot lavender bath, drink a bottle of Malbec, anything to get her mind off this case—and more importantly, off Marcus.

An hour later, she dropped the towel from her shower and stepped into a pair of black boy-cut underwear. She put on an oversize cotton T-shirt and sighed. The soft fabric hugged her. She'd just flipped her head over to dry her hair when the doorbell chimed. *Who in the world?* She tugged on a pair of yoga pants, tied her hair up in a messy bun and walked to the window. Pushing aside the sheer curtain, she peered outside. She dropped the curtain as if it had seared her hand and took a step away from the window.

Marcus's car was parked at her curb.

Her stomach cartwheeled and tumbled. She yanked off the T-shirt and tossed it on her bed. She threw on a black bra, grabbed a black tank from her chair and put it on. Not the best outfit, but better than nothing.

The doorbell chimed again. She took one last look at herself in the mirror, then ran down the stairs, unbolted the door and pulled it open a crack.

"Marcus, hi." She peered around the door at him. "I

didn't expect to see you tonight. What are you doing here?"

He grinned down at her. *Oh, crap.* That wasn't good. Was it?

CHAPTER SEVENTEEN

MARCUS WASN'T SURE what he'd expected, but it wasn't to see her with wet hair. She'd clearly just gotten out of the shower. Even without a stitch of makeup on, she was stunning.

"For you." He handed Evelyn a bottle of wine. She took it, looked at the label and smiled.

"Thanks. I undeniably need this tonight."

He leaned against the door frame, crossed his arms and studied her sweet face. "No doubt, after that blowup."

She cringed and looked away. "Yeah. Sorry about that."

"Nothing to be sorry about. From where I was standing, Sanderson was out of line."

She looked up and mustered a small smile, rendering him speechless. He cleared his throat and pushed off the door frame. "May I come in?"

She hesitated, and Marcus's heart dropped. He held his breath and waited. *Open the door, Evelyn. Come on, let me in.* After what felt like a million years, she nodded, opened the door wider and stepped back.

He entered, the nervous tension returning. He heard the click of the dead bolt behind him as he surveyed her home.

The main living space was open. Beautiful hardwood floors lined the house from the front door to the back. A fire crackled in the huge fireplace that sat in the middle of the wall to the right. It was flanked by two floor-to-ceiling windows. A large white sofa sat facing the fireplace. Two overstuffed chocolate-brown chairs sat at each arm, a white throw tossed over the back of each. An old wooden shipping trunk, acting as a coffee table, sat on a throw rug. *Coastal Living* magazines were piled at one end. The living room seamlessly moved into a large eat-in kitchen. Someone had poured a lot of sweat and time into remodeling this small home to make it feel so open and warm.

He glanced at her. "You eat yet?"

"No." She cradled the wine to her chest.

He walked toward the kitchen. "May I?"

She titled her head, and her eyebrows creased.

"Cook you dinner. We Morettis make a mean Italian meal."

"You want to cook me dinner?" Her voice rose in surprise. She followed him and reached for a corkscrew to open the wine.

"Do you mind?" he asked, already rolling up his sleeves.

"No, that sounds lovely." She smiled, then pulled out the cork, brought the bottle closer and reached for a glass.

"Great. Sit."

She sat, then poured the red liquid into two glasses. She handed one to him.

"I'm mortified you had to see that today. It's just this case. It's eating at me."

He swirled the glass, brought it to his nose and inhaled deeply, then sipped. "You sure know your wine."

"Ryan?"

Marcus laughed and nodded.

Evelyn chuckled. "He knows me well."

Marcus figured Evelyn would shoulder most of the responsibility for tracking their killer. She was still a mystery—one he'd enjoyed unfolding and discovering—but he'd known from the beginning that she demanded more from herself.

But to think she was solely responsible for capturing the killer was ludicrous.

"You know you're not working solo, right?"

"Yeah, but I should have already figured this guy out. Gotten inside his mind. Something." She shook her head and reached for her wine. "Each time I look at the profile I've put together, something changes, something shifts and I have to rework it. It's maddening."

"Eve—"

She jumped up. "Enough about me."

Marcus bit back a smile. *Fair enough.* Clearly talking about the case—or more importantly, her frustrations with it—was off the table. He'd go with it. For now.

She grabbed two plates and some utensils. Once the places were set on the granite counter, she picked up her glass and pulled up a stool. "So why this case? Why Seattle, and why now?"

Marcus glanced up from rinsing the baby spinach he'd pulled from the fridge. "Justice runs in my blood and has for generations. When duty calls, I answer. This case called. So here I am."

It wasn't the full truth, but now was not the time to bring up his ulterior motive. When the mayor called in a personal favor to consult on this case, Marcus hadn't hesitated. He wanted Evelyn on his team at the Bureau. Ryan had smelled that the first few days on the case.

She, on the other hand, hadn't said anything to him yet. She was smart. She had to know his endgame. But now things had gotten a bit…complicated.

Turning back to the sink, he swallowed hard. Her softness more than intrigued him. So yes, he wanted her on his FBI team, needed her on his team, but he *wanted* the woman in front of him. And he couldn't separate those two things, so instead he focused on the truth that'd never change—that justice ran in his blood.

She took another sip of Malbec and studied him over the rim of her glass. "So it had nothing to do with my multiple rejections of the Bureau's offer to join their elite team."

He dumped the toweled-off spinach in her white ceramic salad bowl and beamed. "Busted."

"I'm not leaving my team."

"You haven't even heard my offer." He grabbed a knife and chopped the almonds he'd scrounged up, threw them in the salad. Next, he sprinkled dried cranberries into the mix.

"Marcus, I'm not leaving my team."

He shrugged, then grinned at her. "A guy could dream."

She laughed. "Fair enough. Tell me about your family."

A shadow passed over her face. He felt a twinge of sympathy for her. Just as quickly, though, the darkness passed, and she smiled at him.

"I have three siblings. Two brothers and a younger sister."

She tipped her glass to him. "Where do you fall in the lineup?"

"Second oldest, by forty seconds."

"You're a twin. Oh, your poor mother." She groaned. "I can't imagine a second Marcus running around. Somehow, I can't see the world being big enough for *two* of you."

He chuckled. "My twin and I are nothing alike, in case you're wondering. My family is currently scattered across the country, but we try to get together as often as our schedules allow. My easygoing Italian father—"

Evelyn's eyes raised skeptically.

"I know, I know. *Italian* and *easygoing* aren't exactly two terms you normally hear together, but that's my dad. He's currently working on his second retirement as a history professor and soccer coach."

He set the salad in front of her, grabbed the seat next to her and raised his glass. "Bon appétit."

Following suit, she raised hers and tipped her head. "Bon appétit."

"My older brother, Derek, retired from the Air Force a full bird colonel and is now at the Bureau. Cole, my younger brother and twin, well…he'd literally have to kill us if he told us what he does. But we all have our suspicions." Marcus chuckled.

She waved her folk in a small circle. "Go on."

"My mother, Charlotte, was an Air Force flight nurse."

Evelyn openly stared at him as she swirled her glass. "Wow. So your family bleeds red, white and blue."

"Always have. Always will."

He chewed slowly and glanced over at Evelyn. *He'd never met a woman who'd so quickly gotten to him. He'd never met a woman like Evelyn, period.* Not only did she match him stride for stride, but she also spoke his family's language. He hadn't seen that one coming.

"You were saying about your mom?" she prompted.

"My feisty Spanish mother met my father on a flight. He never really had a choice but to put a ring on her finger." Marcus leaned back in his chair and beamed. "And then there's my baby sister, Alexis."

"So who does she take after? Your feisty mother or your laid-back father?"

"Oh, she puts my mother to shame in the feisty department. That one has kept us all on our toes. She's in her last year at MIT. The agency's been champing at the bit to get her on their dime, but school's important."

"They sound lovely."

"They are. I'm lucky." He put down his glass. "What about yours?"

He watched her closely. A shadow passed across her face again. He knew he'd hit a nerve and hated the idea of bringing up anything that caused her pain. She fisted her hands in her lap. He cringed inwardly, but waited for her to speak. After the crazy showdown in the bull pen, he wanted answers. No, he deserved answers, both personally and professionally. She'd made him swear there'd be no holding cards in this investigation. And while he suspected she had her reasons for keeping her background close to the chest, he needed to know. He had to make sure that emotional outburst wouldn't repeat itself.

The vein in her throat jumped. She tucked a strand of hair behind her ear.

"They were killed fifteen years ago." She didn't look at him. "Their case was never solved."

"I'm sorry."

"It happened a long time ago." A deep sadness

crossed her face and tears glistened in her eyes. "Can we change the subject?"

Marcus nodded, wanting to take her in his arms to keep her grief at bay. But he didn't, too intrigued by what she kept hidden. "Fair enough. So, what makes you tick?"

She shrugged. "Easy. Justice. All victims deserve justice."

He was surprised at how quickly she responded. "I agree, but something makes you tick on a deeper level. What is it?"

She folded, unfolded and then refolded her napkin. Without looking up at him, she rolled it between her fingers and shifted in her seat. Fascinated by the internal struggle he was witnessing, he waited. She sighed and flicked the napkin aside, and picked up her glass.

She took another sip of her wine and stared at the red liquid. "You really want to know what makes me tick?"

"Yes." He reached for his own wine.

She gently lowered her glass to the granite counter and reached for his hand. "Come with me."

Startled, he put his glass down and pushed back from his chair. She led him up the stairs, her hand warm in his. He shot a quick glance into her bedroom, spied the unmade bed and had to rein in the wild images that bombarded his mind. Given their conversation downstairs, sex was clearly the last thing on her mind. She stopped and faced the closed door to their right. She dropped his hand and glanced up at him. He couldn't help noticing the fear and uncertainty in her eyes. *What in the world?*

"This is what makes me tick, Marcus. Like it or leave it." She pushed open the door, then flipped on the lights.

Grisly crime scene photos, Post-it notes with hand-scrawled questions and newspaper clipping covered the largest wall. Perplexed, he looked at her for a moment before moving toward the wall. A calendar with one date circled in red jumped out at him. He walked up to it and stared. Was that the date of her family's death? His head spun. If so, it was only a couple weeks from now. How the hell was she working this case? Why had no one mentioned this before now? He stepped closer, grimacing at the violent images.

Glancing over the old photos, his attention landed on the smiling face of a girl who remarkably resembled Evelyn. The photo butting up to it showed the same girl, hunched over a woman, bloodied, her throat slashed. He put two and two together. His chest tightened and his throat closed with unspoken emotion. The thought of losing his baby sister in such a violent manner made his stomach roll. *What kind of hell had Evelyn lived through?*

"I'm surprised you don't know already," she said from behind him. "Though I'm grateful Ryan and the captain kept their mouths shut."

"I tried to get it out of Ryan, believe me. But the guy's a vault." Marcus glanced over his shoulder. "Though, I must admit, I'm surprised and a bit annoyed no one thought this important enough to mention to me."

She leaned against the door frame, her arms wrapped tightly around her waist.

"What's this all about, Evelyn?"

"You might want to sit." She pulled out the large leather office chair and patted it.

He sat, and she plopped herself onto a small white

sofa. Tucking her feet underneath her, she stared at the wall full of painful reminders.

"I had just landed a multimillion-dollar modeling deal and was at my first runway show in Milan."

He whistled, though it didn't surprise him. She was a knockout, the type who didn't realize it, who walked around oblivious to how her looks affected people.

She rolled her eyes and a smile tugged at her lips.

"I received a DVD in the mail. My family sent them to me all the time. It was their way of keeping me connected, I guess. A few days prior, my sister had mentioned she'd be sending something, so I didn't think anything of it. So here I was, eighteen, in another country, and naive as hell. I'd just gotten home from my first runway show and popped this DVD in, expecting to see my sister's latest cheerleading event and my family's smiling faces." Her voice cracked. She cleared her throat. "Instead, I watched my family being brutally butchered. My sister was already dead. He'd slashed her neck from ear to ear before hitting Record. I was powerless to do anything as this faceless monster riddled my mother's body with bullets, then sliced open my father's throat. He bled out right before my eyes."

"Holy shit." Marcus tore his gaze from her for a brief moment to glance at the grotesque crime scene photos. *How had she even gotten ahold of those? What heartless moron had hand-delivered a constant and brutal reminder of the darkest day of her life—to a teenager?*

"In that moment, my life shattered into a million tiny pieces." She spoke quickly, her voice barely more than a whisper. "The cops never found the guy, and by the time they saw the video, the press had already labeled my father a family annihilator. My family's memory was ruined, and I lost everything."

He moved—professional lines be damned— and crouched in front of her, cradling her face in his hands. He brushed away her tears, wanting to pull her into his arms.

She bit her lip and drew back. "I'm sorry. How embarrassing."

"There's nothing to apologize for." He covered her hands with his and squeezed.

Marcus couldn't believe it. Here she was, opening up about her family's gruesome murder and apologizing for the emotions that came with it. He'd been impressed with her from day one, but he'd had no idea just how remarkable she was until this moment. He'd never met a stronger, braver soul in his entire life—doubted if he ever would again. He was falling hard for her, and there was nothing that could stop his free fall now.

She laughed through the tears. "My therapist kept telling me I needed to share my story with people other than Kate and Ryan. That it'd be good for me, for my healing and all. Who knew that someone would be you?"

She pulled her hands from his. He instantly missed her warm touch. Stepping away to give her space, shock ripped through him. *Had he just been granted access to her inner circle?* His palms got clammy.

"I think I need another glass of wine." She rose and walked to the door.

He followed her. He had so many questions, but she'd shared all she could right now. He sensed that in the way she moved to distance herself from the wall, the memories. He'd respect her privacy.

She let him leave the room in front of her, then flipped off the light and tugged the door closed. They stood close in the tiny hall.

Tipping back her head, she looked up at him, eyes misty. "Tread lightly, okay?"

She turned and went down the stairs in front of him. *Tread lightly?* Of course he'd tread lightly. She'd endured more pain, more heartache at the tender age of eighteen, than most people experienced in a lifetime. The sheer thought that she'd have to endure any more made him see red. He'd kill anyone who tried to hurt her.

They sat in her living room. He lounged in one of the armchairs. She was curled up on the sofa, cradling her Malbec, her feet tucked up underneath her. The fire crackled in the fireplace as they finished the wine. His mind reeled at what he'd just seen in that room, at what she had gone through and how extraordinary she was.

There was still just one question that bothered him. He didn't want to push, but she'd let him into such an intimate, precious part of her life already that he couldn't see her minding just one more question. At least he *hoped* she wouldn't. He swallowed hard.

"None of that's in your file. Why?"

"I know." She ran her finger around the edge of her glass. "It was part of a two-part deal to come here."

He cocked his head. *Two-part deal? What the hell?*

"I'd been in San Diego, a fresh-faced rookie. My captain kept mentioning how much potential I had. Coming from my background, you have two choices—let it cripple you, or harness it and *you* define it. I'd chosen to take my experience and channel it into my job. It seemed simple to me. Apparently my captain saw me as his golden child."

That same coolness he'd seen when she'd gone toe-to-toe with him that first day in the conference room descended now.

"Then my training officer found out about my past and everything changed. When other people, especially other law enforcement agents—male, female, it didn't really matter—found out about my past, I changed in their eyes, went from being this sought-after officer to a helpless victim. Infuriating. But, human nature, or so at least I'm told." She rolled her eyes and took another sip. "I don't know if it's because we've all seen so much evil on this job that it's hard to believe anyone can separate themselves from such personal horror. But I hate it."

He couldn't blame her.

She stared into the fire. "Anyway, my captain in San Diego and the chief here, who was a captain then, are great friends. He asked me to think about transferring to Seattle under Diaz. I agreed to come here as long as that part of my past was classified. It wasn't meant to be misleading or deceitful. I simply wanted the opportunity to stand on my own, to prove myself as a solid cop, because of who I am *now*. I didn't want my past clouding people's perception of me."

Marcus nodded. "That seems fair."

She shook her head and laughed. Then she set her glass down and smiled at him. The tender look melted his insides. He wanted this woman more than he'd wanted any other woman in his life. It took every inch of willpower not to go to her right now.

"Thanks for stopping over tonight, Marcus."

And just like that, he knew she'd ended their evening.

He sighed. *Probably for the best.* If he stayed much longer, he'd be taking her back upstairs, and that would most definitely be crossing the professional boundary she'd so firmly set in place.

There would be time for that. He'd make sure of it.

He put down his glass on the side table, got up and stretched. He grabbed his jacket on the way to the door, but before he turned the knob, he said, "I can stay."

Smooth, Moretti. Smooth.

"Marcus." His name came out in a soft whisper, one that held so much promise and so much pain.

He turned, could see her internal struggle and felt like a jackass. He knew she held herself responsible to these families. Hadn't she just finished telling him so not two hours ago?

She twisted her hands in front of her. "I want you, too. I do. But not until this case is closed. I couldn't live with myself if this—" she motioned between the two of them "—whatever this is, jeopardized the case."

A strange mixture of disappointment and pride crushed him. He wanted to stay, to take her in his arms and take away the hurt she'd carried all these years. But he also respected her too much to ask her to choose between her dedication to this case and him. So he'd wait.

Her inner strength amazed him. She was definitely worth the wait.

He nodded, then opened the door. "Okay, then, after this case."

"Marcus?"

He turned.

She stepped onto the porch. Shutting the door behind her, she walked into his embrace. He wrapped his arms around her and pulled her close. She smelled like lavender. He breathed deeply, seared this moment into his mind. He felt the rapid drumming of her heart, its beat matching his own.

How was it that he'd fallen for this woman so completely?

She sighed into his chest, drew back and looked up at him.

Screw the professional line. He cupped her chin with his hands, stared into her eyes and got lost in their sapphire depths. He lowered his head and pressed his lips to hers. He wasn't sure how she'd respond to his kiss, but he sure as hell wasn't expecting the reaction he got. Instead of withdrawing from him, she threw her arms around his neck, pressed her body close, with no hesitation, and returned his touch.

He came up for air first, then grinned at her. She sheepishly returned the gesture, color staining her cheeks.

"After this case," he said. It was a promise.

Her eyes lit up. "After the case, then."

She laughed, the sound light and free in the cool air of the quiet street. Fumbling for the doorknob behind her, she opened the door with one hand, without breaking his gaze. She stepped over the threshold, touched her lips, playfully winked and shut the door.

CHAPTER EIGHTEEN

EVELYN SLUMPED AGAINST the closed door, heart pounding. She hadn't been prepared to rehash her family's murder tonight. But Marcus had come after her, to check on her despite that ridiculously embarrassing blowup with Sanderson, hadn't he? And seeing his car at the curb had not only shocked her—if she were being completely honest with herself—but had also sent a thrill down her spine. She could have ignored the doorbell and all that followed, including the conversation that ripped her heart to shreds—again. She could have. But she hadn't. She'd made a decision to open the door. With that one motion, he'd walked straight into her home. And her heart.

She couldn't blame him for asking what made her tick. She'd have done the same. And she could've given him some stock answer. But he'd been sitting there, looking all handsome, kind, *safe*.

Not to mention that she'd been the one demanding they lay everything on the table when it came to this case. And this—the pain, the brutal memories, the blackest recess of her soul laid bare—was part of that. That wall and what it represented made her the woman she was, the detective she was. Over dinner, she'd known she needed to come clean and let him in.

And she didn't regret that decision. She just hadn't

realized that, with each word she spoke, a hot dagger would slice deeper and deeper into her heart. Then he'd been there, not shrinking back, but moving toward her, touching her, giving her the thing she craved the most. Soft human contact.

Her heart had surged when he'd asked to stay. She wanted him to, more than she'd wanted anything in a very long time. She'd let him into her past, and that meant something. But she wasn't sure she could let him into her present. Not with her family's case still cold. She couldn't ask him to walk that with her, could she? So she'd said no.

Kate's question—*Isn't that his choice?*—had played back in her head as she watched him walk out her door. So she'd moved to him, into his arms and off a cliff.

Now she was falling. She hoped he'd be the man she thought he was and catch her.

She leaned her head against the door. She'd just let the sexiest man she'd ever laid eyes on walk out the door. *After* he'd asked to stay. Clearly she was insane.

What the hell was wrong with her?

"Just open the door, Davis," she mumbled, eyes still closed. "It's not rocket science."

The job had always taken precedent over every area of her life. And if it wasn't the current investigation that denied her the soft contact she secretly craved, it was her family's cold case that separated her from the rest of society, left her alone. She'd never thought it an issue.

Until now. Until Marcus.

But it didn't have to be. At least not tonight. It *was* his choice, and he'd asked to stay. So why the hell was her door still shut? She took a deep breath, threw open the door and flipped on the porch light.

"Marcus?"

He stopped and turned around. His head cocked to the side, but he didn't move. Her heart sank at his hesitation. *Please come back*.

He walked toward her, his gaze never leaving her face.

Her stomach tightened. "Marcus, I—"

His mouth found hers. A helpless breath escaped her as Marcus reached under her tank top and caressed her ribs with one hand. She hadn't realized how much she wanted him—needed him—until his lips met hers. A sharp desire surged through her. Her skin burned where he touched.

Showering her with kisses, Marcus pushed her inside, kicked the door closed behind them and nuzzled his lips against her throat.

She pressed herself closer. She couldn't tell where her body ended and his began. Marcus pulled back. A soft whimper of protest bubbled up from her. He tipped her head up and locked eyes with her. Everything else fell away as she got lost in the fire staring down at her.

"You sure?" His voice sounded hoarse, strained.

She looked up at him and studied his face, then nodded.

Passion pooled like dark ink in his warm chocolate eyes. She'd never noticed the tiny flecks of gold that flickered in the deep brown before. Then again, she'd never been this close to him, either. His five o'clock shadow peppered his face and emphasized his strong features. This was exactly where she wanted to be: with this man, in this moment. Nothing else mattered but being here with him. She needed him, craved not just human contact, but *his* contact. A deep, primal hunger to be touched and loved by him sent tremors through her. She stretched out her hand tentatively.

He seemed to sense her need and cupped her face, gently kissing her. She wasn't sure what she'd been expecting when she'd asked him to stay, but the soft, tender touch surprised her, propelled a wave of electricity through her. Every cell sizzled, burst with desire. She couldn't move.

"Evelyn." He dropped his hand.

"Don't talk." She shook her head, reached for him. "Just kiss me."

Burning, possessive lips crushed hers. His heart hammered against her chest, and she felt his heat pressed against her. All hesitation vanished. Her mouth parted, inviting him closer. He didn't waver, answering ravenously. She sensed his feverish pitch and matched him.

Passion for passion.

She shoved off his jacket, went for his shirt, then his belt. They stumbled and fell into a heap on the sofa. He slid his knees on either side of Evelyn, pinning her underneath him. She smiled, reached up and lowered his face to hers. Kissing him hard, she tasted the tartness of her favorite Malbec and felt the softness of his tongue. He murmured her name against her mouth as she entwined her fingers in his curls, tugging him closer.

He stopped, yanked his shirt over his head and let it drop on the floor. Eyes locked with hers, he stood and kicked off his shoes, then unzipped and slipped off his jeans. Her mouth dropped open as she blatantly stared.

His broad shoulders rose and fell with each breath. Tight muscles rippled down his perfectly proportioned frame. He was beautiful. He was all man.

And all hers.

She sat up and extended her hand toward him, desperate to touch the bronzed, solid body in front of her. Mesmerized, she rose from the sofa and yanked at her shirt, anxious to feel his skin against hers. He grabbed her hand and pushed it away.

Her brows furrowed. Was he changing his mind?

He shook his head and grinned. "I'll take care of that."

She smiled and raised her arms, allowing him to slowly pull her tank up and off her body. His fingertips skimmed her skin, the feathery touch sending heat through her veins. Without breaking her gaze, he tugged her yoga pants off, then her panties. The air felt cool against her exposed skin.

His hands slid down her arms. He brushed his fingers along her waist, back up her ribs and skimmed his hand between her breasts. Evelyn squirmed as with one hand, he swept his fingers down her hips. He cupped her breast with the other. She shivered at his light touch and reached out to stroke his taut stomach. She tried to move closer, eager to feel his body against hers—skin to skin.

He shoved her hands away again, lowered his head to her neck and trailed his lips from her ear down her throat. A soft groan escaped her as she went from simmering to boiling in T-minus two seconds.

Marcus lowered them to the plush carpet in front of the fireplace. He pushed her onto her back, crawled after her and gently spread her legs wide with his knee. She threw her arms around his neck and hungrily tugged him to her, kissing him with a ferocious desire she didn't know she possessed.

And she was. Possessed. By him.

As the fire crackled, he caressed her face, looking into her eyes before devouring her mouth again. He matched her passion, satisfied her need. She pulled away, breathless. Her fingers followed the muscles in his shoulders as his lips memorized every inch of her body.

"You're so beautiful," Marcus whispered into her ear.

He caught her wrists in one hand and yanked her arms over her head. Pinning her, he lowered his head and kissed her again. Then traced her collarbone with his tongue. Her body arched at the sensual touch. He peppered her with soft kisses and worked his way south. Her breath hitched.

She couldn't wait. Wanted more. Craved it all. Now.

Wriggling free of his grasp, she reached down and pulled him back up to meet her mouth. He held his rock-hard body over hers as she kissed him. He was close enough for her to feel his warmth without overwhelming her under his weight.

But that wasn't enough. She needed him on her, in her, surrounding her, filling her.

"I want you now." She clutched his neck and crushed him to her, kissing him hard.

He chuckled against her lips. He drew away, looked down at her and grinned. "With pleasure."

She wrapped her leg around him and lifted her hips as his hard body crashed into hers. They moved as one in perfect sync, as if they'd always known each other. Heat tore through her, melted her insides. Desperation drove her against him.

Their shared rhythm intensified, and they rode the swell until it exploded. Evelyn moaned a helpless cry of release, pushing harder, and dug her nails into Marcus's back. She held on as if he were a lifeline. Marcus dropped his head to her shoulder and shuddered.

Her blood thumped loudly in her ears as she caught her breath. Marcus kissed her forehead, then gently lowered himself onto her. She breathed in his smell and they lay like that for a moment before he rolled to the side, wrapping his arm around her and tucking her against him. Evelyn's body curved into his and he kissed the top of her head.

"Whoa," he murmured into the back of her neck.

Evelyn smiled, turned over and snuggled herself into the crook of his shoulder. She lazily traced her finger across his chest muscles. She felt his heartbeat skip, then steady and fall in line with hers. The fire popped and hissed. She smiled. *Whoa* was right. She couldn't have agreed more.

He gently swept her hair away, exposing her bare shoulder, and gently pressed his lips to her skin. The touch was feathery and he traced his fingers down her side, following the curves of her body. Then he shifted, and her eyes widened as he stood. Her heart took off as she sized him up and saw his eagerness. "Really? Again?"

"Really."

A startled gasp escaped her mouth as he suddenly scooped her into his arms. "Sweetheart, that was just to get it out of our systems. Now I'm going to show you a really good time."

Because that wasn't a good time? Holy crap.

She threw her arms around his neck, showering him with tender kisses as he carried her up the stairs.

THE NEXT MORNING, Evelyn woke with a start. She groaned. What had she done last night? Marcus walked in from the bathroom half-naked, answering her silent question. Vivid memories flooded her mind, and her skin tingled as she stared at his toned body. She sat up, hugging the sheet around her, suddenly shy.

"Morning."

"Morning, sexy." He tugged on his shirt, leaned over and softly kissed her. The gentleness morphed into something more, something hot. He pulled back, grinned down at her. "As much as I want to tumble into bed with you and repeat last night's performance, I need to go. Showing up at the station together may set tongues wagging. And the only tongue I want to set wagging is yours."

"That would definitely complicate things," she whispered. *As if this isn't complicated enough.*

"Not for me, it wouldn't." He chuckled and kissed her again. "I'll see you soon."

Evelyn watched Marcus leave. She touched her lips again, remembering the heat of his goodbye kiss, then did something she hadn't done since she was eighteen. She flopped back onto her pillow and giggled.

CHAPTER NINETEEN

EVELYN STEPPED OUT of the elevator. A yellow envelope hung limply from her hand. Marcus did a double take. When he'd left her this morning, her cheeks had been flushed, her eyes alive. Now, her creamy skin was pale and clammy, and the corners of her eyes pinched together, strain pulling across her face. She looked like she'd seen a ghost. He sprung from his chair and was beside her in two strides. He gripped her elbow and pulled her to her desk.

"Evelyn. What—"

She handed him the envelope.

He dumped the contents onto her desk. He stared down at the bloody hunting knife and a photo of the two of them embracing on her front porch. The hair on the back of his neck bristled.

The photo had a hole in the middle where the knife had clearly pierced it.

"What the hell is this?"

"What is what?" Ryan joined them, coffee in hand.

Marcus flipped the photo for Ryan to see, then motioned to the hunting knife.

Ryan's eyes darkened. His jaw twitched. He snatched up the photo. "What. The. Fuck. Where did that come from?"

"I found it pinned to my door with the knife."

Marcus's head snapped up. "This morning?"

His skin crawled as she nodded. Marcus's stomach sank to the floor. Someone had been watching Evelyn, waiting for him to leave.

"If there was any question about my being in this sicko's crosshairs, it's been answered," she said with an irritated tone.

"What the hell were those idiots on detail doing? Sleeping through their shift?" Ryan reached for his phone. "Lazy sons of bitches."

Marcus corralled Evelyn away from Ryan as he yelled into his phone.

"You okay?" Marcus asked.

She shook her head. "I'm fine. Just a bit rattled."

A bit rattled. Who was she kidding?

"Evelyn."

"Fine. I'm pissed. Is that what you want to hear?" She glared up at him, her eyes moist. "Well, I am. I'm pissed. At this psychopath for besting me time and time again, and at myself for letting him."

"Whoa. Wait a minute. You can't possibly think—"

Ryan burst into another fit, his brutal tongue-lashing escalating. They both glanced at him, then moved farther down the hall.

Marcus took a step toward Evelyn, closing the space between them. He lowered his voice. "You can't possibly think that all this is your fault. You aren't in it alone. We're a team, Evelyn. And this asshole is not going to get away with this."

She closed her eyes, took a deep breath. She opened them again and locked onto him.

"This whole thing is spinning out of control. We need to do damage control, and we need to do it now."

Marcus studied Evelyn's face. She shifted, but didn't break eye contact. Somehow he didn't think she was talking about the case. He scowled. *Oh, no. You aren't going to drop me that quickly, sweetheart.*

"Did you see anyone when you left this morning?" she whispered.

"Not even the detail." Marcus lowered his voice. "About last night—"

"It was unprofessional."

"A hell of a lot of fun is what it was."

She shook her head, crossed her arms. "It can't happen again."

"Evelyn, stop. It doesn't need to be like this."

She went to open her mouth when Kessler stuck his head out of his office. "Get in here. Now."

Ryan slammed down his phone and grumbled. "How those assholes even got a badge is beyond me."

He glanced up and shot her a troubled scowl. He tapped the photo and the knife. "This isn't over."

Evelyn nodded. Marcus slid the knife and photo back into the envelope and tucked it into his briefcase. The three of them walked into Kessler's office.

His face was drawn. "We have another murder."

"Another family?"

Evelyn's voice sounded faint. Marcus glanced over and noticed that her face had grown pale. His fists balled together. When the hell would they catch this guy?

Kessler shook his head. "A mother and daughter, but similar MO. It's on Mercer Island. I want you three to head over to see if it's our guy. If it is, maybe you'll get lucky and find something on this asshole."

THE SILENCE WAS PAINFUL. Evelyn knew Ryan was furious with her. Uncertainty clawed at her. Was Marcus? It wasn't her fault their unsub had slipped past the guys on detail. But it was her fault they were there in the first place. If she wasn't so stubborn, she'd have been in a safe house, and he wouldn't have been able to get to her again. She glanced in the rearview mirror, but couldn't read Marcus's stoic face, and that made her heart ache.

The warmth of last night seeped away with each passing minute of silence.

At the address, Ryan threw the car into Park and got out without a word. They signed the log, then walked into the stunning three-story town house. The entire back wall was nothing but glass. Through it, Lake Washington glistened as sunbeams broke through the familiar Seattle cloud cover.

CSI agents scrambled around like an anthill had been stepped on. Her team followed the commotion to the left, toward the open kitchen. Ryan led the way. Evelyn was right behind him, taking in as much information as she could. A woman lay sprawled out on the Italian tile floor, a pool of blood collecting underneath her crisp, toffee-colored suit. Evelyn pulled up sharply. Marcus bumped into her.

He leaned closer. "What is it?"

She turned, horror in her eyes. Her hand fluttered to her mouth. "I know that woman."

"What?"

She felt the color drain from her face. Her hands were clammy, her knees weak. "I know her. That's Anastasia Kulik. At least, that was her name the last time I saw her."

"Which was when?" He glanced past her.

"Fifteen years ago, in Milan. She was my roommate, the one the modeling agency assigned to me. Sweet girl. I haven't seen her since Milan, or spoken to her since I left. I'd put that part of my life out of my mind."

Marcus scrubbed his hands over his face. "Ryan—"

Her partner joined them. "What's up?"

Evelyn didn't want to tell him, but she wasn't about to lie to Ryan now. She compartmentalized her emotions, channeling them into pure and unadulterated focus. She took a deep breath. "That woman. She was in Milan with me."

"Shit." Ryan ran his hand through his hair. "We need to fill in Kessler ASAP. Between the photo and the woman, this is hitting too close to home."

"I couldn't agree more," Marcus said.

THAT EVENING, THE five o'clock news dubbed the serial killer the Seattle Slayer.

"Can we not put a gag order on these idiots? Do they not know they're only fueling this guy's ego? Encouraging him to kill again?" Evelyn said, fuming.

Neither man had allowed her to stay at the crime scene. She'd argued and lost. So she'd pulled out her working profile. Something was off. She didn't want to pull on the golden string right in front of her, but she didn't think she had a choice. Not when so many pieces connected back to her…or at least appeared to. So she worked and reworked the profile, scribbling down notes in the margins.

The killer had to know her. Any doubt had been shredded when she'd stared down at Anastasia's body. Evelyn tapped the pencil against the desk, then scribbled "how close?" in her notes. Was he a copycat killer or…

She scribbled "could it be him?" in the margins, then scratched it out.

Evelyn wasn't willing to go there.

Yet.

At least not in public.

Bone-aching weariness washed over her. Irritated, she grabbed the TV remote and stabbed at the mute button. She had a job to do, and being chained to this desk for the past several hours wasn't helping her attitude.

She swirled in her chair and tried to make out the tone of the conversation that was going on behind closed doors. Marcus had been in with Kessler for over an hour.

"It's their constitutional right, Evelyn," Ryan said in a tone that indicated he was still pissed at her.

"Don't give me that shit. I know what their constitutional rights are."

He didn't look up from the file in front of him.

"Seriously, you're ignoring me now?" She couldn't believe how childish he was being.

"Ignoring people seems to be the going thing the past few days."

"Excuse me?" Her blood simmered.

He threw his pencil down and glared at her. "You ignored both Marcus and me, and put yourself in harm's way. Come on, Evelyn. You can be so bullheaded at times. It's infuriating. I can't do my job if I'm worrying about you. Help me out here."

She glared back at him, but he didn't waver as he stared her down. Finally she felt herself cave. He was right, after all. She could be stubborn. And had been from the very beginning of this case. She cradled her head in her hands. "I'm sorry."

And she was. She'd let her emotional high get the best of her last night. She'd known not to cross that line with Marcus, yet she'd done it anyway. In that moment, it had felt right. But the instant she opened her door and saw that photo of the two of them, she'd known she'd made a mistake.

"Sorry enough to stop this shit?"

She threw Ryan a tiny smile. "Yes."

He returned the gesture. "Good. Now I can call her off."

"Huh?"

"Kate. She almost drove to the station to kick your ass this morning."

Evelyn rolled her eyes. What a freaking mess. She threw a worried look toward Kessler's office, then turned back to the TV. Seattle Slayer Eludes SPD was scrolling across the bottom of the screen.

"We can't fuel this guy. We have to let the public know who they're dealing with—the real facts, not the sensationalized ones. The public needs to be diligent about keeping their families safe. If we can have the whole city on the lookout, he'll have fewer chances to slip through the cracks."

The captain opened his office door and poked his head out.

"Davis. O'Neil. My office, please. I want you to hear Agent Moretti out for a moment."

Ryan rose and grabbed his mug. Evelyn followed suit. *Agent Moretti?* The formality in Kessler's tone couldn't be good. They walked in and sat. Dark bags rested under Kessler's eyes. He'd aged years in the past three weeks. Evelyn flicked her eyes to his hands. *Shit.*

He was running his forefinger over the top of his thumb again.

An awkward silence hung in the room. Marcus eyed Evelyn, then took a deep breath. "This guy is targeting you, Evelyn."

"Yes, I would say that's obvious."

She'd had her suspicions since the second murder but had brushed them off, blaming her edginess on the quickly approaching date on the calendar. She didn't need to consider his statement, not with the photos and the knife. Her stomach pitched, her mind playing back a colorful image of what she'd witnessed on Mercer Island. Poor Anastasia.

"I don't want to be the guy who points out the elephant in the room...." Marcus said.

She crossed her arms. "Then don't."

"These murders all have a familiar tone. One that's remarkably close to your family's case. I don't think it's wise to have you as lead—"

Her back stiffened as all the muscles in her body constricted at once. Her stomach rolled as the floor dropped out from under her. Her fists balled, nails cutting into the flesh of her palms as she stared at Marcus. Shock ripped through her, followed by crushing disappointment. She hadn't expected him to throw her family's murder in her face. Not after last night. She'd trusted him with the most vulnerable, delicate part of her soul and then shared her bed with him. Heat rushed to her cheeks. And now he squashed that trust by questioning her ability to keep from blurring the line between her family's murder and the current case. Humiliation wrapped around her heart and squeezed tight. How could she have so wrongly judged him?

"Please…don't say another word."

"He has a point," Kessler said.

"Captain, you can't be serious."

"But I am. Special Agent Moretti has a point that I refuse to ignore, especially at the risk of one of my people. Until further notice, I want you to take a step back," Kessler said.

"What?" Angry tears sprung to her eyes.

"I didn't say step out. I said *back*. You aren't being demoted."

"It sure feels like it."

Kessler dismissed her with a flick of his hand. "I know how hard you've fought to be seen as an equal within this department, how hard you've worked to keep your past where it belongs—in the past. But I won't risk your life, or the life of your partner, in order to appease your feelings. No matter how justified they may be."

Evelyn stole a glance at Ryan. *Why wasn't he defending her?* He stared straight ahead, shoulders back, spine straight, refusing to meet her eyes. Her stomach sank even further. *Did he agree with Kessler? With Marcus?* She shook her head and bit the inside of her cheek to keep the angry tears at bay. She couldn't pinpoint which hurt worse: Marcus's blatant abuse of her trust, or Ryan's silence.

"Agent Moretti, give your men the green light to follow up with your theory."

Kessler glanced at Ryan. "Detective O'Neil, you're now SPD point. I do not, under any circumstances, want Detective Davis in the spotlight."

"Yes, sir." Ryan nodded.

Evelyn's mouth dropped open. No argument, no pushback, nothing. Her partner had just singlehandedly railroaded her. She pressed her lips together and silently fumed.

Kessler turned his attention to Evelyn. "And you. I still expect 150 percent from you. You're still our best profiler and closer. Get inside his head. Figure him out, shut him down, just do it under the cover of silence. We're all on the same team. So let's—"

"With all due respect, sir, he's hijacking our investigation," she interrupted.

She saw Marcus open his mouth to speak. Ryan shook his head. A quick nod from Marcus acknowledged their brief exchange, and he snapped his mouth shut. She bristled.

"Enough." Kessler slammed his hand on his desk. The vein in his neck bulged.

She jerked back as if she'd been struck. She'd pushed him too far.

He pinned her with steely eyes. "This isn't a discussion, Detective Davis. This is happening. And I expect your full cooperation. Do you understand me?"

She looked at the floor, wished it would open up and swallow her whole. Heat flooded her face and burned her cheeks. "Yes, sir."

"Good. Now take a walk. Get your head around this and be back here in an hour. Got that?"

Evelyn nodded. She rose without a word and stormed out of the captain's office, heading for the stairwell.

Ryan followed her. In three strides, he was next to her. "Ev..."

"I don't have to take this, not now. Especially from him." She refused to look up.

"Why are you so hot under the collar, Davis?"

"Agent Moretti can't come in here like he owns the

place. How dare he suggest I be sidelined. It's ridiculous."

"I agree with him."

"What?" She stopped short and glared at him. She knew he agreed with Marcus—his silence in Kessler's office had screamed louder than his words did now. But his admitting it out loud felt like a punch in the gut. "Why?"

He leaned against the door, blocking her escape. He ran his hand through his hair. "Because, Evelyn, this prick's targeting you."

She knew the killer was targeting her—even if she refused to admit it aloud—and she didn't want Ryan to say the words. Make it real. If the tables were turned, and their unsub had Ryan in his line of sight, she wouldn't hesitate to pull Ryan. It wasn't safe. She got that. But she couldn't hide. Wouldn't hide. The killer didn't care about any of those people he'd killed. He cared about *her*. He wanted *her*.

And that pissed Evelyn off.

"Ryan—"

"No. Stop. I know it here." Ryan struck his fist to his chest. "Over my dead body will I let some psycho take you out, Ev. I won't have people saying 'the dead don't lie' about my friend because she's too stubborn to admit when she needs to step back. Damn it, Ev. You of all people know better."

She sagged against the wall. Marcus was right in requesting she be removed as lead. It was the smart move, the right move—for the investigation, for the victims' families. It would have been the move she'd suggest if things were different, and she wasn't so invested in this case. But she was invested, and she just wasn't ready to admit that he was right.

"Why didn't you say something sooner?" The question came out in a soft whisper. She should've known he'd have come to the same conclusion she had. Hadn't they been in sync since day one?

"Would you be stomping around here like this if I had? Shit. Better to keep it to myself until I'm sure."

"I would've listened to you." And she would have. Despite the emotional tug of this case, she'd have listened to him. She'd follow him through hell and back. She'd do anything for Ryan, for his family.

"Why?"

She shrugged and closed her eyes. "I trust you, trust your gut."

"So why are you flipping out now that Marcus has brought it up? Because he mentioned your family?"

Her eyes snapped open. She hadn't expected him to bring up her family this close to the bull pen. No one acknowledged their conversation, everyone up to their eyeballs in reports and files of their own.

"Walk with me." He pushed open the door to the stairwell.

He let the door close behind them before continuing. He rubbed his hands over his face. "Look, I know this case has been rough, especially with the date right around the corner—"

"No, it's not that."

"Then what is it? Help me out here. I don't understand why you just crushed Marcus's balls in there."

"I don't…" At a loss for words, she grasped for anything. "I don't trust his motives."

Rare anger flashed in his face. "Come on, Evelyn. Give me a fucking break."

His outburst shocked her. She'd seen him lose it before, just not at her.

"You have to learn to trust someone other than Kate and me. You have to let other people in." He paced. "Marcus isn't trying to take over this investigation, humiliate you or any of that other horseshit that's running through that pretty little mind of yours right now. He's trying to help us nail this bastard. And protect you in the process."

"He—"

"Stop. Do you hear yourself right now? This sick murdering bastard is fixated on you. He's already murdered fourteen people just to get your attention."

Her stomach rolled as his words sunk it.

"Taking you out of the public equation is not an attack on your ability. It's good police work."

She slumped against the door. "Marcus came over last night."

"I know. I sent him after you."

"Yeah, I figured as much." She managed a small smile. "Thanks for giving him the wine tip, by the way."

"Always the best for you, sweet cheeks." He winked.

Her eyes filled with tears. "I let him in, Ry. And not just into my house. But really in."

Ryan shook his head. "Not following you, Ev."

"I told him about my family last night. I showed him my office."

Ryan whistled. "And him bringing them up in front of Kessler like he did, without first bringing you up to speed, felt like a violation of your privacy and your trust."

She nodded, wiping her eyes with the back of her hand.

He studied her for a second, then chuckled.

"This may come as a huge surprise to you, seeing how awful you are at noticing these things. But he isn't just watching out for you professionally, Ev. The guy really cares about you."

"Yeah, I got that last night." Her head tilted to one side as she eyed her partner. "But you can't possibly know that."

"Yes, actually, I can. I asked. He told." He grinned.

Horror washed over her. *Had Marcus told him about last night? Already? He wouldn't. Would he?*

"Relax. It's my prerogative as your partner to know if some guy likes you."

"When did he tell you?"

"The other day." Ryan's brows scrunched together.

She turned, leaned her head against the cool, pebbled concrete wall and closed her eyes. *Ryan didn't know about last night.*

"Why do I get the feeling we aren't talking about the same thing?"

She opened her eyes and sheepishly grinned.

"He stayed. Didn't he? Atta boy! I knew it!" Ryan hooted, then grew serious. "If the man stayed last night, do you really think he's trying to do anything other than protect you? Don't be a moron."

Evelyn shook her head. She was being an idiot. She'd realized that he cared the moment she'd opened the door and he'd come back and kissed her, but she'd still second-guessed it—until now. And she'd all but thrown it back in his face. She cringed. Great. She looked up into Ryan's laughing face.

Why was he smiling? This wasn't funny. She grimaced. "I need to go apologize to him."

"I'm coming with you."

She tilted her head, eyebrows arching. "Totally not necessary—"

"Oh, I know."

"Then why?" She shook her head. "I don't need you to hold my hand. I know when to take a step back and admit to being ridiculous."

"I know, but it happens about as often as Halley's Comet flies by. I don't want to miss it."

CHAPTER TWENTY

EVELYN PUT DOWN the report, looked up and sighed. Marcus, Kate and Ryan sat around Ryan's table, case files spread over the polished wooden surface. The kids had long been asleep. Kate and Ryan sifted through the information in front of them. Evelyn sat staring at Marcus, head bent over his file. Perplexed. She'd expected him to rub her emotions in her face when she went to apologize. He'd extended grace instead. Professional, yet warm. Kessler had smiled and gone back to work.

Kate demanded Evelyn stay with them. Concerned for the kids' safety, she had argued...and lost. But not staying at her place was the right move. The photo and the knife had rattled her more than she'd let on.

Marcus insisted on driving her to her place to pack a small overnight bag before they drove together to Ryan's. He'd kept his distance at her home. But before they'd walked into Ryan's, he'd leaned over and kissed her in the car. Once again leaving her breathless...and confused. Despite her hot and cold signals, he was persistent. *What was with this guy?*

He put the folder down, looked up and caught her staring. He smiled.

Flustered, she set her wine down, got up and paced.

"I still can't figure out how this guy would even know about me. It's not like I live a flashy life."

"You can say that again," Kate said, not even glancing up from the file in front of her.

"You wouldn't necessarily need to have a flashy lifestyle," Marcus said.

Ryan tossed down the case file he'd been scrubbing, laced his fingers behind his head and leaned back. "Probably just an accident."

"That's actually what I was thinking," Marcus said.

Ryan sat up, surprise and curiosity on his face.

"Crossing paths with him at one of your regular places was just plain old bad luck," Marcus said. "Wrong place, wrong time. He could've fixated on anyone. This time around, it was you."

"How fabulous for me."

That wasn't what she wanted to hear. How many times was life going to deal her a crap hand? There had to be some limit to the amount of grief one person could be dealt, right? She stopped pacing. Dread filled her veins as the same question bubbled up again, sending her heart off at a gallop. There wasn't any way this could be the same. *No. Not possible.* It was ridiculous to try to connect them.

That couldn't be possible. Could it?

"Is it too far a leap to think he knows about my family? These murders have a similar tone." She'd tried to keep the tremor out of her words, but her voice rebelled by cracking as her sweet sister's face flashed in her mind. It wasn't the exact question her mind had landed on, but she still couldn't voice it. Having this psycho be her family's killer was too much for her mind to settle on. She glanced around the table. Ryan and Kate nodded. Marcus slowly shook his head.

"I'll have someone look into that, but right now, we're working under the assumption that he didn't."

The muscles in her neck relaxed. That was a fair statement. No use getting everyone all worked up for nothing. She nodded.

"But you must've somehow triggered his fixation. Once he locked eyes on you, he started obsessing—" Marcus stopped. "You okay?"

"Yeah," she said, willing herself to smile. "It's just a little overwhelming. I'll be fine."

Kate glanced up. Evelyn caught her concerned expression and forced the feeble smile to stay put. Kate didn't look away, nor did she appear persuaded. *Crap.* Evelyn could see she wasn't convincing Kate of anything and broke eye contact first.

"You know as well as I do that he would have begun digging into your life immediately," Marcus said.

Evelyn sank into her chair. Marcus was right.

"So going with the wrong-place, wrong-time theory, he would have needed to start digging immediately in order to satiate his primal urge, his obsession, to know everything about me. I get that." Evelyn pinched the bridge of her nose and squeezed her eyes tight. "In that psychopathic mind of his, *I* belong to him. He's possessive and has to know everything about me." She looked up. "Doesn't mean I have to like it."

"This working theory is good," Ryan chimed in. "I can't see how he'd know about your family. Your records are sealed."

Marcus raised his eyebrow. "But what about in Phoenix?"

Evelyn shook her head. "Evelyn Maslin no longer

exists. She vanished fifteen years ago. I can't see with sealed records and a new last name…"

"No." Kate pointed at Marcus. "He's right. Your family's story was all over the newspapers, and that's public record. It would probably only take a little digging to connect the dots between Evelyn Maslin and Evelyn Davis. It might not be that difficult. Not in this day and age. And *especially* if you know what you were looking for."

"Shit." Ryan scratched his head. "Of course. We do that kind of background digging on a daily basis."

"But why kill these families? Why make them look like family annihilators? There has to be—" Kate's voice trailed off as she locked eyes with Evelyn. With each question, the tension in Evelyn's shoulders twisted deeper.

Marcus sighed. "It was the only surefire way to get your attention. You're a homicide detective. It's not a hidden fact that you're the best closer for the psychologically dark cases. Wasn't there a whole write-up about you and your closing rate just last year when the mayor tried to gain public support for a larger law enforcement budget?"

She nodded, then grimaced. That stupid story. She'd known it'd been a bad idea from the get-go and had fought the chief on it. The spotlight was the last thing she wanted. She was perfectly happy doing what she did best, under the cover of anonymity. The chief had pushed back—the SPD needed the good press, the mayor, another gold star. So her hand had been forced. *Wait.* Tilting her head, she looked at Marcus. *How did he…?*

"That story would do it," Kate said, interrupting Evelyn's silent musing.

"If he's truly obsessed with you, Evelyn, he'll do anything to get your attention," Marcus said.

Her heart threatened to break. She felt the searing pain, the endless heartache of the family members left behind with each syllable he uttered. Her hand fluttered to her throat as bile rose and choked her.

Marcus reached over and touched her hand. "Evelyn. It's not your fault. *None* of this is your fault."

She felt helpless. Again. The realization that this psychopath had homed in on her made her skin crawl. Him baiting her with the gore and those poor families' untimely deaths made her sick, angry.

She pulled away from Marcus's touch and switched topics. "So why are you throwing all your muscle at this case? Surely there are other cases that need your attention."

Ryan and Kate glanced at each other, then refocused on the files in front of them.

Marcus leaned back. "I already told you why I'm here. Last night. Remember that conversation? When we were sitting in your kitchen, drinking wine and enjoying a home-cooked meal together. The call came, I answered."

She crossed her arms.

"Not everyone has an agenda, Evelyn. Though I must admit, aside from wanting to lock this bastard up for good, I have one small angle now."

"Figures," she muttered under her breath.

He raised his glass, took a drink, then pinned her with his gaze. "You."

She choked on the liquid in her mouth. Kate quickly

raised her glass to her lips, but not before a tiny smirk appeared. Ryan's only tell that he was a bit taken aback was the tiny movement of his eyebrow.

"And why shouldn't you be?" Marcus asked. "You're strong, sexy, stubborn and smart as hell. If I had any doubts about your character and strength before, they're gone now. And after we arrest this guy, and we will, I have every intention of finishing what we started last night. Right now, he's made you his target. Therefore, you just became *my* priority. You may not have figured this out yet, but I'm also strong, smart and stubborn as hell. So, don't even bother arguing with me about this. You're my priority now. Get over it."

"Well, there you go." Ryan chuckled. "Although, you forgot to add sexy onto *your* list, Mr. Secret Agent Man."

Marcus shrugged, a slight smirk pulling at his lips as he refocused his gaze on Evelyn.

"Yes, indeed." Kate's eyes twinkled.

Evelyn had walked into that one. *Damn it.* Not willing to deal with his statement or the emotions they'd evoked within her, she changed the subject again. "Okay, so what's next?"

"We hold a press conference," Marcus said.

"What?" She flinched back as if struck in the face. "Absolutely not. The captain won't sign off on that."

"He already did."

She stared at Marcus. The emotional whiplash this man induced startled and infuriated her. She struggled to get her frustration under wraps. She had to rely on her gut. And her gut told her to trust this guy, even though her impenetrable wall was still up, the years of automatic self-defense still screaming at her to do the opposite.

"My take on the killer's profile is fluid at best. I'm not certain I've locked it down enough. Are you sure a press conference at this stage in the game is the best direction to take?" Evelyn shifted uncomfortably in her chair. She hadn't been able to lock in the profile, and that ate at her. Going to the public with something so uncertain made her extremely nervous.

"It has the potential to cause mass chaos," she said.

Marcus opened his briefcase and pulled out a file. "Actually, your profile is better than you think. I called my brother, Derek, who's a forensic psychologist and one of the lead profilers at Quantico. I asked him to write up a profile based on the information we had on this guy."

"And?"

He slid the file across the table and smiled. "Your profile matched his. Exactly."

Evelyn didn't miss the pride in Marcus's voice. She scanned the file, her face growing warm from the heat creeping up her neck. Ryan threw a knowing glance toward Kate. Their eyes met, and her lips curled.

"So, no," Marcus said. "A press conference at this stage won't cause mass chaos, if done properly. And it's needed."

"We can't stay quiet on this thing any longer, Evelyn," Ryan said.

Marcus nodded. "It's imperative we downgrade the celebrity factor of the Seattle Slayer and bring to light the severity of this case. Put all of Seattle on alert. Plus, we need him to know that we have his scent."

"But we don't…" Unease settled into the pit of her stomach. She couldn't see any good coming out of this.

"But he doesn't know that," Ryan said. "Having Marcus and I give a press conference to alert the city will rattle him, knock him off his game."

"Ahhh," Kate said. "It'll fluster him, especially if Evelyn is nowhere to be seen."

Marcus grabbed the file. "He'll want to know—need to know—why you aren't on the case any longer. Did you get hurt? Did you pull yourself off?"

"Or he could retaliate." Evelyn wouldn't put it past him, if for no other reason than just to prove he could.

"Hopefully he'll get sloppy and make a mistake in the process of trying to figure it out and reconnect with you. Then—" Ryan slapped his hand on the table "—we'll nail his ass."

Marcus picked up his Malbec and took another swig. He set it down, then looked at Evelyn. "Yup. We'll nail the bastard's ass."

"You know I want this guy as much as any of you, probably more. I'd like my life back. But this still seems a bit fast to me. This guy is extremely volatile. A public display of strength on SPD's part could very well push him to lash out again." Evelyn couldn't shake the unease working its way up her spine. "Did the chief really sign off on this?"

Ryan nodded.

"It's been approved all the way up the chain to the mayor," Marcus said. "It's happening tomorrow."

"I get the need to calm the city. But this…" She bit her lip.

"Ev." Ryan picked up his beer and tipped it toward her. "It's the right move."

Somehow she doubted it.

CHAPTER TWENTY-ONE

A WARNING RANG somewhere in the deep recesses of Evelyn's subconscious, screaming at her. *Proceed with caution. Proceed with extreme caution.* Calling the press conference was the right thing to do. Her profile being confirmed by the guys at Quantico solidified that. They needed to educate the public not only to keep them safe, but also to reassure them that the SPD was doing its job. She got that. In any other case, she'd have been the first one to suggest it.

Still, something made her pause.

She stared blankly at her computer screen. Kate plopped down on the edge of Evelyn's desk, startling her. Her friend held out a steaming cup of coffee. "Where's my hunk of a husband?"

Evelyn took the mug and sipped the hot brew. They'd all stayed up late going over the files, throwing hypotheses at the wall, reworking them. She hadn't slept after Marcus left. Every time she closed her eyes and started to fall into a fitful slumber, gruesome images flashed against her eyelids. In vivid detail, she saw the Garlands…the Middletons…and Anastasia. Every time her mind's eye would land on the most precious, familiar crime scene photo, and sharpen focus on her family, she'd jolt awake. She knew the current murders only mimicked her family's to grab her attention. But still, the subconscious tie disturbed her.

Hence the need for a caffeine fix.

"They just left to meet with the mayor's office before the press conference." Evelyn took another sip of the rich liquid. A contented sigh slipped from her lips.

"That's nice." Kate crossed her legs. "I actually came to see you."

"Oh, yeah?"

"Yep." Kate set her coffee down. "Tell me the truth. How are you holding up?"

Evelyn studied her friend for a moment and debated whether or not to be honest with her. *What the hell.*

"This case is kicking my ass. And I hate that. Every time I shut my eyes, I'm bombarded with flashes of all these gruesome crime scenes." She picked up the stack of photos next to her, held them up and let them fall from her fingers. She shook her head, then pinched the bridge of her nose.

She looked up to see Kate's brows scrunched together. Worry simmered in her eyes.

"And I feel it all." Evelyn pressed her hand to her heart, agony washing over her. "All the pain, all the heartache, all the worry. All the fear of those families' loved ones. I feel it all. Every second I work this case, every moment I spend with a loved one, my heart gets filleted. Slowly. Plus, now that they've decided to backseat me...well, I feel like I've failed them. The families, I mean."

Kate shifted her weight, uncrossed her legs and hooked her ankles. "You haven't failed them, Evelyn. And you haven't been backseated. You're still an important part of the team. But given the recent developments…"

Evelyn's eyes widened.

"Ryan told me last night about the knife and photos." Kate's pursed her lips. "First, I'm a bit surprised—and pissed—that you didn't tell me yourself. And second, did you really think he'd keep that from me?"

Evelyn cringed, then shook her head. She'd thought about calling Kate, then that second had passed and the nightmarish day kept right on rolling. After Marcus read Kate in on the case last night, she'd just expected Ryan to fill her in on all the nasty little details. Including the bloody hunting knife stuck in her front door. Evelyn squirmed. *That* little detail should've come from her. As her best friend and the closest thing to a sister she had left, Kate deserved that much.

"I meant to tell you about the knife. Sorry."

Kate shrugged. "It's okay. But for the record, I think it's smart. That you're keeping a low profile."

Evelyn leaned back in her chair and stared up at the ugly ceiling. "It's infuriating. And crippling. And demoralizing. How can I help if an invisible ball and chain is shackling me?"

"Come on, Ev. There's no invisible ball and chain unless you've put it there. You're fully capable of performing that magic of yours, whether you're front and center or right here. If the powers that be didn't think you could handle it, they'd never have brought you and Ry on as lead." She leaned closer. "And the only reason you're being asked to take a more invisible role now is because they care about you. They're protecting their own. Besides, you'd do the exact same thing if you were in the chief's shoes, and you know it. You're invaluable to the team. Don't forget that. And as far as your heart goes, I'd be worried if you didn't feel it. It's what makes you so good at your job. Don't discount it now."

Evelyn smiled. "Thanks. I seriously don't know what I would do without you. You're a pillar of strength for me."

"Me? A pillar of strength? For you?" Kate laughed. "How can you be so brilliant and so not, all at the same time?"

Evelyn cocked her head.

"You've got it all wrong. Don't you get it? *You* are the pillar of strength here. Not me, not Ryan. *You*." She picked up her coffee and carefully sipped as she scrutinized Evelyn. Worry and fatigue washed over her beautiful face. Kate sat her mug down. "We aren't going anywhere, sweetie. So stop worrying about that. Focus on the case."

Evelyn grimaced. "I'm not feeling very strong lately."

Kate stood, then smoothed her jade-toned pencil skirt. "You're stronger than you think, braver than anyone I've ever met or will ever meet. I'm certain of that. So don't doubt yourself. No one else does."

CHAPTER TWENTY-TWO

LATER THAT AFTERNOON, back at work, Evelyn paced as she watched the TV screen. Her head throbbed and her heart pounded against her ribs. She wiped her palms against her pants. Any minute now, the press conference would start. On screen, the mayor's chief of staff gave a brief introduction before the mayor and her team walked to the stage. Evelyn sat on the edge of her desk and observed as the mayor straightened his tie.

"Good afternoon. Thank you for joining us today. With me are Chief Diaz and FBI Special Agent Marcus Moretti. Agent Moretti's been consulting with the Seattle Police Department on this unfortunate series of murders."

Evelyn snorted. *Unfortunate. That's the only word you could come up with?*

"To his left is Detective Ryan O'Neil. He's our Seattle Police Department lead, who is heading up this investigation. After working with the local FBI office and Special Agent Moretti, the SPD is closer than ever to finding the killer the media has dubbed the Seattle Slayer. We've called this press conference to calm and educate the people of Seattle about the true facts of this ongoing investigation."

He turned toward Marcus and nodded. "Now, I

would like to turn the podium over to Special Agent Marcus Moretti."

Marcus looked handsome in his dark blue suit and yellow tie. She rolled her eyes. *Oh, good grief, really?* Even on TV, he made her heart race. Her cheeks flushed as her mind replayed his gentle caresses.

"Stupid man." She twirled her chair in a circle.

Marcus cleared his throat. "Thank you, Mr. Mayor. This individual is most likely a white male in his late thirties, early forties. He'll be very well-educated and, at first glance, easygoing and approachable. However, he most likely has extensive combat training and is very dangerous. If you suspect anything unusual, do not, under any circumstances, approach this individual. Call 911 immediately. Let us apprehend him. The most important thing is to stay calm, be diligent and watch for unfamiliar activities or anything unusual. We're working tirelessly on your behalf."

He turned toward Ryan. "Detective O'Neil."

Ryan nodded at Marcus, then stepped up to the podium. He was also sharp in a black suit and blue tie. "Thank you. As Special Agent Moretti already confirmed, we're working diligently toward finding this suspect. We're confident our team will apprehend him quickly. Until then, we're asking the public to report any suspicious activity to our hotline."

Evelyn got up and paced like a lioness in an iron cage. She should be at the press conference—bad idea or not—showing the city of Seattle that her team wasn't scared, that they were upholding their promise to protect and serve and that they were a strong, impenetrable, united front. She should be there, standing shoulder-to-shoulder with Marcus and Ryan. She turned back to the TV, her mind landing on Ryan. He'd stopped talking.

"Detective?"

Ryan pointed to the rear of the room. A young reporter's face lit up as he straightened and held out his recorder. Evelyn went back to pacing.

"Detective, what else can you tell us about the Seattle Slayer?"

"The Seattle Slay—"

Evelyn slammed to a halt. Her head snapped up and she spun around, catching the subtle twitch in Ryan's jaw. His knuckles grew white as he gripped the podium. Her heart pounded so hard against her rib cage she thought her chest might burst.

"Don't." She pleaded to the screen. "Please, Ryan, don't."

His face hardened, eyes darkening. "Let's call this what it truly is, folks. This guy is a psychopathic killer, not a celebrity."

The reporter shrank back, all light gone from his face.

Evelyn's heart sank, afraid of what he'd say next.

Ryan stared directly into the camera. "We know you're watching, and we have a message for you—"

"No, we don't," Evelyn yelled at the TV. Marcus threw Ryan a startled glance. She stood alone, powerless in the empty bull pen, as Ryan threw down an invisible gauntlet to the monster terrorizing their city.

"We *will* find you. You can't hide from us forever. You'll make a mistake, and we'll nail your ass."

Marcus leaned toward the podium and put one hand on Ryan's shoulder. "That's all, folks. Thank you."

She slumped into her chair and dropped her head

into her hands as her stomach plunged to her toes. *What had Ryan just done?*

The rest of the briefing came and went. Evelyn didn't even listen. She sat at her desk, fuming. She'd gone from horrified to pissed in all of about two minutes. She didn't even bother turning off the TV after Marcus and Ryan exited the stage. She'd known this press conference was a bad idea. Everyone was on edge. *Why had no one listened to her?* Wasn't she supposed to be the resident badass who could get into the mind of a killer, close the impossible cases? Wasn't she the one who was being poached by the Bureau because of that exact skill? So why the hell hadn't they listened? Calm the city, yes. Spit in the face of this killer, no.

"WHAT THE HELL was that, Ryan?" Evelyn asked the moment he and Marcus stepped out of the elevator.

Ryan pushed past her. He sat at his desk and answered with a sheepish shrug. "I got a little carried away. It won't happen again."

"You got—" She choked on her words. "You got a little carried away? You shouldn't have gone off like that."

"Ev, it won't happen again. I've got this." He loosened his tie and unbuttoned the top button of his shirt. "Calm down. It'll be fine."

"Don't tell me to calm down," she snapped. "And no, it won't be fine. You just publicly challenged him. If he was watching—"

"Which he was," Marcus interjected.

"—you all but personally invited him to prove you wrong."

Ryan's face went white. "Shit."

"Yes. 'Shit' is right."

Marcus leaned against the wall. "We've got to think about doing damage control on this before he retaliates."

"Not tonight, Marcus." She sank into her chair. "If we go back on the air, it'll appear we've made a mistake. Which will only fuel him further. Tonight, we sit on it."

He shook her head. "I don't like it. But you're right."

"So now what?" Ryan asked.

"You go home." Marcus said it so quietly, Evelyn almost missed it. Her eyebrows shot up.

Ryan rose. His eyes flashed. "No way. Look, I saw red at the thought of glamorizing this bastard targeting Evelyn, and I responded. I'm sorry. I didn't think, just reacted. It won't happen again."

Marcus put his hand on Ryan's shoulder. "I know. Believe me, I want this guy just as much as you do. But you're too worked up about this. Go home. Tuck the kids in bed. I'll drop Evelyn off in a bit. Then we'll regroup tomorrow morning, first thing."

Ryan threw a pleading look at Evelyn. "Ev—"

"It's okay, Ryan. Go home."

A mixture of emotions flashed across his face. Evelyn recognized the remorse and frustration. She bit her lip. Now was not the time to go soft on her partner. He needed to cool down, for all their sakes.

Without another word, Ryan turned and stormed to the stairwell. He slammed his open palm into the door, which bounced off the wall as he exited. And just like that, he was gone.

Marcus walked over and sat in the seat Ryan had vacated.

"Did you know he was going to go off like that?" she asked.

He raised his hands in defense, then shook his head.

She sighed. Of course he didn't know. She'd seen the startled look on his face as Ryan went off on his tangent. That wasn't something you could fake.

"How bad is it?" he asked.

"He'll be fine. He cools off quickly. Kate, on the other hand, may be pissed at you for stirring him up by sending him home. But you made the right call."

She pushed her chair back and stretched before grabbing her jacket and putting it on. "I need a drink. Since you're my taxi service tonight, care to join me?"

Marcus grinned. "You know I do."

CHAPTER TWENTY-THREE

Coffee at Starbucks wasn't exactly the type of drink Marcus had in mind when Evelyn invited him to join her. He'd hoped for something more. But she'd been right in insisting that it be coffee, not hard liquor, that pacified them tonight. He didn't care really. As long as he got to spend time with Evelyn, he was one happy man.

So here they were, tucked securely in the far corner, backs to the wall, eyes on the door, silently nursing their drinks. Old habits died hard, and every muscle in his body was taut, ready for action if called upon.

"Sorry about Ryan." Evelyn looked down and swirled the steaming liquid. "He can be a bit of a hothead."

Marcus chuckled. "You think?"

Her gaze snapped to his face and her eyes flashed. "He's a good cop."

"Easy, tiger. No need to defend him, Ev. Ryan's solid."

Marcus should have been pissed that Ryan mouthed off on live television, but he wasn't. How could he be, when Evelyn's partner had merely beaten him to it? The very idea that this sociopath still ran loose sent chills down Marcus's spine.

The door chime sounded. Both Evelyn and Marcus glanced over as a younger couple walked in.

"It's almost as if these murders are fueling him." Evelyn took a sip of coffee. Her face grew hard. "But what's the trigger? Why is the rage intensifying? Is he searching for revenge? For a release? Nothing makes sense with this guy, and it's driving me insane."

Marcus needed to change the subject, and fast. Even the best needed a break, a moment to give their brain time to reboot. He'd hoped to give that time to Evelyn now, not rehash pieces of the case.

"Tell me about this fed friend of yours."

She sat back, clearly startled at the about-face in conversation. "Not following."

"The friend you talked about the first day we met. In the conference room." He winked at her and motioned with his hands. "I think your exact words were, 'I don't think FBI agents are idiots, *Special* Agent Moretti. As a matter of fact, one of my closest friends is FBI.'"

"Oh, yes." Evelyn laughed. "You must mean Fiona?"

Marcus reached for his steaming cup of coffee and scanned the room before returning his gaze on Evelyn's face. "So, where is this friend of yours based out of?"

"San Diego. She's the Bureau liaison with ICE's Human Smuggling and Trafficking Unit."

Marcus's eyebrows shot up. *ICE?* Sex trafficking was organized and violent, particularly along the border. Would-be terrorists and criminals often accessed the same routes as the traffickers. Working in that unit required a thick skin and some serious skill—both in combat and in brains. Somehow it didn't surprise him that one of Evelyn's best friends would be working in such a capacity. It seemed everyone in Evelyn's inner circle was a step above the average Joe. Would this woman, casually sitting across from him, ever cease to amaze him? He smiled. Probably not.

"Impressive."

"You don't even know the half of it. She's amazing. Her strength inspires me." Evelyn's eyes softened. She took another sip of her latte. "She's a bit like me— survivor turned champion of other victims."

"How so?"

He wasn't sure he wanted her to answer him. If Evelyn had survived her family's murder and become a homicide detective, her statement could only mean that Fiona had been a victim of the sex trade herself. Bile rose up in his throat. No one should have to survive that type of brutal horror.

"She was sold," Evelyn said softly. "She was only eleven."

"Eleven?" The word came out in a primal growl. Marcus felt his blood boil.

She pursed her lips. "I know. Disgusting, right?"

"There are no words."

"We met a year after she'd escaped, at a youth hostel in San Diego."

"She escaped? How?" Marcus knew the stats. The majority of trafficked victims didn't escape.

"Sorry." She shook her head. "Some stories aren't meant to be told."

"Fair enough. Go on."

"So here we are, two broken, grieving, angry teenagers, trying to figure out what to do with the remaining pieces of our lives. If it hadn't been so sad, it would've been a bit comical."

She shifted in her seat and tucked her leg underneath her. "A sweet volunteer at the hostel recognized the signs of trauma we were both clearly exhibiting, and somehow, bless her soul, convinced us to see this counselor friend of hers who specialized in youth trauma. The volunteer opened her house to us, and we both spent the next two years healing. Our friendship blossomed. Ultimately, our goals took us in different directions."

She smiled, looking nostalgic. "There's this bond between Fiona and I that distance can't break."

"You're pretty incredible. You know that, right?"

The blush creeping up her neck surprised him. He swallowed the chuckle in his throat. It hadn't gone unnoticed to him that she'd opened up. Let him in to her inner circle. And now, willingly talking so candidly about her past, she'd let him even further into the secret chambers of her heart. He didn't take that lightly. Nor did he want anything—even a well-meaning, affectionate chuckle—to ruin that. Especially when he had every intention of staying in that inner circle for good. There was no better time than now to test the waters with just how far she'd let him wander into that gorgeous, generous and strong heart of hers.

"And to be completely truthful with you, Detective Davis, I'm falling for you." He all but whispered the words, his voice raspy. He studied her face, watching for a reaction.

She put down her coffee, wove her fingers together and leaned her chin on them. Blue eyes sparkled with a fascinating combination of reservation and excitement. Marcus's heart jumped into his throat.

"Well...don't let it go to your head, Special Agent Moretti, but I'm beginning to think the same about you."

She threw him a coy smile, then winked before picking up her latte and taking another sip.

His heart kicked into overdrive. *Be cool, man, just be cool.* Promise shimmered in her eyes. He wanted nothing more than to know all of her. Marcus shifted in his chair. He couldn't wait to nail this psycho and wrap up this case.

CHAPTER TWENTY-FOUR

RYAN BLINKED. THE tiny movement sent excruciating agony through every part of his body. Pain and confusion clouded his mind, making his thoughts muddy. He blinked again and tried to get up off the floor. Why was he on the floor? What was that putrid smell? Why did everything hurt? He shook his head to clear his mind, then vomited as the room began to spin. Pain boiled over, searing every nerve ending. He managed to pull himself up to his hands and knees and cried out before collecting his breath. Crimson droplets and tears fell from the tip of his nose and dripped onto the floor. He tasted copper in his mouth.

Blood was everywhere.

The room spun, tilted on its axis. Speckled lights flitted in and out of his vision. With each ragged breath, his chest convulsed in violent spasms. He felt as if he were breathing through Jell-O.

What was happening?

Nothing made sense.

When he'd left Kate and Ava in the kitchen, they were devouring vanilla gelato straight out of the container. The last thing he recalled was kissing Liam and laying him down to bed. He remembered turning on the sound machine, then softly pulling the door closed.

Then he'd felt searing pain in his back.

He'd turned. Another jolt of pain had hit him as a blade plunged into the softness of his belly. His breath had left him, but still he'd fought hard, Kate and Ava on his mind. He had to get to the kitchen. Protect his family.

He'd twisted and rolled away from another swing of the knife. Protecting his family was his sole goal. He'd driven his shoulder into the hooded man, then tackled him. They'd tumbled down the stairs and landed hard. He'd looked up and seen the butt of a gun come down. Then darkness.

Soft cries from the kitchen screamed for his attention. Panic tore into him. He dragged himself from the dining room, a trail of blood following behind his wrecked body. Pushing through the torture, he crawled down the hallway toward the quiet, desperate pleas. Kate. He could hear Kate begging someone. *Who was she talking to?* Suddenly, she cried out. A single gunshot exploded in his ears. His wife's hysterical sobs echoed in his mind, then went quiet. Too quiet.

He tried to stand. His legs buckled, betraying him. Collapsing against the wall and gasping for air, he put his hands on his knees, then struggled to right himself. A figure loomed over him.

Ryan gathered his waning energy and lunged, desperate to get to his family. He needed to see them. Protect them. The figure sidestepped Ryan's feeble advance. He fell. The figure's boot came down and cracked against Ryan's skull. His face exploded in blinding pain. He tried to raise his head, but the movement sent an electric surge through his body.

He opened his eyes and stared through blood and tears. "Why are you doing this? What do you want?"

The man knelt in front of him. His head cocked to one side, and his eyes narrowed into tiny slits.

"What do I want? I want Evelyn to know that she misjudged me. She should've taken me more seriously. She can't take from me and expect me not to take from her." He sneered at Ryan. "So I'm sending a message."

He leaned into Ryan's face and pressed his hand into one of Ryan's knife wounds. Ryan swallowed the moan in his throat.

"Do you think Evelyn will get this one? That I stole the only family she had left?"

"Evelyn?" Ryan's mind was muddy, hazy, but he knew he had to keep the bastard talking. "What do you have against her?"

"She lived. My family died, but that bitch lived. It's her fault. She was supposed to pay then. She got lucky. Her family didn't. But I'm collecting now."

"You're…" *The man who killed Evelyn's family.* He couldn't bring himself to say the words. And just as she'd been powerless to save them then, he was now helpless to save her or his own family. His heart stuttered and dropped. His body sagged as despair ripped through him.

"Yes. I'm…I'm…" He mimicked Ryan in a singsong voice. "I've tracked her for fifteen years. But now I've got her. And there's not a thing you can do about it."

A cruel smile spread across his dark features. He raised the gun.

Ryan stared down the cold metal barrel. Hope trickled out of him. His chest constricted and his breath caught in his throat. He'd lost his wife. Pain gripped his heart and squeezed. He couldn't lose Evelyn, too; he needed to warn her. But he knew he couldn't. He'd failed her, failed them. He turned his face toward the kitchen that held his broken, bloodied family. Sorrow tore at his soul. A series of sharp cracks exploded into the still air.

Then Ryan felt nothing.

CHAPTER TWENTY-FIVE

THE EVENING HAD been perfect. Marcus wanted to prolong it and take Evelyn down to the local hole-in-the-wall pub he'd discovered, then continue talking over a nice bottle of wine. But with a sweet smile, Evelyn had insisted on going back to Ryan's. So here he was, opening the car door so he could take her back to her partner's home. How did this woman have such an effect on him? He grinned. He liked it.

She turned, reached up and gently put her hands on either side of his face. Marcus's pulse took off. Without a word, she pressed her lips softly to his. Disappointment shot through him when she pulled back. He wanted so much more.

"I'm glad you're here, Marcus." Evelyn smiled up at him, her eyes twinkling. "Let's close this case already."

She winked and slid into the passenger seat, then looked back at him, her eyes soft, warm and trusting. His heart jumped. Had she just…? Yes. He could see it in her body language, her face, her expression. She'd just let him in—completely. He'd thought it was coming, felt something shift between them during the evening. But it still somehow managed to leave him speechless.

Evelyn Davis had just let him into her heart.

As he shut the door, he grinned like an idiot, then walked around the front of the car and got in. She locked eyes with him again and he forgot to breathe. Swallowing hard, he turned the key and the engine rumbled to life. He checked over his shoulder, then pulled into the light traffic on Pike Place.

He grabbed her hand. "You know, all I want to do right now is take you to my place."

Color stained her cheeks and a surprised, nervous laugh bubbled out of her. After a brief pause, she smiled at him. "And all I want to do right now is say ye—"

His police scanner squawked, interrupting her. "Shots fired. We have a possible oh-ten at 5345 Southwest Admiral Way. All available units respond immediately."

The color drained from her face. She pulled her hand from his and lunged for the purse sitting at her feet. She frantically rifled through it until she pulled out her phone. "No, no, no."

Marcus yanked the wheel hard, slammed on the brakes and threw the car into Park. "What? What is it?"

Her fingers shook as she hit the number one on her speed dial, then pressed the phone to her ear for a moment. She hung up, then hit redial. "Come on…come on…don't give me voice mail. Pick up!"

"Evelyn. Talk to me. Now."

"It's going directly to voice mail." She stared straight ahead. "That's Ryan's address."

Marcus's eyebrows knit together. Before she could utter another word, he threw the car into Drive and, tires squealing, pulled a U-turn in the middle of Pike Place.

"He's not picking up." Terror was etched in her face. Her eyes turned turquoise as tears threatened to overflow.

He flipped on his siren and lights. The siren screamed as he gunned it.

"Call again."

She grabbed the dash as he weaved, dodging traffic. She hit the next number on her speed dial and clutched the phone.

"Kate isn't picking up, either," she whispered.

Marcus heard the panic in Evelyn's voice. It sent cold fear down his spine. *Please, God, let them be okay.*

"Call again."

She punched at the phone and hugged it between her ear and shoulder, then pointed at the looming green street sign. "Take Western to Lenora, then hang a left. Get onto Alaskan Way. Go, go, go!"

With surgeonlike precision, Marcus maneuvered his car through the throng of traffic toward Western. Dread snaked its way around his heart and squeezed.

"Without traffic, it'll take at least ten minutes to get there."

"Yeah, if you're driving like a fucking civilian," Marcus said, pressing the accelerator farther to the floor.

"Get onto West Seattle Bridge."

The car flew over the wet concrete. The streetlights flashed by in a blur. The minutes crawled, each second more agonizing than the last. His mind tumbled over itself, endless possibilities emerging for him to filter through. None of them good.

"Take Admiral. Follow it around," she shouted.

The force of gravity pushed them into their seats as his car hugged the curve, topping ninety.

"Oh, God, please don't let us be too late. Please..." She whimpered against the back of her hand pressed firmly to her mouth.

His heart pounded. He wanted to take it all away:

the fear, the panic, the pain. If he could, he'd absorb it all into himself.

Marcus pressed the pedal harder and the speedometer flashed past ninety-five. He should slow down. The road was hazardous enough without adding the slickness of the falling rain, but he ignored the warning bells clanging loudly in his head and inched the car toward one hundred. Instead of speaking to Evelyn, he focused on driving, on getting them to Ryan's house.

Besides, what was he supposed to say? That everything was going to be okay? That maybe it was a mistake? How could he say any of those things when none of them were true? His gut twisted as he thought about Ryan, Kate and the kids.

What the hell would he and Evelyn find waiting for them?

Up ahead was the flashing light of a cop car. He took his foot off the accelerator, letting the vehicle slow itself down. "Evelyn. Let me go in—"

Evelyn whimpered again and angrily dabbed at her eyes before glaring at him.

"No way. I'm going in. We don't know anything yet." She unbuckled her seat belt and stared straight ahead as they approached. One hand rested on the door handle, the other tightened into a fist in her lap.

He pulled up to the house, stomped on the brakes. "Evelyn, wait for me."

But before the car settled to a stop, she'd grabbed a set of latex gloves from her bag, thrown herself out of the car and raced toward the open front door. Marcus slammed his hand against the steering wheel. Nothing good could come out of this.

CHAPTER TWENTY-SIX

EVELYN IGNORED MARCUS and ran to see Ryan and his family. She shoved down the emotions that threatened to engulf her. The panic. The fear. Now was not the time or place to lose her edge—she owed it to them to do things right. She'd seen her share of crime scenes, but this would be different. She took a deep breath and quickened her stride, slipping on the latex gloves as she went. She took the stairs to the front door two at a time and flashed her badge to the uniform standing guard, then muscled herself through the door.

There was blood everywhere.

Deep crimson pools stained the off-white carpet in the dining room. It splattered the hallway walls, and bloody handprints smeared the staircase railing leading upstairs. The stairs no longer looked white. Large stains marred them in an odd pattern, as if someone had thrown a basketball coated in red paint down them.

DEATH HIT HER like a wrecking ball. Skidding to a halt, she covered her mouth to keep the cry from escaping her throat. *My God, what happened?* She stood horrified, her eyes sweeping the scene.

She glanced to the left, to the right, but her feet refused to move. She didn't know where to go first.

She moved to go upstairs, then she saw him.

Ryan.

He was slouched against the wall at the far end of the hallway. He wasn't moving.

"Oh, God, please, no." Without hesitation, she ran to him. She stared down at him, her stomach heaving. He was barely recognizable, his body riddled with bullet holes. His head was down, chin resting on his right shoulder, and his arms drooped limply at his sides. His left eye was swollen shut. An angry gash split open his bottom lip. A large red stain covered the lower part of his shirt.

Despite what she saw, she crouched down and put her fingers against the side of his throat.

Nothing. There was nothing. No pulse. No hope that he could be saved.

Ryan was gone.

She hung her head, pushing against the advancing pain and the sorrow threatening to consume her. *God, please, not again.* She squeezed her eyes shut and shuddered. Blackness swarmed the edges of her vision, eager to pull her to its waiting black pit. She dropped to her knees, cradled her head in her hands and focused on breathing. In. Out. In. Out. She couldn't pass out now. With each measured breath, Evelyn shoved back the advancing darkness until it was a mere shadow at the edge of her consciousness.

Marcus came up beside her and dropped to his knees. He caught her in his steady gaze, his eyes soft, searching. She couldn't deal with his warmth. If she gave in to it now, she'd never recover. Evelyn shook her head. He nodded and looked past her to the kitchen, his face hardening.

She didn't need to go to the kitchen to know what

she'd find. One of Kate's feet, now bloodied, stuck out from the kitchen door frame, her perfectly manicured toes marred with dark stains. Evelyn bent over Ryan, her body slumped. *I can't do this, not again.*

She looked down at her gloved hands. They were covered in blood. Ryan's blood. Her heart stuttered. She shouldn't have touched him. A visual exam would have confirmed what she'd already known.

Ryan was dead.

"I just need a moment," she whispered, reaching for Marcus's hand.

"You got it."

And that's all she took: a moment. A moment to collect herself, set aside the pain, banish the fear, bridle the grief.

She knew from experience that it would all be there when this was over. But for now, she pushed it aside, locked it away.

A commotion to her right pulled at her. She opened her eyes. Officers rushed into the house and slammed to a halt. Silence engulfed the house. Evelyn rose and glanced around. She cleared her throat. All eyes were on her.

She took a deep breath. "Listen up, everyone. This isn't just any crime scene with unknown victims. This is Ryan, his family. My partner. They're our own. Family. Right now, I need the best from you." Evelyn looked from face to face, locking eyes with each of the officers in front of her. "If you can't be here, and I mean all in, I understand. This is hard for everyone. But if you can't, please leave now. No one will think less of—"

She hadn't even finished before the newest member of the force shook his head, mumbled a sorrowful apology and walked out. Watching him go stung, but she understood. She nodded, then turned to the rest of the cops. "Anyone else? It's okay."

No one budged.

"All right, then." She pointed to the officers closest to her. "You two, upstairs. Phelan, take three guys and canvas the area. This bastard could've stuck around to see the show. But this isn't a show. This is *our* family. And we *will* find the guy who did this."

Marcus handed her a new set of latex gloves. She yanked off the set covered in Ryan's blood, pulled on the fresh ones and moved toward the kitchen, bracing herself for what they might find.

Ava lay half in Kate's arms. A single bullet hole was in her young forehead. Blood soaked the floor beneath them. Relief washed over Evelyn. Ava hadn't suffered. *Thank you, God. That little girl hadn't suffered.*

Then Evelyn's heart slammed to a halt. The blood in her veins turned to ice. "Stop. Everyone stop moving, now! Where's Liam?"

"What?" one officer asked.

"Liam. Ryan's little boy. He's not here. He's not in the kitchen."

The officer shrugged. "Jones did the upstairs walk-through."

"Find Jones. Bring him to me. Now!"

Frantic now, panic flooded her like a tidal wave. Was he hiding? Was he hurt? Waves of grief and fury surged through her, rolling over her with each heartbeat. Blood pounded in her ears, its roar deafening.

Jones rushed up. "Detective, we checked the upstairs level. No one was there. Both children's beds were empty."

"Then where is he?"

"I don't know. Lemme check with Phelan. Maybe they found him outside."

"Go. Check in with him. I want an immediate report."

Marcus came up next to her.

"Marcus, you don't think that bastard took—"

"No, Evelyn. Stop. Don't go there. We'll find him."

She took a deep breath. Steadied the wild dark thoughts swirling in her mind. Marcus was right. She couldn't go there. Wouldn't go there.

Evelyn turned back to Kate, the closet thing she'd had to a sister. Her stomach rolled, threatening to empty its contents.

She rubbed her temples. "Get someone from the D.A.'s office on the phone."

"That might take a while. It's late. Will anyone be there?" Officer Massey asked.

"I don't care that it's late. Get someone on the phone now. If you have to drag the D.A. himself out of bed, do it."

Bile rose into her throat as she knelt beside her friend. Evelyn knew the killer had come after Ryan's family to show that he was more powerful and in charge. She knew it.

Careful not to contaminate anything, Evelyn inspected Kate. There were multiple stab wounds to her back. Cuts and bruises covered her forearms and hands. Evelyn managed a tight smile. "Damn, girl, you put up a fight, didn't you? Good for you, giving him hell."

She wouldn't have expected anything less from her feisty Irish friend. But her smile vanished as she reached for one of Kate's hands. Averting her eyes from the deep, angry, crimson gashes along her friend's back, Evelyn focused on Kate's fingertips. "Now, tell me, sweets, did you tear into him?"

What a nightmare.

"I need forensics in here," she called down the hall as she stood.

A young officer scurried into the kitchen.

"Can you check her now?" Evelyn asked, pointing to Kate.

He nodded and knelt. She watched him study Kate's fingertips with one goal: to find human skin, hair, blood, something, anything, under her nails. But deep cuts tore at the soft flesh of each fingertip.

He looked up and shook his head. "There's nothing here but bloody pulps, Detective. It looks like whoever did this took a knife and removed any evidence."

Evelyn's blood boiled. The killer was smart. She straightened up. But she was smarter.

"Anything yet, Massey?" she asked the officer, who was on his cell.

He looked over his shoulder and shook his head, clearly irritated.

Another officer appeared beside her. "Umm, Detective Davis?"

"Yes, Stevenson, what is it?"

Her eyes darted past him, back to Massey huddled in the corner, phone lodged between his shoulder and ear. Tearing her eyes back to the officer next to her, she waited for him to answer her.

"I think you need to see this."

"See what, Stevenson? Spit it out," she snapped. She said it more sharply than she'd intended to, but her nerves were raw, her filter gone.

Cheeks flushed, he held out an evidence bag.

She snatched it from his extended hand and read the crudely scrawled note inside.

Don't underestimate me, Evelyn. This one's on you.

She spun around and vomited into the kitchen sink.

The room spun. She gripped the sink's edge to keep from sliding to the floor with the note clenched in her hand. The scrawled words tore at her, ripped through the softest parts of her, each word an angry, painful thrust.

This hellish nightmare couldn't be her fault. Could it? Could the horrible, violent deaths of the people she loved—of the only people she called family—be her fault? *Please, please don't let it be true.* Her stomach heaved again as the darkness advanced, and her knees buckled beneath her. She tightened her hold on the cool black granite countertop.

A soft pressure on the small of her back brought her back to the present. She lifted her head and was captured by Marcus's strong, concerned face.

"What is it?" he asked.

Evelyn held his gaze, drank in its unwavering strength. She never wanted to let go of him, never wanted to be away from that strength. The thought warmed and terrified her all at once. She forced herself to glance away. She had a job to do.

Hand shaking, she gave him the evidence bag and turned to the young officer, managing a small comforting smile. "Thank you, Stevenson. Can you show me where you found that note?"

He nodded and motioned toward the hall.

Marcus read the note. "Son of a bitch."

"What the hell is going on here?" Kessler hollered, storming in. "Moretti, get her out of here. Now!"

"What? No! Captain, I need to be here. He's my partner. Those kids and his wife, they were the closest thing I had to a family."

Kessler shook his head. "That's exactly why you *can't* be here."

"Sir, you need to see this." Marcus handed the evidence bag to him.

Kessler scanned the contents. His face blanched. He looked at Evelyn.

Tilting her chin, she stared back at the captain. *Don't send me away, please.*

"She needs to be in protective custody," Marcus said.

"No. Absolutely not." Evelyn crossed her arms over her chest. "I'm fine."

"I agree," Kessler said to Marcus as if he hadn't heard her. "I'll speak with the chief to set it up. Starting immediately."

"That's not necessary. She can stay with me. No one knows where I live. It's a sublet."

Chief Diaz stormed into the house and slammed to a halt. He glanced between Kessler and Evelyn, his face darkening. "What's she doing here? Kessler, I told you to keep her out of here."

Marcus stepped in. "I'm taking her to my place now, sir. For all practical purposes, it's as good as any safe house we can get."

The color in the Diaz's face drained. "Safe house? Kessler. Davis. *What* is going on?"

Kessler wordlessly handed the evidence bag to Diaz. He scanned the note. A string of colorful, deadly words flew out of his mouth. Eyes hard, he looked at Evelyn.

"I'm fine, really," she said.

"Evelyn, no one here is questioning your ability," Diaz said. "But you're going with Agent Moretti."

"Sir, that's not necessary. I said I'm fine."

Who was she kidding? She wasn't fine. But she needed to be here.

"This isn't a suggestion, Detective Davis. This is an order," Diaz said in an authoritative voice. She couldn't remember him ever using that tone with her before. That alone snapped her back to reality. The painful, soul-shattering reality that more people she loved had been ripped from her life. Tears flooded her eyes. She bit her lip to keep them at bay, then squared her shoulders.

"You'll stay at Agent Moretti's house until further notice. You won't leave his property until I've given the order. From this moment forward, I want you to all but disappear until we know more of what we're dealing with. You're my responsibility, and I won't have you putting yourself in harm's way. Do I make myself clear, Detective?"

Her jaw dropped. Had he just put her on house arrest? She suddenly felt very tired. As in, she might just slump onto the tile floor in front of all her colleagues, curl up and drift off into a deep, dark, endless sleep.

Before she could respond, Diaz turned and stepped close to Marcus's face. "As for you...I'm holding you fully responsible for the well-being of my officer. Anything happens to her, and I mean anything—a hangnail, a stubbed toe, anything—and you'll be answering directly to me. Believe me, you don't want to go there. Do you understand, Special Agent Moretti?"

Despite her current hell, a small smile crept onto Evelyn's face at the chief's fierce protection of her. Up until recently, he and Ryan were the only ones who knew her whole story, yet they never treated her differently, never coddled her. Her heart constricted as she thought about Ryan, and how much she already missed him.

"Chief." Her voice sounded strange, quiet, meek.

All three men turned to her, eyes filled with unspoken grief.

"I'll go with Moretti, but I need to be part of the team that finds this guy. And I need to find Liam. Please." She held her breath as the chief struggled with her request.

She was too close to the case, too emotionally involved. Emotions got people killed. But, hopefully, the chief wouldn't deny her request, her need to be in the thick of things, her need to put this asshole away for good. Would he? How could Diaz, Kessler or Marcus argue with such a request? Chief Diaz sighed, then rubbed his hand over his face.

"Fine." He grimaced slightly. "Against my better judgment, I'll allow it. But here are my conditions— you stay behind the scenes, and no one other than these two men are to know about this."

How could she possibly stay on the case if she couldn't be seen by anyone?

"I'm not kidding. Nothing public, Evelyn. You follow Agent Moretti's orders without hesitation. Do you understand?"

"Yes, sir."

Diaz put two fingers between his teeth and whistled. All movement stopped. All noise halted. Every eye in the home turned to face him. "Listen up, people. Evelyn is going to give you a description of Ryan's son. Take notes. I want every available officer out there searching for him. He's our number-one priority until he's found."

Evelyn took a deep breath and squared her shoulders. "Liam is sixteen months old. He has jet-black curls, blue eyes and dimples in both cheeks when he smiles." Her voice cracked. Marcus stepped close and put his hand on the small of her back. She cleared her throat. "He's about twenty-five pounds and roughly two and a half feet tall."

With every word she uttered, her heart broke all over again. She shouldn't be reciting Liam's stats to all these officers solemnly staring back at her. She should be cuddling him to her chest, assuring Ryan's sweet baby boy that everything was going to be all right.

That he would be all right.

But she couldn't.

And that pissed her off and broke her, all at once.

She yanked out her phone and pulled up her screensaver. The sight of Liam and Ava grinning up at her hardened Evelyn's resolve. She held up her phone. "Here is a recent photo of Liam. I'll send it to Captain Kessler and have him distribute it to everyone."

She paused for a moment, struggling to stay strong. "He's just a baby. We need to find him."

Diaz put his hand on Evelyn's shoulder and squeezed. "We will have all of SPD out looking for Liam. You have my word."

She bit her lip, fought to keep her composure. "Thank you, sir."

"But hear me, Evelyn. If for one second I think you're endangering yourself or this investigation, I won't hesitate to yank you from it so hard that your head will spin. Go. Now."

Diaz looked at Marcus. "Get her out of here. I'll be in touch."

With a curt nod, Marcus took Evelyn by the elbow and led her away. Away from the house, the blood, the death, the horror of what lay behind the walls.

She let him direct her. He opened the car door and held it for her. She stopped to look back at the house that had once held so many beautiful memories. Tremors tore down her spine. Her lips quivered.

"Evelyn," Marcus said softly. "Sweetheart, we need to go."

Tearing her gaze from the house, she let him help her into the car. She stared straight ahead, eyes focused on nothing.

CHAPTER TWENTY-SEVEN

MARCUS RAN HIS finger along the door seam of his penthouse apartment and checked the seal he'd installed before leaving that morning. Why did that feel like a million years ago? How could so much happen in such a short time?

The smooth seal was still intact. He sighed. At least this place was still uncompromised. He punched in the seven-digit code, then held open the door for Evelyn. She entered his apartment in front of him, still not speaking. He didn't like the silence. He understood it, but he didn't like it. Not one bit. He watched her move slowly, as if in a trance, through the door. She hadn't even made it past the foyer when she stopped cold.

"Evelyn?" Marcus spoke her name softly, quickly stepping around her to look her in the face.

Her eyes had glazed over.

Not good. Not good at all.

"Evelyn, sweetheart, come back to me."

Her eyes refocused. She looked down at her hands and a soft cry escaped her tightly pursed lips, almost like the meow of a newborn kitten.

Marcus cringed. He needed to get her clean. She was covered in blood—Ryan's blood, Kate's blood. She trembled.

Gently, without breaking eye contact, Marcus reached for her.

"Let's get you cleaned up. Okay? You can take a warm shower. Then sleep."

Still she didn't say a word. *Was she in shock?* "Evelyn?"

She blinked, then nodded.

It wasn't words, like he wanted, but it was something.

He took her elbow in one hand, letting his other hand rest on the small of her back as he steered her down the hall. He moved past the second bathroom just around the corner from the open kitchen. It was small, ordinary; not what she needed right now. Instead, he headed for the master bedroom. He'd move his stuff into the other bedroom later. His main focus was on getting her clean, getting the blood off of her body. The smell would linger in her nostrils, and the images of Ryan, Kate and Ava's broken bodies would be forever seared into her mind. And as much as he wanted to take those things from her, rid her of the pain they would undoubtedly cause her, there was nothing he could do.

He hated that.

But at least the master bathroom would give her the space and privacy to clean the part of her that she could.

He directed her into the bathroom and, without letting go of her elbow, he pulled the shower door open. With one hand, he reached inside, careful to keep contact with her, and turned on the faucet. A strong stream of water poured from the showerhead. Steam rose, lazily filling the room.

"Take as long as you need. I'll bring you something clean to wear, okay?" He didn't want to, but he finally let her go.

She walked to the sink and leaned both hands against its ledge, head down. She stood that way for what seemed like an eternity.

He paused at the door. Maybe leaving her alone wasn't the smartest thing. She was strong, but how strong? Had she hit her breaking point? If only he could get inside her head right now to find the correct thing to say, the precise thing to do. Did she need space, like so many of his buddies did when dealing with death on such a personal level? Did she need to talk it out like his oldest brother did after a grueling investigation? Or did she need human contact to remind her she wasn't alone, that she was alive and loved? He felt lost and helpless—something he wasn't used to feeling. More than ever, he wanted to do right by her, be there for her, whatever *that* looked like, however ugly it got. Because it could get ugly.

He would've been surprised if it didn't.

"Evelyn?" he asked in a soft voice.

"Right, right. 'Course." She nodded, wincing as she focused on her reflection in the mirror for the first time.

The woman in the mirror stared back at them, her blue eyes dark with panic, almost wild. Mascara and streaks of dried blood streamed down her face. She looked as if she'd just come from battle in a war-torn country and barely survived. Pieces of her jet-black hair clumped together. Evelyn tilted her head, gingerly reached up and touched a mass that had fallen in front of her eye. She brought the strands to her nose, jerked back and dropped them like a hot coal. Marcus's heart heaved. He knew her hair smelled like blood.

She gripped the ledge. Her knuckles turned white as

she dropped her head. He went to her and put his hands on her shoulders.

She pulled away from him. As she glanced at the bloody palm prints she'd left on the white countertop, a small wounded sound bubbled from her chest.

"Oh...no...no...no..." She held her hands out in front of her in horror, violent tremors shaking them.

Her breath came in shallow gulps as she bent over the sink, frantically grabbed the faucet and turned the hot water on. A tiny whimper escaped her as she viciously scrubbed her hands, pumping the soap dispenser, pushing her hands under the steaming water, repeating the motion over and over. He tried to touch her again, but she shied away from him.

She finally shut the water off and turned, shoving her hands behind her back. "I can't... I need... Please—"

It wasn't necessary for Evelyn to say anything more. Marcus leaned against the door and gave her space. "I'll just be outside, if you need anything."

He left the door slightly ajar, then sat on the edge of the massive, California king bed. Propping his elbows on his knees, he waited. He listened for the sound of the shower door opening and closing. And after what felt like a million years, the sounds he'd really waited for, hoped would come, drifted to his ears.

At first, the noise came out in tiny whimpers. Then it grew. And grew. Her deep, guttural sobs echoed in the stillness of the room, tearing at him, shredding his heart to pieces. But she needed the release. And as much as it hurt him to see her in this much pain, he had to allow her this time alone. He clenched his fists, got up, paced. He cast anxious glances at the small opening with each pass.

He reached for the door handle, then stopped. What the hell was he doing? He couldn't walk in on her. No matter how innocent his intentions were, it would still be inappropriate, especially given her current state of hell. He rested his head against the door frame and listened to the gut-wrenching sobs that refused to let up.

After thirty minutes, he couldn't stand it any longer. He turned and left the room, careful to keep the door open. In the hall, he pulled out his phone and dialed.

"You okay?" His brother answered on the second ring, voice groggy from the three-hour time difference.

"Derek, I need you—"

"What happened?" His voice switched to full alert mode.

"There's been an accident." Marcus's voice cracked. He cleared his throat, then walked down the hall, away from the sobs still coming from the bathroom. He entered the kitchen before continuing. "Scrap that. There hasn't been an accident. There's been a development on the case."

He stopped again. What was he even saying? *Accident. Development.* He took a deep breath to regain his focus. "Evelyn's partner and his family were found murdered in their home tonight. We were second on the scene."

Derek whistled softly into the phone.

"That's not all, as if that weren't enough." His voice grew hard, fresh anger springing up inside of him. "The prick left a note for Evelyn. We're on lockdown with her. She's here with me and isn't going anywhere until we've got a better handle on this situation, but I could really use a pair of fresh eyes."

"Say no more. I'll be on the next plane."

Marcus rubbed his face with one hand. The tension in his shoulders diminished. His pulse calmed. Maybe with his brother here, they could finally get the upper hand on this guy. "Thanks, man."

"Marcus," Derek said. "I know this goes without saying, but keep a close eye on her. She may be strong—I'm not discounting that—but most people couldn't handle what's she's been through once, let alone twice. Everyone has a tipping point."

"What are you saying?" Marcus barely breathed the question as he glanced down the hallway, listening until he heard her sobs.

"Nothing, nothing," Derek said. "I'm not saying she'll do anything to herself. I'm only saying that sometimes the brain, in order to protect itself, will go into its own sort of lockdown. Just keep an eye out for that."

"I will." If he had his way, he wouldn't leave her side until this whole disaster was over. He didn't scare easily, but the idea of anything happening to Evelyn scared the shit out of him.

Marcus hung up and pocketed his phone. Stillness greeted him. He stood motionless in the kitchen, barely breathing, only listening. Silence was not good, not good at all. He sprinted down the hallway and burst into the bedroom. The sound of running water floated out of the bathroom. But nothing more. He scanned the room. The oversize shirt he'd pulled out for Evelyn was still neatly folded on the edge of the bed where he'd left it.

He moved toward the door, then stopped. He wanted to respect her privacy and give her whatever space she needed, but he'd also promised the chief, Derek and—most importantly—himself that he'd keep her safe at all costs. And as hard as it was to imagine, if that meant keeping her safe from herself, so be it. *Screw the line.*

He took a deep breath, then inched the bathroom door until it stood wide-open. Steamed rolled out in huge waves. The mirror and shower-stall door were fogged up. It took a minute for his eyes to adjust and see past the steam. Evelyn sat in the middle of the massive shower, her back scarlet from the scalding water pounding down on her. Her knees were pulled up to her chest, her ankles crossed. She was shivering in the still-steaming water. Her arms were wrapped around her legs, and her right cheek rested on top of her knees as she stared into the air in front of her, focused on nothing.

Marcus's heart lodged itself in his throat. He reached for a plush oversize towel and tentatively walked toward her.

"Ev…" His low voice sounded loud, even to his own ears. "Evelyn, sweetheart. Let me help you get dried off and into bed."

She made no move to cover herself.

"I can't," she whispered, tears springing to her eyes again, making them look aqua.

He crouched just outside the glass door. "Yes, baby girl, you can."

She shook her head slightly. Dark strands of soaked hair fell into her face.

"But I can't. I don't know how to…how can I possibly…" Her voice trembled. "How can I come back from this? It hurts, Marcus. Everything hurts. I can't see how I can."

"I know you can."

"I don't… I can't…not this time…" She started to

cry again. Big teardrops mixed with the warm water showering down on her. "Not this time…"

He was angry at himself for not seeing this coming, for not realizing how incredibly fragile she was before this very moment—and for leaving her alone, despite his instincts telling him not to. He was pissed at the bastard who had taunted her for weeks before delivering such a heart-wrenching blow, and at her for not fighting back. She could fight back. She'd proven that once already, hadn't she?

He needed her to fight back. Now.

"Yes, you can, Evelyn. You radiate life and strength as if it were a life force. Tap in to that. Believe in yourself. Trust yourself. You can. And you will. I promise."

She shook her head again. "How can I, if moving from this very spot feels impossible?"

And then she rested her cheek on her knees again and closed her eyes.

Marcus's pulse went into overdrive. He could see her giving up, giving in. *Like hell. Not on my watch.*

"If you don't come out right now, I'll come in and get you." His tone, though still warm, held a tiny warning.

Her eyes popped open. "You wouldn't."

His answer to that small challenge was to move toward her. With a sigh and a silent prayer that this wouldn't come back to bite him in the ass later, he opened the door and, towel in hand, walked into the shower.

She let out a tiny squeak of surprise, but didn't move. As she stared up at him, he realized that although her eyes were wide, they weren't frightened. That gave him some relief as he moved closer to her, reached through the warm spray and shut the water off. He bent low and, in one fluid motion, wrapped her in the towel and swung her into his arms.

"I told you I would," he all but growled into her ear as he carried her into the bedroom. "You aren't alone in this, Evelyn. I'm not going anywhere."

Evelyn flung her arms around his neck, buried her face in his shoulder and wept.

He sat on the bed and cradled her on his lap, holding her to him. Without releasing her death grip, she wept and wept, giant sobs wracking her body. He held her until the weeping subsided.

"I don't know if I'll ever be okay again, Marcus," she whispered into his chest.

"We both know that's not true. You're stronger than you give yourself credit for."

"I may have been. But I'm not anymore. That bastard took that from me."

"Look at me."

She raised startled eyes to him.

"You're still the same powerful, intelligent, feisty, stubborn, incredible, sexy woman you were the first time I met you."

Her lip trembled, and it took all his willpower not to kiss her right now.

He cleared his throat. "We'll find this guy. He'll make a mistake. And when he does, we *will* get him. You and me. We'll take this guy out."

"There was so much blood." She squeezed her eyes tight.

"No more talk tonight. You need your sleep, Ev." He shifted her off his lap.

She curled her legs underneath her and pulled the towel tightly around her.

Looking at her sitting there, so small and fragile, made his heart break. He'd never seen her this vulnerable before, and it worried him. He grabbed the shirt he'd laid out for her. "Put this on."

He turned to give her privacy while she slipped into the shirt.

"Stay with me tonight."

As much as he'd wanted to hear those words before, he wouldn't let his mind go there. She wasn't asking him to sleep with her. She wanted his companionship, the comfort of his arms around her as she fell asleep. And that he could give.

"You aren't alone, Evelyn. You sleep under the cover, and I'll sleep on top of the sheets."

Despite the fatigue and sorrow, a tiny laugh bubbled out from her as she crawled beneath the heavy down comforter. "What? Are you frightened I might try to take advantage of you and that smoking hot body of yours?"

He couldn't believe it. He was trying to be a gentleman, and she was laughing at him. Well, better to laugh than be consumed by grief. He couldn't help the smile that tugged at his mouth as he looked at her snuggled under the covers. Just like his shirt, the bed swallowed her.

"Something like that."

CHAPTER TWENTY-EIGHT

MARCUS AWOKE WITH Evelyn's face nuzzled into his neck and one of her arms thrown over his chest. She'd hooked her leg around his. The edge of her shirt was hiked up past the top of her thigh, exposing her mile-long legs. At some point during the night, he'd managed to get under the covers. He rubbed his free hand over his face. *Right. Managed.* He sighed. He needed to put some distance between the two of them.

Without waking her, he unhooked their legs and slipped from the bed. As he stared at the sleeping beauty in his bed, his heart filled. The anguish, the fatigue and the pain from last night lay hidden beneath the veil of sleep. She looked so peaceful, but he knew it was only a facade. When she awoke, the horror of the past twenty-four hours would come crashing in, and he wasn't sure how she would handle it. He wanted nothing more than to protect her. But would she let him?

FILES, HANDWRITTEN NOTES, photos and lab reports were tossed everywhere. He'd been working on the case since early morning, juggling the items in front of him with the endless calls that flooded in. Two soft knocks at the door interrupted him. He grabbed his .45 and unhooked the safety before moving to the door.

He tapped back: *tap tap-tap tap tap*. With the single tap in return he relaxed.

Derek.

He swung open the door and smiled at his big brother. Derek's friendly face set him at ease. "Hey, man, thanks for coming."

Derek pulled his brother into a bear hug. When he released him, Derek glanced at the weapon and raised an eyebrow. "What's with the piece?"

"What's with not calling first?" Marcus flipped the safety and tucked the gun into his waistband.

"Oh. Good point." Derek laughed. "Sorry. Well, thanks for not shooting me. Mom would've been pissed."

Marcus locked the door behind Derek.

"Where's Evelyn? I expected her to be up."

"She locked herself in the bedroom." Marcus ran his hand through his hair.

Derek looked down the hallway. "When?"

"This morning. She came out and asked if they had found Liam yet. When I told her they hadn't, she went back in and shut and bolted the door. She's been in there the rest of the day."

Marcus's phone chirped. "Sorry, it's been nonstop today."

"Rightfully so."

"Moretti," he said into the phone.

"Agent Moretti, this is Officer Sanchez."

"What have you got?" he asked quietly, running his free hand through his tousled hair.

"Two things. We haven't found Liam yet. Nor are there any current leads."

"You sure…" Marcus's stomach rolled. He knew the

odds: time was not on their side. They needed to find that child. Fast.

"Sorry, sir." Sanchez sighed. "I wish I had better news."

"Not your fault. And the second thing?" Marcus asked, already back to pacing.

"CSI found a partial print on the banister that doesn't match any of the O'Neils."

Marcus pulled up short. A spark flickered in his chest as he turned and grinned at Derek. His brother stared back at him, brows pinched together in a silent question.

"You sure? I need some good news here, Sanchez."

"Yes, sir. Kessler had us double-check before I was cleared to call you."

"Does it match anything in our system?"

"A match hasn't popped yet, but we're still running it through all available databases."

Marcus nodded. "Okay, fine. Keep me posted. And Officer Sanchez? Do not, under any circumstances, contact Detective Davis about this. All updates on Liam come directly to me. Do you understand?"

"Yes, sir."

"Great. Excellent. Let me know when anything pops. Also, send a copy of the print to my email now. Thanks." Marcus pocketed his phone.

"We caught a break. Finally. That bastard left a partial at the scene."

Derek whistled, low and slow. "He's getting sloppy. That last kill was a knee-jerk reaction, not something planned."

"I know." Marcus nodded. "I hate the circumstances around it, but we really needed this."

"Marcus, I get that she's locked herself away, but she needs to know. You have to tell her."

"What she needs right now is space to breathe," Marcus said. "You haven't seen her. Last night, she held her partner in her arms and saw her best friend sliced to pieces. She's a complete wreck."

"Fair enough. That's normal. I'd be concerned if she *weren't* a wreck. But she could very well be the last piece of the puzzle. There might be something sealed inside her head that'll tip the scales in our favor."

"She needs time."

"We don't have time. And besides—she can't stay holed up in there forever."

Marcus groaned. "I know that."

"You need to get her ou—"

Marcus blew out a frustrated breath. "Derek. I know. I'll tell her—"

"Tell me what?" a familiar female voice asked.

Both men looked up. Evelyn stood where the hallway met the open kitchen. Still beautiful and doll-like, despite the fatigue and sadness, hope shone brightly in her eyes. She'd pulled her hair into a messy bun on top of her head and was still only wearing Marcus's large shirt.

Derek's eyebrows arched. He threw a quick glance at his brother. Marcus ignored him.

Confusion washed over her face. "Who's this? And what did you need to tell me?"

"Evelyn." Marcus went to her. "Can I get you anything? I—"

She raised her hand to stop Marcus. "I heard your phone ring. Was that news on Liam?"

"Yes and no. They're still searching, but they haven't found him. Yet."

Tears sprung to her eyes.

"I should be out there hunting for him." She rubbed her eyes with the heel of her hand.

He wished they could have this conversation elsewhere, wanting to give them privacy. Marcus felt the need to protect her, shelter her. He took a step toward her.

"Not going to happen, Ev."

He saw her eyes flash. Good. At least there was still some fight in her. At least he hadn't lost her yet.

"So while Liam is out there, somewhere, alone and scared, I'm a prisoner here. Great. Thanks."

She turned, walked down the hall and slammed the bedroom door.

Marcus glanced at Derek. "I'm sorry about that. I've never... She's never... Sorry, man."

Derek shrugged. "Don't be. I'm not. It's a typical reaction, really. Could you imagine if it were you who was in here on 24/7 watch, unable to do the very thing that has kept you going for so many years? Wouldn't you be angry and frustrated? I would be."

CHAPTER TWENTY-NINE

EVERY CELL IN Evelyn's body was on fire, burning her from the inside out. Grief and fear played tug-of-war with her mind. Agitated, she paced the room like a caged animal. She should be out there looking for Liam, not holed up in here. Glancing around, she searched for an escape, then halted. *Escape? What the hell was she thinking?*

Marcus wasn't keeping her a prisoner. He was trying to help her, throwing her a lifeline.

All she needed to do was reach out and grab it.

She had a job to do and refused to let that monster shackle her, no matter how much it hurt. She'd powered through the debilitating grief before, and she'd do it again. Especially with Liam's life on the line.

It was time to finally voice the nagging thought that had pounded the recesses of her mind for far too long.

Evelyn took a deep breath, opened the bedroom door and headed toward the voices in the kitchen. Both men looked up when she walked in and stopped talking.

Marcus set down his drink. "Evelyn."

"I'm sorry, Marcus. You've been amazing through all this, and I honestly don't know what I'd have done without you."

He opened his mouth to speak, but Evelyn held up her hand. If she stopped now, she wouldn't be able to finish, and she needed to explain, needed someone else to understand.

"It's not an excuse, I know. But I feel this loss, this pain, and I can't get away from it. It's embedded into my soul, permanently parked right here." She put her hand over heart, pooled tears threatening to escape down her face once more. "I can't escape it any more than I can escape my own skin. I battle it every single second of every freaking day. But I was out of line. And I'm sorry."

"Ev—it's okay. I get it." He tipped her chin up and smiled down at her, the gentleness in his brown eyes warming her down to her toes. "I'm not going anywhere. Got it?"

A sense of wonder washed over her at the goodness he had in him. Without even knowing it, he'd become her lighthouse in this nightmarish storm. He'd rendered her speechless, so she did the only thing she could do— she threw her arms around his neck, buried her face into his warm chest and hung on for dear life.

Until an awkward cough brought her crashing back down to reality.

She let go of Marcus and turned, coming face-to-face with a man who could only be Marcus's brother.

"Oh, my, sorry about that." She stuck out her hand. "Evelyn. Evelyn Davis. My apologies for the ice-queen welcome earlier."

"Derek Moretti." He smiled softly and shook her hand, his blue eyes soft. "And the pleasure's all mine, Evelyn. No need to apologize. I'm amazed you're even out here."

Yep, he definitely came from Marcus's DNA pool.

He extended the same grace and compassion she'd come to love from Marcus.

"I have a thought I want to run by you," Evelyn said.

"Let's hear it." Marcus sank to the stool.

"What if this—" Evelyn pointed to the mass chaos in front of them "—started differently than we thought?"

"Not following."

"We're assuming all these murders are connected to me because of my own family's murder, right? A way to get my attention, draw me out. But what if it goes back further than that? What if we've been looking at the wrong trigger all along?"

Derek's eyes grew wide. "Holy shit."

Evelyn glanced between both men. "Following now?"

"I think so, but go on." Marcus waved his hand in the air.

"I think we should broaden our search to a homicide that *seemed* like a family annihilator case around the same time frame as my family's murders."

"What the—Evelyn, are you suggesting what I think you are?"

"I'm not convinced this guy is a copycat stalker."

Marcus stared at Evelyn, the color fading from his face.

Evelyn took a deep breath. "I think we should consider the possibility that this guy is the killer who murdered my family."

MARCUS'S PHONE CHIRPED. He tore his eyes from Evelyn's face. *How the hell had he missed that connection? Better yet, how long had it been since Evelyn made that leap?* He punched in his code, then scanned the email.

He had the partial print now. At least something had gone right this morning. He tapped his phone.

Evelyn frowned. "What did I miss?"

"The killer left a partial at the scene."

Her mouth fell open. "Have we—? Is it—?"

Derek grinned and opened his laptop. "Time to call in the big guns."

Marcus dialed his phone and waited. A soft, feminine voice answered on the second ring.

"Hey, MK."

Marcus smiled at his sister's nickname for him. "Hey, sweetheart. You have a second?"

"For you? Always."

"Great. I need red." Red was their term to go secure on any line. His genius baby sister had figured out a way to scramble their calls without needing a special phone. It had saved all the Moretti brothers at one point or another.

"Go ahead," she said, her voice high with excitement.

Marcus rolled his eyes at Derek, who smiled. They knew she loved when her brothers called, especially red. If her parents hadn't demanded she finish school, she'd be running circles around them at the Bureau—or gone deep and silent with some black ops group.

"You're on speaker. Derek and Evelyn are here, as well."

"Howdy, folks."

Evelyn smiled and tipped her head to the side. Marcus hit the send button on his phone. "I'm sending you a print now. It's only a partial, but it's all we've got. I need you to run it through every agency that you can get into. Be discreet—"

"When am I not?"

He could almost see her eyes rolling now. He'd seen her do it a million times before. Her tech skills were legendary and highly sought after. She'd been able to hack into the FBI database without leaving any type of footprint since she was fifteen.

"True. But it needs to be discreet *and* fast. This guy's had us running for over a week now. I'm tired of it. He can't be a ghost. His prints have to be somewhere."

"It may take me a few days to run this through, but I'm on it. We'll find something. And MK?"

"I know, I know." He smiled. "Be careful."

"Actually, I was going to ask, when do I get to meet Evelyn?" Alexis laughed then hung up.

MARCUS'S PHONE CHIRPED ONCE. He jolted awake. The red digits on his side table glared at him—3:48 a.m. Whoever was calling now had better have a good explanation. He rolled out of bed, careful not to disturb Evelyn, and reached for his phone, entirely conscious—one of the few benefits of having lived in the sandbox.

"Moretti." He headed for the bedroom door.

"We found him," the voice on the other end of the line said. No introductions, no salutations.

Marcus's pulse jumped. "Who? Our print guy? And who is this?"

"Sorry, sir, this is Officer Sanchez. We found Liam."

"What's his status?" Marcus quietly padded down the hallway, past Derek, who was sprawled on the plush sofa. Softly snoring now, the man would be fully awake in a second. Marcus swore his brother always slept with one eye open.

"Alive."

Marcus closed his eyes and blew out a loud breath.

His stomach uncoiled as relief washed over him, followed by instant concern. "Officer Sanchez, I need more than one-word answers. Tell me everything you know. Now."

"Sorry, sir. A priest down at St. James Cathedral on Ninth just called it in. Apparently a masked man came into the cathedral, walked straight up to him and handed the child over. He told the priest not to wake the child, turned and walked off."

Marcus paced the kitchen, listening intently. He grabbed a piece of paper and pen, furiously jotting down notes as Sanchez fully debriefed him. "Okay. Where is he now?"

"He's been transferred to Seattle Children's Hospital. There aren't any signs of physical or sexual abuse, but he's not responsive. He's currently in a medically induced coma."

Marcus's heart sank. "Why the hell is he in a coma? Spit it out, Sanchez."

"I'm not sure, sir. That's all the information I have."

Marcus sat at the end of the kitchen island, head in his hand. "I want to speak with the physician in charge later today. Let's make that happen."

"Yes, sir. Kessler told us whatever you say goes." Marcus heard the rustling of paper on the end of the line. "I'll get on that right now."

He nodded. "Great, thanks. And, Sanchez, if anything changes in the next few hours, let me know immediately."

He hung up, then rubbed both hands over his face.

When he looked up, Evelyn was sitting at the opposite end of the counter. Derek leaned against the wall, arms crossed. Both of them stared at Marcus.

"What was that about?" Derek asked slowly.

"They found Liam. He's alive."

"Oh, thank God," Evelyn said. "Where'd they find him? How is he? When can I see him?"

"As far as they can tell, he's fine." Marcus repeated all the information he'd just learned. "The priest said he was preparing for the late night mass when an armed masked man came into the church and came straight up to him with a young child passed out in one arm. When the priest asked the man his name, he apparently cocked the gun, pointed it in the priest's face and told him to shut up. If he woke the child, the man would kill him."

Derek's eyebrows shot up.

Evelyn glanced over at Derek. "I know you've done a lot already, but can you make a call and have your team at Quantico reevaluate the write-up?"

"I was just making a mental note to do that." Derek went to the refrigerator, opened it and grabbed a bottle of water. "We hadn't factored in any sort of empathy. A psychopath having compassion for one child but murdering the sibling not only startles me, but also makes me sick. What kind of twisted person are we dealing with here?"

"Oh, but it gets better," Marcus said. "This masked man then shoved Liam into the priest's arms, turned and walked out. A note was pinned to Liam's onesie that read, 'I'm not the monster. I saved him.'"

"He did what?" Evelyn's eye grew wide.

"Very interesting."

"Interesting, my ass," Marcus said. "Liam is currently at Seattle Children's Hospital."

"Why? Did he hurt Liam?" Evelyn asked, her voice hard. Worry and fear shone brightly in her face.

"I don't know everything yet. There weren't any signs of physical or sexual abuse, but he's not responsive."

Evelyn moved to the window and stared out into the inky night. "I hate not having all the information."

"I know, Ev. I'm meeting with the doctors later today." Marcus turned to his brother. "I want you there with me."

"You got it," Derek said softly.

Marcus felt her steady gaze slicing straight through to his soul. Tilting her head to the side, she stared at him. He knew she was reading him, figuring out what he wasn't saying. He'd seen her in action before.

Then, it was brilliant.

Now, it was unnerving.

"There's something else you aren't telling me, isn't there?" Evelyn moved slowly, closing the distance between then until she stood right in front of him.

Of course she'd sense he was holding something back. *Because he was.* But what the hell was he supposed to do? He'd gotten her to come out of her self-induced solitary confinement. The last thing he wanted was his words to send her running back.

"Marcus?"

He sighed. There was no easy way to bring it up. He scrubbed his hands over his jaw and then locked eyes with her. "The funeral is in two days."

She stumbled backward, as if his words had physically slammed into her. Pain washed over her face as she looked away. The artery in her neck pulsed. He knew how critical it was for her to get up, to choose to be there—even if every movement felt like a hot blade slicing into her heart.

At least then she would remember she was alive.

"The captain is concerned that it will be too much."

She shook her head. "It won't be."

He took another step toward her, watching her closely. She blinked back tears and tipped her head up. *Good girl, be defiant.*

"That's what I told him, too. That you wouldn't let your team down, because you're stronger than you think you are." Marcus stood less than two feet from her now. "I told him you'd show up. That you'd show that bastard that he doesn't get the last word."

"I will. But, Marcus…" Her lip trembled, then a hard mask fell over her face. "I want this prick. I need to find him. And I need to take him down."

He opened his arms and, without hesitation, she moved closer. He wrapped his arms around her and pulled her close, her body melting into his.

"We will."

CHAPTER THIRTY

SHE WOULDN'T BECOME a ghost. She couldn't. She owed them that. Evelyn sank into the chair, stared through a film of tears at the photo of Liam and Ava smiling up at her for a long time. Still clutching her phone, she unlocked it with a swift swipe and dialed.

"Chief?"

With that word, an invisible, internal pendulum swung. Grief still penetrated every cell in her body, but a tidal wave of determination rolled over her: to catch the asshole who took Ryan and his family, to bring justice and closure to the families before them. She straightened.

"Evelyn. How are you?"

She took a deep breath. "Marcus told me Liam was found. When can I see him?"

"I would imagine sometime after the funeral." He hesitated. "But only if you're up for it."

"Yes, I understand, sir." Her chest constricted. "I would like to be there for the funeral."

She could only imagine the look on the chief's face. The long pause on the other end of the line grew. "Sir."

He cleared his throat. "We can arrange that. I'll get a protective detail prepped to sit with—"

"No, no, not sitting in the crowd. I want...I need, rather, to help carry..." She clutched the phone and squeezed her eyes closed. Some faceless monster wasn't going to make her cower like a scared animal. She wouldn't run and hide. She was stronger than that. Evelyn took a deep breath. "Sir, I need to help carry Ryan's casket."

THE SUN SHONE BRIGHTLY, a golden ball of warmth and light. Its rays bounced off the deep waters of Puget Sound, tiny diamonds sparkling and shimmering on its face. Evelyn looked at the brilliant blue sky and shuddered. How ironic. Most days, Evelyn yearned for the sun: for the memories it brought, its warmth, its comfort, its cheerful occupation of the sky. But today, of all days, she cursed the happiness it promised but could not deliver. Why couldn't the familiar clouds—gray, heavy, comforting—occupy the sky, blanketing them in a world of secure gray?

Heaven knew she needed it.

Today, she would bury more loved ones.

Silence fell over the six officers as each of them shouldered an equal share of Ryan's weight. Even with it dispersed, the corner of his flag-draped coffin dug deeply into Evelyn's shoulder. Another wave of anguish washed over her as she took that first deliberate step.

They walked with careful, measured strides over the perfectly manicured cemetery grounds, a soft emerald carpet unfolding before them. The pathway to his final resting spot was lined with uniform-clad men and women—police and firefighters alike, black ribbons strung across their shields, each raising their right hand and honoring him with a silent, crisp salute as they passed. Behind them, the rest of their division split to shoulder Kate and Ava's coffins. There wouldn't be a family gathering afterward. There was no family to gather.

Evelyn tried not to look at their strong, stoic faces. She tried to keep the hurt and sorrow she saw mirrored in her fellow officers' eyes from penetrating the feebly constructed barrier around her heart.

Liam lay in the hospital, but she had yet to see him. It had been agreed that she'd do so after today. So with emotions locked in a vault, tucked deep in her soul, she forced back the advancing pain and focused on the task ahead of her. Foot in front of foot. That's all she could do right now.

Evelyn's request to be part of the funeral procession, to be one of Ryan's pallbearers, was a simple one. She wanted everyone in the world—whoever was watching, whoever cared—to see that even in death, they were still partners. Her city needed it. Her house needed it. *She* needed it.

She'd secretly hoped that the person who had done this, who had taken her partner and his family from her, would see her there, see he hadn't broken her. That her presence would show that bastard she was strong and resilient, and now hell-bent on tracking him down and taking him out.

She knew being at the front corner of Ryan's coffin wouldn't necessarily scream all that, but it would send a clear, distinct message. *You didn't get me.*

So here she was, the edge of Ryan's flag-wrapped coffin resting heavily on her left shoulder.

How fitting. She chewed the inside of her cheek, combating her emotions. How many times had Ryan offered a shoulder for any one of the officers in their house: to cry on when life tried to swallow them, to lean on during an intense and exhausting investigation, to be the calming force in the midst of chaos? He was— had been—steadfast and strong. And now he was gone.

She would miss him, a permanent hole left in her heart.

Biting her lip until her tongue tasted copper, she cursed herself. *Stop. Don't think about that. Get inside that bastard's head and nail his ass to the wall.*

A tiny grim smile tugged at her lips. Yes. If it took her until the day she died, she would find the bastard who did this.

EVELYN'S PRESENCE BY Ryan's casket was brash. And dangerous. Her very public appearance at the funeral could be seen as the equivalent of flipping off the prick who'd left that note.

But they—the chief, Marcus and Derek—had all agreed it was necessary. Not only for Evelyn and the entire SPD, but also for all of Seattle. As hard as they'd tried to keep Ryan's murder out of the paper, it was eventually leaked to the press.

And chaos followed.

In the privacy of the chief's office, it had been agreed that Marcus would protect Evelyn at all costs. His priority—not that he needed the chief's order for that—was Evelyn's safety. He weaved in and out of the crowd, shouldering past the men and woman who served and protected Seattle, following Evelyn closely. It grated on his nerves that he couldn't walk next to her, support her, shield her. But that was out of the question. Although he'd been working closely with Ryan and Evelyn, he was still a Fed—an outsider. And though the chief and the mayor trusted him and wanted him here, not everyone shared that sentiment. There was a look-out team on guard in the case the perp came today. He trusted the team to do their job, as they'd trusted him to do his—guard Evelyn.

So, from the cover of the shadows, he followed and watched.

Back straight, arms tucked tightly to her sides and even with fisted hands throughout the short ceremony, Evelyn stood elegant and beautiful in her crisp, class A uniform. He could see the sorrow, the pain and the rage running through her.

What he saw nearly took his breath away. His mouth twitched in a tight line, pride surging though him. Even now, she was trying to be strong for her team, to let them feed off of her strength—or her perceived strength. She was fighting not to lose it. He could see it in her face, the way she lightly chewed the inside of her cheek, the way she curled her fingers into balled fists. God, she was an incredible woman. Most would have passed on being a pallbearer, allowing their emotions to dictate their actions, to give them liberty to fall apart.

But not this woman.

A slight movement caught his attention. With a deep breath, Evelyn separated herself from her fellow of-ficers and pushed toward the podium. *What the hell? Was she giving the eulogy, as well?* He watched with hawklike intensity as she settled behind the podium, took another deep breath, then looked out at the crowd. Her ability to control her facial expressions prevented anyone from seeing the war of emotions raging inside of her. But Marcus's training kicked in, and he saw it. His heart ached for her.

"Ryan Michael O'Neil was a faithful husband, an

adoring father, a steadfast, loyal partner and the most remarkable cop." A sad smile played at her lips. "Anyone who knew him knew that his wife, Kate, and his children were the absolute loves of his life. He cherished them and ferociously protected them. The job took second place. No one could persuade him otherwise."

Soft laughter rode on the cool breeze as many in the crowd of Seattle's finest nodded.

"Yet he was a man of unending valor, one who attacked each day with a renewed sense of hope and excitement. Everything Ryan did was to one end—to uphold and protect justice. And he did that to his very last breath. The world lost an incredible man—" Her voice cracked. Evelyn tightened her grip on the podium, then bowed her head.

Marcus wanted to go to her, but didn't. She needed to do this on her own, to prove to everyone, including herself, that this would not cripple her. That she was strong enough.

She raised her head and glanced toward Marcus. It didn't surprise him that she'd found him amongst the crowd. The time they'd spent together had only magnified the undeniable attraction between them. But publicly locking eyes with him for even a split second shocked the hell out of him. He'd known how important it was to her to keep the professional line drawn. However, the look she gave him now, her eyes searching and…needy, was anything but.

She took another breath.

"The world lost an incredible man, and his void will forever be felt by those privileged enough to know him, for it's a space that we will never be able to fill." She paused. A small, tentative smile pulled at her lips. "But his legacy will live on. His son will grow up knowing his father inspired many to uphold justice, no matter what the cost. He encouraged people to push past the darkness in the world we see every day and to celebrate the goodness that's evident, if we'd only look for it. His father championed everyone he came in contact with, be it for a moment or for years, to be better men and women. He drew the best out of people, and he saw the good in the world. And that's simply remarkable."

Her eyes flickered to the casket to her right, and her smile faded. Pain flashed across her eyes, and her face blanched for a moment. "An integral, dynamic part of our community has been stolen with his untimely passing. I lost an incredible partner and friend. The SPD will forever feel his loss. But we'll hold his memory close to us and live our lives in honor of Detective Ryan O'Neil."

LEAVING THE PODIUM under the cover of reverent silence, Evelyn passed the casket holding her partner, her friend. Her bottom lip trembled for one brief moment as she stood, back straight, hands fisted, looking down at the flag-draped coffin. Her chest heaved. She dropped to her knees, bowed her head and gingerly placed a hand at the head of the casket. She squeezed her eyes tight, willing herself to be strong. Just a little longer. She was quickly losing the battle that raged in her, especially now that it felt as though every cell in her body wept, collectively grieving for the man she knelt beside. The feebly constructed wall around her heart crumbled, and that terrified her. She rested her head against the smooth side of the casket, shutting out everyone around her.

"I'm sorry I failed you, Ry," Evelyn whispered. Her throat closed around a sob. "I'm so, so sorry."

Taking a deep breath, she stood, composing herself once more. She stepped back, lifted her head and saluted. The rest of their uniformed family followed suit.

An unspoken vow had been whispered in the depths of her being the moment Kate opened her door all those years ago. A vow to love and protect. Although not family by blood, this family had woven themselves into her soul, making her one of their own. She was supposed to protect her own.

Yet three caskets now lay side by side, evidence of three people she'd failed.

Her eyes brimmed with unshed tears. They all tore at her, but it was Ava's tiny casket that ripped at her heart and caused grief to claw at her chest. She pushed back the emotions and commanded herself to keep it together. She'd gotten this far, gotten through the eulogy. She could make it until she got back to Marcus's, until the quiet of his loft provided the sanctuary and privacy she desperately needed.

The groundskeepers lowered Ryan's casket into the ground.

Each shot of the twenty-one-gun salute chipped away at her resolve, tearing into her, ripping apart her already bruised and bleeding heart.

Evelyn clung to her last reserves of composure. She had to get away, needed time to grieve, time to rage, time to fall apart completely, then painfully pull herself together. Because she would track down the man who did this.

And she'd destroy him.

He'd wounded her, yes, but even though it felt as if she would never recover from this tragedy, she knew she would. Someday.

Evelyn glanced over her shoulder toward the three graves. She hadn't let the death of her family devastate her then, and she wouldn't let the death of this family shatter her now.

She couldn't.

CHAPTER THIRTY-ONE

THE MOMENT THEY walked into the warmth of Marcus's home, the makeshift emotional barrier around Evelyn's soul crashed. Grief reached up and gripped her throat. She fought for breath. Paralyzed with raw emotion, she was unable to move from where she stood in the cozy foyer. Panic, pain and rage slammed into her.

All at once. Consuming her.

"Oh." She doubled over, hands on thighs and her head between her knees.

"Evelyn?" Marcus locked the door, then quickly went to her, putting his hand on her shoulder. "Evelyn?"

"Give me a minute." She crumpled onto the hardwood floor, buried her head in her arms and sobbed.

She'd hoped to make it to the privacy of the bedroom. But now, as another wave of sorrow wrecked her, she didn't care that she'd melted down in front of Marcus. Hadn't he already witnessed this once already? She didn't even care. The only thing she could think about, the only thing she felt, was the soul-consuming grief that roared over her like searing lava, blistering everything it touched. She gave in to it until she had no more tears to give.

She lay there, cheek hugging the cool floor, and stared at Marcus. He was leaning against the kitchen counter, giving her space. She loved him for that. She needed to get up, but didn't have the strength. She closed her eyes.

"Okay. Your minute is up."

Her eyes popped open. Marcus crouched down beside her. He gently gripped her chin and lifted her face. With his thumb, he wiped away the mascara streaking down her cheeks. "Talk to me."

"I have nothing to say."

"You don't have to be brave, strong or stoic here, Ev. You're safe. So start talking."

She pulled herself up to a sitting position and drew her knees to her chest. "What good will it do?"

"A hell of a lot. Let it go."

"I can't."

"Why the hell not?"

"I don't think I'll ever be able to recover if I do. Okay, Marcus? If I start talking now, I might not be able to come back from that darkness."

"You'll come back," he said softly.

"I don't know if I want to talk about it."

"Why? What are you afraid of?"

"I'm afraid I won't be able to catch the asshole who did this, that I won't be able to protect Liam or make it right." She started crying again. "That I'll let down more people I love."

Marcus's head snapped up. "You think this is your fault?"

"You read the note, Marcus."

His face hardened. "Just because some sicko wrote a note doesn't mean you're responsible for his actions."

She scrambled to her feet, dragged her hand over her wet eyes. "Doesn't it?"

"No, it doesn't. It means he's a sick bastard. That's it."

"I can't deal with this right now." She stomped down the hall and slammed the bedroom door behind her.

MARCUS SENSED MOVEMENT before his eyes made out the shape standing in the doorway. He grabbed his Glock and flipped off the safety. He didn't know how to move without letting the shadowy figure know he was awake. But he had to, had to get to Evelyn. *He shouldn't have agreed to Derek staying at a hotel tonight. Damn it.* Marcus's pulse took off. He silently swore as he slipped from the guestroom bed and crouched beside it.

"Make a move, and I'll blow your head off."

"Marcus?"

His heart lodged in his mouth. *Evelyn?* He flipped the safety on and stood. "What are you doing?"

He didn't hear her response, just the muffled sobs coming from her. He put his gun on the nightstand and went to her. She leaned against the door frame, heavy tears streaming down her face. Marcus's heart broke as he watched the anguish tear through her.

"Evelyn, sweetie." He opened his arms and pulled her to him. "Come here."

She leaned into him, pressing her body against his. Even through the button-down shirt, he could feel her warm curves. She tilted her face up and her lips found his. Shock tore through him. Sex was the last thing he'd expected from her. He stood still as she slipped her hands around his neck. Then he returned her intensity with his own. *What the hell are you doing, Moretti?*

"Evelyn—"

"I need to forget the pain. Even if it's only for one night. Please."

She found his mouth again, but he stiffened. She pulled back. "You don't want me?"

He brought her into the room and shut the door. He looked at her and almost lost his self-control.

She hugged her arms around her body.

"Of course I want you. I've wanted you every single day since I met you." He rubbed the back of his head. "I think I made that pretty clear the other night. And I haven't been able to get you out of my mind since. But we just buried your partner, your best friend."

She frowned, then shook her head. "I don't understand."

"I don't want to take advantage of you," he said softly.

"Of what? My emotional state? Please don't make me beg, Marcus. I need to forget. I can't think of the pain, the death, the loss for one more minute. I'm slowly losing my mind, my soul. All I can think about is how much I hurt, and it's suffocating. Please. I just need to forget. For one night, I need to forget that the world is ugly, mean and dark. I need to feel alive, even if it's only for one night." Tears rolled down her cheeks. "Please don't make—"

He swallowed the rest of her words as his mouth found hers. He scooped her in his arms, held her to his chest and carried her to the bed. Tonight, he'd make her forget. He'd make her feel how loved she was, how safe she was. He'd deal with the consequences later.

He lowered her to the bed and looked at her. *God, he loved this woman.* The intensity of his feelings startled him. He cradled her face and brought his lips to hers. He showered her with light touches and kissed away the renegade tears that slipped down her cheeks. His stomach tightened. Where he touched her, his skin burned.

Evelyn pushed her body closer to his, seeking his kiss with equal passion, equal fervor. Marcus lowered his lips to hers and pressed lightly, tenderly. He moved to her eyes and kissed softly. She moaned as his lips traveled down her neck. Desire spread through him.

He wanted Evelyn, and he wanted her now.

He reached for her shirt and pulled at the buttons. She raised her arms to aid in its removal. Gently, he tugged it over her head, then threw it to the floor. He kissed her again and traced his lips down her collarbone, past her navel.

She shuddered, pushed closer and reached for his waistband. Her fingers brushed along his stomach, journeyed lower, traveled downward.

Marcus ran his fingers and mouth over her and committed every inch of her body to memory. He made her forget.

EVELYN WOKE UP molded to Marcus's body, her leg draped over his thigh, her face nestled against his chest and her ear tuned into the constant rhythm of his heart. She didn't pull away. She just lay there in the silence of the dawn and enjoyed his closeness.

She'd known what she'd asked him last night. It hadn't erased the pain. It was still there, but so was something else. She felt grounded, bound to something besides the constant dull ache of agonizing grief.

Marcus. She was tethered to him. He gave her strength, courage…hope.

"Morning, beautiful. I was half expecting to wake

up tied to the bed, with you long gone." He kissed the top of her head.

She gazed at the man she'd completely fallen for. "Nope. This caveman I know told me to stay put."

Her head bobbed in time with his laughter.

"Though I'm hoping there's coffee in my future." She sat up and pulled the covers up. "I'd like to go in and speak with the chief about Liam. He said we could discuss it after—"

He gathered her closer to him. "Done and done."

CHAPTER THIRTY-TWO

EVELYN STOOD OUTSIDE her precinct building, frozen. A sense of dread washed over her. The last time she'd been here, she and Ryan had fought about his reaction at the press conference. Her heart sunk. She knew nothing good ever came out of what-ifs, but she couldn't stop her mind from going there, wishing desperately things had gone down differently that night. Marcus put his hand on her shoulder and squeezed. Her pulse quickened. He winked. Her cheeks flamed as memories of the night before rushed to the front of her mind.

She put her hand on his. Now that she'd found him, she wasn't letting him go.

Evelyn took a deep breath and forced a smile. Quietly, she and Marcus walked into the precinct together. The officer behind the front desk glanced up, did a double take, then jumped to his feet.

"Detective Davis, welcome back. It's great to see you, ma'am."

"Thank you." She headed to the stairs and called over her shoulder, "I'm only here for a few minutes. Please continue to forward all phone calls to Agent Moretti."

The young officer nodded. "Yes, Detective."

Captain Kessler met them at the top of the stairs. "It's good to see you, Davis."

"Thank you, sir."

"I'm glad you called. Follow me to the conference room. There's something we need to discuss."

She cast a worried glance at Marcus, then followed Kessler into the conference room. Chief Diaz and another man she didn't recognize sat at the table. Both men stood as she entered.

"Evelyn, it's good to see you. Please…" Chief Diaz motioned for her to sit.

She sank into the closest chair, heart pumping and blood roaring in her veins. The chief cleared his throat.

What was going on? Was this gentlemen Internal Affairs? No, he couldn't possibly be; the Armani suit was too rich for any police officer she knew. *Then who?* She wracked her brain over the events of the past few days. Again, nothing surfaced.

"Liam—"

A startled gasp flew from her lips. "Is he okay? When can I see him? Is something wrong?"

At this point, she didn't care if any of them—the captain, the chief or this mysterious man—thought she was weak or emotional. She was emotional. Her hands fisted under the table. Marcus stealthily reached over and placed his hand on hers. Somehow, she managed to keep the tears threatening to burst at bay.

"Is he okay?" she repeated, harsher than she intended.

"Yes, Evelyn, if you'll stop interrupting me, I can answer your questions," the chief replied. "He's at Seattle Children's Hospital."

"When can I see him? I need to see him."

"There's something you need to hear before you can see him."

Her back went rigid. She tried to see what lay just

behind his eyes. Concern? Grief? Frustration? Try as she might, she couldn't get a read on him.

"This is Ethan Brown. He's a lawyer at Brown and Dover."

Lawyer? She froze. *What the hell is going on?* She threw Marcus a puzzled look, then flipped her attention to the man sitting next to the captain. He hadn't moved, barely seemed to even breathe as his deep, steady eyes studied her. He wasn't from the Pacific Northwest—his deep tan gave that much away. He smiled.

She tore her eyes from his tanned, friendly face and tuned into the chief again.

"I'm sorry, sir. I don't understand." She tucked her feet to the left, straightened her shoulders and clutched her hands in her lap.

Diaz looked at her. "Mr. Brown is the O'Neil family lawyer."

She'd come in today to speak with the chief about removing the protective duty and returning to her house. She hadn't expected to be sitting across the table from Ryan and Kate's freaking family lawyer.

"He's here to talk with you regarding Liam." Mr. Brown cleared his throat. "Detective Davis—"

"It's Evelyn. Please, just Evelyn."

The handsome man smiled. "Evelyn, did Ryan or Kate ever speak to you regarding guardianship of their children if anything were to happen to them?"

"No." She tightened her hands into a death clasp. *Guardianship...what...?*

He brought his brown leather briefcase to his lap, unclasped it and pulled out a stack of papers. He handed an envelope to Evelyn. "This is a personal letter from Ryan and Kate. It might clear up any confusion."

Numbly, she unclenched her hands and accepted the envelope. "Clear up what confusion?"

"Detective Davis, you're Liam's legal guardian now."

Her mouth dropped open for a brief second before she could rein in her response. Her head spun. The room tilted on its edge.

"Me?"

"Yes, ma'am. The letter should explain everything. I have all the documents with me."

Evelyn stared at the pale yellow envelope. She hadn't realized until she glanced down that she'd been gently stroking the paper. She stopped moving and looked at Chief Diaz. "Sir, may I have some privacy with this?"

He nodded, stood before she even finished speaking. "Absolutely. Take all the time you need."

Diaz's crow's-feet deepened as he studied her, turned to the other men and motioned to the door. "Mr. Brown, if you would please follow me. We'll wait in Captain Kessler's office. Kessler, does that work?"

Kessler bobbed his head. "Of course, sir."

"And under no circumstances are you to breathe a word of this to anyone."

"Of course, sir. It's not mine to tell." Kessler turned to Evelyn, a look of fierce protection washing over his face. "But you *are* mine to look after, got it?"

The envelope burned her fingers. She mustered a smile and glanced at Marcus. "I think you'll have to get in line with that one, sir."

"Fair enough." He tipped his head and grinned at Marcus. "I guess you could do worse."

Soft laughter echoed in the room. Then, with a quick

nod from the chief, all three men exited the room. Marcus pushed back from the table.

She looked up, startled. "You don't have to go."

He cupped her cheek with his hand and smiled at her. "I have a feeling this needs to be done alone."

"You're probably right."

"But I'll just be outside if you need me. I'm not going anywhere. That's a promise." He leaned down, kissed her softly and left.

She stared at the envelope for what felt like an eternity, then put it down and wiped her palms on her pants. She got up, walked to the blinds and twirled them shut.

There was no telling what Ryan and Kate had penned, but she wasn't sure she'd be able to keep her emotions in check. She glanced back at the envelope, grief tearing through her, fresh and ferocious. She couldn't imagine Ryan and Kate sitting down to write such a heart-wrenching letter, knowing if Evelyn ever read what they wrote, it would mean *they* were both dead, their children alone.

Evelyn swallowed the sob lodged in her throat and sank back into her chair. She picked up the envelope, used her forefinger to lift the corner of the seal. She fished out the letter, took a deep breath and read:

Dear Evelyn,
I can't even begin to imagine what you're thinking right now. God knows I can hardly put pen to paper and articulate my thoughts with just the idea that one day you may have this in your hands. First of all, I know what you're thinking right now and, no, we aren't crazy.

A tiny laugh bubbled up from her broken heart. She ran her hand across her face, wiping away tears. He was right. She did think they were crazy.

There is no one in the world who loves our children as fiercely as you. We've seen that love in your face time after time: when Ava spit up all over you and you just laughed, the time Liam peed on you when you first changed him—the list could keep on going, but our lawyer told us not to write you a novel.

Another minuscule laugh escaped her lips. She shook her head. "How is it possible you can still make me laugh, Ry?"

Evelyn, all kidding aside…there is no one in this world I would entrust my children to, except to you. They are the best things that have ever happened to us. We know with you, they'll be cared for, protected and loved as if they were your own children, as if you had given birth to them yourselves. Just be glad you didn't. Both put up a fight coming out of Kate, but eventually, she won—Momma always wins.

Evelyn put the letter down and laughed, even as tears blurred the words. She stared at Ryan's meticulously flawless penmanship, envisioned Ryan and Kate doing the same as they put the words to paper. She shook her head in amazement at the strength of her two friends. She picked up the letter and read on.

I hope—we hope—this letter never finds its way into your hands, because if it does, it means we're both gone, and the mere thought of that breaks my heart. I'm confident that if you're reading this, my two babies—my perfect angels—are safe with you.

Evelyn's stomach lurched. *Only one, Ry. I'm so sorry. I saved only one.* She swallowed hard, shoved aside the suffocating guilt and continued reading.

Evelyn, there isn't a woman in this world—aside from my gorgeously stunning wife, of course—who I trust to raise my children in a way that would make me, make us, proud. Except you. Your courage, your strength—God knows, your humor—your love for life, your unwavering tenacity for justice, everything about you screams strength. And if you're reading this, my children will need your strength now more than ever. They'll need you.

She hugged the letter to her chest and bent her head. Tears dripped from her chin and puddled on the table. She rubbed the heel of her hand across her eyes and continued to read.

So please, don't be angry with us for not telling you that you're the one we have entrusted our precious children to. You would have raised hell if you knew. But you would have said yes in the long run.

I don't have to tell you to love them and protect them, because it's you I'm writing to, and
that's a given. But please remind them every single day how much we loved them, how much we
cherished them and that we're watching out for
them—no matter what.

Evelyn could barely make out the last few lines of
Ryan and Kate's letter. She rested her head on the table
and relinquished herself to the pain. Her body quaked
as gut-wrenching sobs shook her. On a relentless, vicious cycle, her heart shattered, put itself back together
and broke all over again. With each successive break,
the agony deepened. Sorrow crashed over her. She felt
like she was drowning in it. The tears fell with no sign
of ending: for Ryan, for Kate, for Ava and for her own
family. After a long time, she lifted her head, wiped
her face with the back of her hands and scanned the
rest of the letter.

We love you, Evelyn Davis, and will be forever
grateful that you blew into this city and into our
lives. Take care of Ava and Liam for us, okay?
Don't let the grief of this tragedy root itself into
either of their souls. It'll rip them apart.
    You, of all people, know that.
    Please, Evelyn. Be strong now. For yourself.
For Ava. For Liam.

Liam.
The letter dropped from her hands. She shot up
from the chair, straightened her clothing, tucked her
hair behind her ears and dabbed the smeared mascara

from under her eyes. She couldn't afford to look like a drunken raccoon. Then she yanked open the heavy, bulletproof conference-room door.

Marcus pushed off from the wall. "Evelyn?"

Without a word, she breezed by him. He fell into step beside her. Refusing to make eye contact with any of her fellow officers as they curiously stared at her, she walked down the hall until she reached Kessler's office. Without knocking, she tugged at the glass door and stepped through the opening. Three startled faces glanced up at her.

"I need to see Liam," she said. "Immediately."

Mr. Brown shook his head.

"Don't shake your head at me, Mr. Brown. That little boy is mine to guard now. And hell will freeze over before I let him be alone for one more freakin' second. Do you understand me?"

Out of the corner of her eye, she saw a smile spread across Marcus's face. She shot him a look. He shrugged, smile still intact.

"Evelyn, I don't think he's trying to prevent you from going to Liam," the chief said.

"He's correct, Detective Davis," Mr. Brown said. "I understand why Ryan and Kate O'Neil named you guardian of their children. With all due respect, ma'am, you're an Amazon."

Marcus brought his hand to his mouth and coughed. "He's right, Ev."

Kessler's eyebrows shot up. Diaz laughed. Evelyn crossed her arms and stared Brown down.

A flush crept into his cheeks. He cleared his throat, grabbed his briefcase and fumbled with the lock. "There's paperwork that must be in place before the guard at Liam's room will even allow you to enter—badge or no badge. Special Agent Moretti's orders."

He glanced between Marcus and Evelyn. "The last time I checked, the Feds trump local police any day, correct?"

"My apologies, Mr. Brown."

"Please, call me Ethan." He gathered the appropriate papers from his briefcase.

"Ethan." Evelyn softened her tone. "Again, my apologies. I have to see him with my own eyes. I need to hold him."

"That's not possible," Chief Diaz said. "Liam's in a medically induced coma."

Evelyn's eyes widened. The emotions she'd locked safely away threatened to unleash.

Marcus put his hand at the small of her back. "Evelyn, Liam is fine. Physically, there was no need for it. But emotionally, the overseeing doctor felt, given the situation, that he should rest until this is all over. The trauma he's faced has been of the emotional sort. He hasn't spoken since the priest brought him in."

Evelyn's gut twisted. *Not spoken? That little chatterbox?* Ryan had laughed, saying that once Liam had figured out how to put sounds together, there was never another moment of silence in their house. Her heart squeezed within her. *What had he seen?* What could he have possibly witnessed that had sent him into utter silence?

"I still want to see him," she said, more sharply than she'd intended. "Where do I need to sign?"

"Evelyn, are you sure about this?" the chief asked. "This is a major commitment. Maybe you should take a few days to think about it."

Her back straightened. "Absolutely not. There's nothing to think about or discuss. Ryan and Kate entrusted me with their children. I'm not going to break that trust, not in this life or the next."

The chief held up his hands in surrender. "I didn't mean anything by it."

"I know, sir. If I can just see him, see that he's safe and whole, then I can focus on the task in front of me."

The chief cocked his head. "Which is what, exactly?"

"To catch the bastard who did this, sir."

He smiled, then rubbed the back of his neck with his hand. "Fair enough. Mr. Brown, what papers does she need to sign?"

Mr. Brown slid a piece of paper and a pen toward her.

She followed the movement of the paper floating across the mahogany conference table and felt as if someone had kicked her in the gut. *One piece of paper. One lousy piece of paper to represent all the memories, all the laughter, all the love that had surrounded the O'Neil family?* She felt sick. She grabbed the heavy, expensive pen, bent over the table and signed the paper.

"Sir, I just need a few hours. Then I would like permission to return and work from here, with the team."

Diaz looked at Marcus. They shared some unspoken conversation, and Diaz nodded. "Take all the time you need, Evelyn. No one is going anywhere. I can promise you that. But my ultimatum still stands when you return. The moment—and I do mean the very moment, Evelyn, so don't push me—I believe your judgment is impaired or shaken, I'll pull you from the case, no questions asked. Do you understand?"

She nodded.

CHAPTER THIRTY-THREE

THIS CHANGED EVERYTHING. Whatever *this* thing was or wasn't between her and Marcus, wherever it might have been, was gone. She didn't—couldn't, really—expect him to feel the same responsibility for Liam that she did. And he certainly hadn't raised his hand to parent a child. *Oh, good grief, Evelyn, parent a child? You barely know the man.* She squeezed her eyes tight and banished the childish daydream from her mind.

In his uncanny way, Marcus seemed to sense her internal struggle. He reached across the central console and folded his fingers through hers. Without a word, he pulled their joined hands to his mouth and gently pressed his lips to her knuckles. Her throat closed around raw emotions as she looked out the window. The headlights of the oncoming cars flashed by as they sped to Seattle Children's Hospital—to Liam.

The car hugged the curves, oblivious to the rain-slicked roads. She snuck a look at her companion. If Marcus noticed, he didn't let on.

How was it she'd experienced so many life-altering moments in such a short amount of time…in this car, with this man? Better question. What the hell was she doing? She hadn't had the time or emotional space for anyone two weeks ago, and she sure as hell didn't have it now that she was Liam's guardian. She took another peek at Marcus, took in his strong profile and, despite the emotional wasteland she currently navigated, her heart jumped. *Crap.* Everything about him pulled at her, enticed her to stay, to not run away but turn and embrace this.

Whatever this was.

Enough! Her emotionally wrecked psyche pushed at the sapling hope, latching on to the dull pain. She sighed, twisting back to look out the window at the passing lights. She rested her head against the glass and closed her eyes.

Life could be so cruel, so incredibly cruel. She didn't want to have to choose between the man sitting next to her and the little munchkin battling to stave off the trauma of the past few days.

She'd fallen in love with Marcus.

There. She'd admitted it. She loved him. His mere presence was a calming force. She couldn't imagine her life without him in it. Didn't want to. But, if she had to choose, if she had to decide between protecting Liam or satisfying her newly found libido, it wasn't even a question: she'd choose Liam.

MARCUS PULLED UP to the hospital's valet and threw the car into Park. He got out, tossed the keys at the attendant and ran to catch up with Evelyn. Once again, she'd sprinted toward the door without him.

"Evelyn, stop."

She did, though he could see it cost her. The anguish and sorrow reflected in her eyes haunted him.

"We do this together." He grabbed her hand. "Besides, the guys upstairs are mine. You wouldn't get within ten feet of Liam's room without me."

"Your guys? I thought SPD was standing guard."

He shook his head. "I pulled them."

"You what?"

"I wanted men that I knew, trusted." He shot her a look. "Not that I don't trust SPD. I just wanted my team."

"Your team of Bureau guys."

He cleared his throat. "Yes, my team. I trust them with my life. No one else would do."

She laughed, then a sad smile crossed her face. "It'll be nice to meet them. Maybe they'll be mine, too."

Marcus froze. *Her team, too?* Had she just said yes to his offer? His heart took off into a wild gallop. No, she'd just made an offhand remark. Right? He cast a quick glance at her. Her face was pensive. *Oh, to get into that mind of hers right now.*

Marcus led her to Liam's room. Two massive men stood outside his door, flanking it. Marcus smirked. They appeared scary as hell with their arms crossed and guns strapped to each thigh. Good.

Evelyn's grip tightened as they approached. Neither man moved or smiled.

"Gentlemen, this is Evelyn."

The tall bald one broke his stance first. His face lit up. He grabbed Evelyn and pulled her up into a bear hug. She glanced at Marcus, eyes wide.

The man set her down, his eyes soft. "Your little man is safe with us. Hell would have to freeze over before anyone got past us." He turned to his partner, nodded his head and winked. "That's Roger. He's not very affectionate or expressive."

Roger smiled. "And that's Azza. He doesn't understand the concept of personal space or boundaries."

Evelyn laughed, shook her head, then grew serious. "Can I see Liam now? I need to make sure he's okay."

Roger opened the door. She walked in. Marcus followed closely behind her. He stopped and put his hand on Roger's shoulder. "No one in until she's done."

"You got it, boss." Roger crossed his arms and fell back into position. His face went blank.

Azza looked into the room, then back at Marcus. "Has she said yes?"

Marcus shook his head. "No, but she's been through a lot. I'm not asking her anything yet."

Azza nodded. "Got it."

Evelyn sat next to Liam. He laid perfectly still, a sleeping angel. She reached out to touch him, then hesitated. Her face crumbled.

"Oh, little man. I'm so sorry you had to go through this, so sorry you were alone and scared." Her voice cracked.

Marcus stood behind her. Close enough to remind her that she wasn't alone, but far enough back to give her space.

"I promise, I'll make it up to you. You'll never be alone again. It's you and me, bud." She stroked his curls and ran her fingers over his baby-soft skin. "Oh, my precious little man. We're going to get through this."

She looked up. "Has the doctor said when he thinks Liam will be strong enough to leave?"

Marcus shook his head. "Not that I've heard. But I can check."

"Thank you." A sad smile twitched her lips. "You being here with me, with us, means more than you will ever know."

"I'm not going anywhere."

A shadow crossed her face and then quickly vanished. But Marcus caught it and his stomach clenched. *She thought he was punching out. Leaving. What? Because she'd just inherited a child? Like hell he was.* He closed the distance between then, cupped her chin in his hands, tilted her chin up and locked eyes with her.

"Evelyn Davis, I'm not going anywhere. Do you understand me?"

She nodded. Tears sprung to her eyes and a guarded look descended. He knew she was pulling into herself, trying to put distance between them. No doubt to protect that tender heart of hers. Didn't she know that she no longer needed to protect herself? That he would die before he let anyone hurt her? Didn't she see that? The haunted eyes, veiled in pain and looking up at him, answered his unspoken question.

He lowered his head and gently kissed her. The touch was light, but it still sent his pulse racing. He pulled back and smiled down at her. "I'm not going anywhere."

She reached up and placed her hand against his cheek. She stared at him for what felt like a million years, but said nothing.

Marcus swallowed hard. What would it take for her to realize that she'd stolen his heart and forever changed him? Life without her—and now Liam—just wasn't a life. Complicated? Hell yes. Anyone with half a brain could see that what lay in front of them wouldn't be easy at all. It would be hard as hell. But was it worth it? Was she worth it? Of course. And if he had to spend the rest of his life proving that to her, he would. Because a life without Evelyn Davis was a life he didn't want.

She dropped her hand and turned back toward Liam. The heat from her touch vanished. He hated that.

She sat and rested her head on the bed next to Liam, stroked his chubby little hand. Her eyelids fluttered closed. He smiled. He'd let her sleep. Then he'd take her home.

Marcus moved into the hallway and shut the door firmly behind him. Roger glanced at him and tipped his head. "Boss."

"When did the doctor last make his rounds?"

Roger glanced at his watch. "About two hours ago. Why? Do you need him?"

"Yeah. Track him down for me, will you?"

Roger nodded and walked off. Azza filled the vacant spot flanking the door, folded his arms and settled into a don't-mess-with-me stance. They silently stood that way for several minutes. Marcus leaned his head against the wall and shut his eyes.

"Permission to speak freely, sir?"

Marcus opened his eyes and looked at the tall bald man. "Of course. Go ahead."

"How are you holding up?"

Marcus felt his eyebrows arch. What was this, a counseling session? "I'm holding up just fine, given the circumstances. But somehow I'm sensing there is more going on in that head of yours than concern for my emotional well-being. Am I right?"

"When will you be back?"

"When this case is over," Marcus said flatly.

"With or without the girl?"

Marcus straightened. The hair on the back of his neck bristled. He pinned Azza with his eyes. "The *girl?*"

"Sorry." Azza's face flushed, and he rushed to continue. "Evelyn. With or without Evelyn?"

Marcus looked through the glass window and studied the two sleeping forms. *Good question.* He didn't know what her answer would be, but he knew the only answer he'd settle for. He watched as Evelyn, without opening her eyes, reached for Liam's hand. Marcus's heart lurched. "With. Definitely with."

"Does *she* know that? Will she even leave this place now? And if she does, in what capacity—as a team member or something different?" Azza was peppering Marcus with questions. "I know she's good, but—"

"She's the best profiler the Bureau has come across in over ten years. She's not just good, Az, she's the best in her field."

"I agree," Azza said. "But this whole complicated mess is a cluster. Can she even be part of—"

"I'm not rethinking my offer to join our team, Az. And I'm not leaving her. So back off."

Azza stepped back and raised his hands in surrender.

"I wasn't suggesting you take back your offer or leave her, boss. She's good people. I was only pointing out that this—" he pointed toward Liam's door "—complicates things."

"I've very aware of that," Marcus said gruffly. The atmosphere in the hallway intensified as the two men stared each other down. Marcus was a tall man, but he still had to look up at his teammate. Azza didn't blink. Marcus's blood boiled and his temper flared. *What was this? He was the boss. Not the other way around.* He pushed his shoulders back and stepped closer. "Is there anything else you'd like to get off your chest? Maybe in regards to how I run this team?"

"Shit, sir." Azza's face fell. "I'm not questioning your judgment. Sorry if it came across that way."

Marcus took a deep breath. He'd given Azza permission to speak freely, hadn't he? No need to be an ass toward his teammate just because he didn't like what Azza said.

"No." Marcus hung his head and shook it. "No, I know. I'm being an ass."

"I was not calling you an ass. Sir."

Marcus had to swallow the laugh that lodged in his throat. The giant of a man in front of him, who could kill someone with a single, deadly blow, genuinely looked like he was about to vomit. *Oh, hell.* He needed to fix this situation. And fast. Marcus put his hand on Azza's shoulder and squeezed.

"You're a good man. There's a reason I requested you to accompany Roger." He winked. "And it's not because of your good looks."

That broke the tension, and both men laughed. Marcus patted Azza's shoulder and grew serious. "I trust you."

Azza jerked his head in quick acknowledgment and cleared his throat. "Thank you, sir."

Marcus dropped his hand and turned, once again studying Evelyn through the window. He was being an asshole. Azza's hard questions were spot-on. And if Marcus was being honest with himself, he'd ask the same questions if the roles were reversed. Like it or not, Liam did add an element that could change what Evelyn contributed to the team. *Maybe she could consult for him and stay home with Liam?* He shook his head. No way he could see her puttering around the house with an apron on. No. He wanted—needed—her on his team.

Complicated or not, he and Evelyn would work it out.

THEY WALKED DOWN the hall, Evelyn tucked under Marcus's arm. Exactly where he wanted her. He and his team were back on the same page, all signs of the earlier tension gone. Liam quietly rested in his little bed. Satisfied with Marcus's team and their protection, Evelyn agreed to leave Liam in their capable hands.

Marcus chuckled.

"What's so funny?"

"You."

Her eyes widened as she pulled away to look at him. "Me? Why?"

"I wish you could have seen their faces when you stepped up to them."

She shrugged. "I was just making sure that both Azza and Roger understood the importance of their assignment."

"By telling them you'd cut off their balls and shove them down their throats if anything happened to Liam?"

She smirked. "It got the point across, didn't it?"

He laughed. "Yeah, I'd say you got that point across."

"I wasn't that bad."

"You definitely made a lasting impression."

"I—" A yawn ripped through her and cut her off.

Marcus pulled her close and tucked her under his arm again. "Don't worry about it. They loved you. I could tell. Now, I'm taking you home. You need to rest tonight. We can go through your old case files tomorrow."

THE SHUTTER RAPID-FIRED three frames per second, capturing Evelyn as she exited the hospital. He lowered the camera and slammed his fist into the steering wheel. *Why the hell was she smiling? How could she be smiling after he'd taken so much from her?*

Stupid bitch thought she was safe. Thought the man

draping his arm over her shoulder could protect her from him.

But she wasn't.

She'd never be safe from him. He'd been at the funeral, only then the scope he'd used was his sniper scope. It was tempting, but no. A single bullet through the heart wouldn't suffice.

Not for her.

That bitch deserved far worse. And she'd get it. When he was good and ready. And he was close.

Those damn reporters questioned if he was done, if the killer had gone to ground or, better yet, left Seattle altogether. He gritted his teeth and brought the viewfinder up to his eye and pressed the shutter again, firing off more photos.

Stupid people. He wasn't done.

Far from it.

He was merely gearing up for the grand finale.

CHAPTER THIRTY-FOUR

LATE THAT NIGHT, Derek walked into Marcus's apartment. Closing the door, he pulled his .45 out, checked
the safety and put it on the kitchen counter. He looked
around and frowned. "Where's Evelyn?"

"Sleeping. Where've you been?"

"Really?" Derek's eyebrows arched. "That surprises
me."

"It's been a long day. She was tired."

Derek threw his jacket over the back of the sofa,
walked into the kitchen and sat. A used tea bag sat on
the edge of the sink.

"Marcus, tell me you didn't."

"I didn't."

"You don't even know what I'm going to say."

"So then say it."

Derek got up, leaned over and grabbed the tea bag.
He let it hang from his forefinger and thumb in front
of Marcus's nose.

"It's a used tea bag," Marcus said. "She wanted a
cup of tea before bed. And I, being the good man I am,
fixed her one."

Derek swung the tea bag back and forth. "Tell me
you didn't drug Evelyn."

"Oh, come on, Derek." Marcus rubbed his hand over

his face, then peered up at his brother. "When you say it like that…"

Derek laughed and shook his head. "She's going to kill you, man. And rightfully so."

"She's been having trouble sleeping." Marcus shrugged. "I'll take my chances."

"And I thought I was bad—"

"What? Sitting around studying psychos, desk-bound? Somehow I don't think—"

Derek tossed the tea bag in the sink and raised his hands. "Easy, tiger. This isn't a pissing contest. Tuck it back in. Besides, being desk-bound has its perks."

He opened the fridge and pulled out a Guinness. "Want one?"

"I'll pass," Marcus said.

Derek went back to the table and sat. He took a sip of beer and eyed the papers thrown about. "Any progress?"

"Actually, I was just about to call Lex." Marcus grabbed his phone and dialed. "Here's to hoping."

"MK."

"Talk to me, sweetheart." He hit a button, then put the phone on the counter in between him and Derek. "I have you on speaker. Derek's with me."

"D!"

"Hey-a, gorgeous." Derek smiled and leaned toward the phone. "We need something to break here, Lex. We're running on fumes."

She sighed. "I wish I had better news for you guys, really I do. I'm still combing through files and have all the big mamas working."

Marcus shook his head. He didn't know anyone else who gave their supercomputer hacker systems pet names. He rolled his eyes. Derek chuckled.

"Boys," Alexis said. "Focus."

"Yes, ma'am," they said in unison.

"Like I was saying, no hit yet on the print you gave me."

"Damn." Marcus tilted his head back and squeezed his eyes shut. He just needed one lousy break. Was that too hard to ask?

"But…" She took a deep breath. "I did, however, find some interesting old case files for you, Derek."

"What?" Marcus opened his eyes.

"I had her look into Evelyn's hypothesis." Derek shrugged, took a sip of his Guinness and grinned. "I trust our guys at the Bureau and at the SPD, but…"

"But he didn't want to be an old man before he got the information, so he called me," Alexis said.

"And?" Marcus stared at the phone.

Alexis laughed. "I found a handful of murders around the same time of Evelyn's family that had a similar MO. I'm doing a multipoint cross examination between those cases and Evelyn's. I haven't hit on anything yet, but I can't shake this gut feeling that I will. Just give me time, gentlemen."

Marcus slumped onto the chair next to Derek. "Okay. Not the information I hoped to get tonight. Keep digging. And be discreet."

"When am I not?" She laughed, then hung up.

Marcus grabbed his phone. "Why didn't you tell me about this?"

"You've kinda had your hands full, Marcus. And I assumed that's why you called me here." He gave his brother a dirty look. "To help."

CHAPTER THIRTY-FIVE

MARCUS AND EVELYN stepped out of the elevator together. She avoided looking at Ryan's desk. Being back was hard enough on her torn heart. A strange sound slapped off the concrete walls, followed by another. What was that? She froze. Every member of the homicide department stood, clapping. Her heart jumped into her throat as she stared in awe at the standing ovation her team threw her way. Tears sprung to her eyes. She smiled, willing herself to keep it together.

The elevator's soft chime interrupted the sacred, warm moment. Officer McBride stepped out, then stopped. He glanced over at Evelyn and Marcus, then did a double take.

Evelyn steeled herself for some emotional response from an officer she barely knew. She couldn't deal with that. Not today. She gritted her teeth, plastered a smile on her face and waited for it.

Instead, McBride stepped next to Marcus.

"Special Agent Moretti, I was going to call you today."

"You've got good news for me?"

The young officer shook his head. "No, sir. We haven't gotten a hit yet—"

"A hit on what?" Evelyn glanced between the two men. McBride's young face flushed.

"On the partial print," Marcus said.

"Right." She nodded and smiled at McBride.

"Ma'am. Are you okay? You sure you want to be back here today?"

And there it was. "Thank you for the concern, Mc-Bride. I need to be here. The chief cleared it."

"Understood. I'll let you know as soon as we have anything."

"Thank you." She smiled, trying to settle the under-lying current in the room. "Shall we?"

MARCUS, EVELYN AND Derek were holed up in the con-ference room. There were other murders in Seattle that needed to be attended to, so they'd been moved from the bull pen and settled in a more sequestered location. Not that Marcus, or anyone for that matter, minded. With Ryan's murder, the nature of the case had become more delicate and he'd demanded the privacy. He'd quietly studied Evelyn as she'd gathered the case files from Ryan's desk. She'd kept the stoic look on her face, but he'd seen the tiny tremble of her lip.

They'd set up their own separate command center and spread out. The murder board took up one whole wall. Photos and notes lined its smooth surface. Derek and Marcus huddled together, talking quietly amongst themselves. Evelyn scanned a stack of crime scene pho-tos, then flipped through them a second time.

She jumped up, a photo in hand, and left without a word.

Derek looked at Marcus. "She okay?"

"Not sure, actually."

"You need to go after her?"

Marcus thought a moment, then shook his head. "No, if she needs to talk, she will."

She walked back in, nodded to Marcus, then stood in front of the murder board and stared. She sat and studied the photo in her hand. A few moments later, she let out an exasperated sigh. "Nothing's popping."

"Something will," Derek said. "Always does."

"Yes, but before he hits again?"

"Something will pop."

Derek returned to his files. Marcus glanced up from the report in front of him and observed Evelyn. Once again, she looked like a black panther coiled to spring. She tapped the edge of the photo against the table and repeatedly glanced at the murder board. She leaned back in her chair and stretched her arms over her head, then stood. "I need a break. I'm heading to Starbucks for some coffee."

Marcus and Derek both glanced at her. She stared back at them without blinking, her face set. Marcus knew that look.

"Can't you get some in the bull pen?" he asked quietly, though he already knew the answer.

She pursed her lips, then shook her head. "*That* is liquid dirt, not coffee. So no, I can't. Right now, I need some real coffee."

He tightened his lips and studied her. This was not a fight he would win. She stared back, unmoving. There was something just beyond her veiled eyes that he couldn't put his finger on. He sighed. This may not be a fight he could win, but he wouldn't let her go alone. Besides, he needed coffee, too. He stood and reached for his jacket.

She shook her head. "That's okay. You and Derek

are in the middle of something. I'll be fine. I'll bring you both back some. I'll take Fin with me. It's only a few blocks away."

Yes, something was definitely not right with this picture.

Derek looked up, his brows scrunched together.

Marcus sat back, crossed his arms over his chest and eyed her suspiciously. Something was undeniably off. He just couldn't put his finger on it. He glanced from the murder board back to Evelyn. What had she seen? What was he missing? "I don't know if that's the—"

She cocked her head. Her eyes were warm and... strangely apprehensive.

"Seriously, Marcus. It's just a few blocks away. I'll be fine. Fin's a good cop." She walked to the door and pushed it open. "Fin, can you come in here?"

Rookie Benjamin Findley, aka Fin, pointed to himself. "Me?"

Her smile grew, lighting up the entire room, and instantly put Marcus at ease. Maybe she *did* just need some coffee that tasted better than burned dirt. He got that. He nodded his approval—not that she needed it. She'd have gone either way. He smiled at her. The fight in her that he was so terrified had seeped out and gotten lost down the shower drain that first night was back. And it had come roaring in, full force. He liked it.

"Yes, Fin. You. Care to go for a little drive?"

He nodded.

She grabbed her jacket and called over her shoulder as she headed toward the stairs, "Great. Let's go, then."

The young rookie stumbled over himself as he followed Evelyn out the door. Marcus chuckled. *Poor kid.*

CHAPTER THIRTY-SIX

FIN WAS HERE to placate Marcus and Derek, nothing more. If it were up to Evelyn—and clearly it wasn't—she wouldn't need a babysitter. But they apparently didn't share her sentiment. So here she was, driving Fin around. She didn't want to pull him into this. But she'd seen Marcus's face, seen the way he stared at her, studied her. Probably trying to see past her thinly cloaked desire for coffee. She knew that he'd keep pushing until he landed on the truth. And she was going on pure intuition, nothing more. So she'd returned his stoic look, silently holding her breath. She'd panicked a little when he stood to go with her. He clearly wasn't about to let her leave on her own, so she'd grasped at straws—or, more accurately, Fin. She needed to get to her house and take a look at something, and fast. Her heart accelerated.

Fin was quiet as she drove. *Good.* She needed silence, not interruptions. She concentrated hard and tried to summon the shadowy memory.

Fin sat up, startled. He twisted in his seat and glanced over his shoulder. "Um, ma'am, you just missed the turn."

"I'm not going to Starbucks."

Finn cleared his throat nervously. "With all due respect, Detective, Special Agent Moretti is going to kill us. Where are we going?"

"Home."

"Oh, no. No way. I was given *strict* instructions to go to Starbucks and Starbucks only. Going to your home was definitely not on the short list of approved movement, ma'am."

She took the next exit. "I outrank you. And stop calling me *ma'am*."

The words came out blunt, cold. She didn't care. There was something in her files at home that wouldn't leave her alone. Something about the knife wounds in the crime scene photos from the Middletons' had sparked an old memory, and she couldn't shake the feeling that she'd seen the same photo before. Only it wasn't. She shook her head to clear her thoughts. She needed the files at home. She wasn't going to take no for an answer.

"Yes," Fin said. "You do. It still doesn't make this a good idea."

"Good idea. Bad idea. It doesn't really matter at this point. We're going to my house. It'll be a quick grab and go. You can stay in the car if you'd like. I need to get a file from my home office, and this is most likely the only time where I won't be under strict supervision." She cast a sideways glance at him. "No offense."

His shoulders sagged. "None taken, ma'am."

But she knew she'd cut him to the core. He was a rookie. She was a detective. She sighed. "I'll be quick. I promise. And then we'll go to a drive-thru Starbucks before we head back to the station."

"So we don't have to tell anyone we went to your

house? Won't this mysterious file showing up kinda give you away?"

A small smile tugged at her lips. "What file?"

Evelyn pulled into her driveway, then cut the engine. She got out and surveyed the street. As usual, it was quiet. Not that she was expecting anything different. Keys in hand, she walked up the steps, unlocked the door and pushed it open. But before she could enter her home, Fin was beside her. He grabbed her arm.

"You might outrank me, Detective Davis, but I'll go in first to clear the house."

"That's not—"

"Necessary or not, it's happening. I'll be right back. Stay."

Fin went through the front door, gun drawn. Evelyn slowly pulled hers from her holster, flipped the safety off and tucked it by her side. As Fin cleared the first floor, Evelyn looked down the street again, keenly aware of how much she'd missed this place. Home.

"Clear," Fin called, walking down the stairs.

"See. Nothing here but you, me and the cobwebs. Stay there. I just need to grab something."

She dashed up the stairs to her office, turned on the light and stared at the wall. Her heart shattered all over again. *How many times can one heart break before it can't be put back together?* Not wanting Fin to walk in on her, she quickly made her way to the wall and scanned it. *There. There's the photo.* She reached up and snatched it off the wall, eyeing it closely. Her heart sank. *The knife pattern was identical to the Middletons'.* It was subtle, but it was there—and as unique as a fingerprint.

Holding the photo, Evelyn started to turn away from

the wall when the calendar caught her eye. Seeing the circled date, she sucked in a breath. *How could that have slipped her mind?*

Today. The anniversary was today.

A soft thud echoed in her ears. She stopped moving, fully alert. Folding the photo in half, she pocketed it and glided stealthily across the floor. Pushing up against the wall, she raised her .45. "Fin?"

Nothing.

Her pulse jumped. *If that kid's playing a joke on me, I'll have his badge.* "Damn it, Fin, answer me."

Still nothing. She took a deep breath, exhaled, then swung into the hall, gun ready. Out of nowhere, a bolt of lightning ripped through her, 50,000 volts of electricity rendering her useless. She couldn't talk, couldn't breathe, couldn't control her muscles. Pain was everywhere. Another jolt from the Taser tore through her and she collapsed, staring up at the man who bent over her.

"Hello, Evelyn."

He brought the butt of his gun down. Her face exploded with blinding pain, then she felt nothing.

CHAPTER THIRTY-SEVEN

MARCUS'S PHONE RANG. His heart lurched. *Evelyn.* He reached for it, glanced at the number and frowned. He didn't recognize it.

"Special Agent Moretti."

"Agent Moretti, this is Detective Josh Sanderson."

Marcus sat up. Why was he calling? And how the hell had Sanderson gotten his number? "What can I do for—"

"Listen. A call just came over the radio that there's an officer down at 2141 Seventh Avenue West. With a request for immediate backup."

"That's Evelyn's place." Marcus jumped up from his chair. His stomach dropped. The blood roared in his ears and pounded against his head "Who's down?"

"Officer Findley. He's been shot."

"Is Fin okay?"

"Yes. His vest took the brunt of the bullet. The kid's just rattled."

Marcus leaned his hand against the table and squeezed his eyes shut. The throbbing in his skull subsided. Just a fraction. *Evelyn was okay. How else had the call come in?* He glanced up and jerked his head toward Derek. Marcus snapped his fingers, then pointed to his vest.

"Shit." Derek threw Marcus his vest, pulled one over his head and checked his gun. In all of five seconds.

"I'm en route now," Sanderson continued. He hesitated a moment, then added, "But there's more, sir."

Sir? Marcus chest constricted. That couldn't be good. What more could Sanderson possibly say? "Spit it out, Sanderson."

"Evelyn is missing."

Marcus's throat tightened. He couldn't breathe. *Missing?*

"Fin found her forty-five abandoned in the house. I'm sorry, sir."

They both knew. A cop never abandoned a weapon unless under distress.

"I'll meet you there in ten." Marcus hung up, shrugged into his vest. His hands shook. Every muscle in his body tightened. His head spun. *Evelyn was missing.* The blood in his veins froze and his heart turned to ice.

"What's going on?"

Marcus reached for his jacket, refusing to look at his brother. If he spoke, he'd lose it. *Evelyn was missing.* He knew he shouldn't have let her out of his sight, let alone leave the building. *Damn it.* He grabbed his spare gun, tucked it into the back holster and moved toward the door. He'd never forgive himself if anything happened to her. He shook his head. *No. He'd find her.*

Derek grabbed his brother's arm. "Marcus, what the hell is going on?"

"It's Evelyn. Fin was shot. She's gone." Marcus shook off Derek and marched into the bull pen.

Derek swore and followed Marcus through the door.

Marcus and Kessler made it to the bull pen at the same time.

"Take the lead on this, Moretti," Kessler said, face set. "Bring Evelyn home."

Marcus nodded, then turned to the mass chaos and whistled. All movement stopped. Every eye bore into him.

"Listen up," Kessler said. "Agent Moretti is no stranger here. I've asked him to take lead on this. Anything he says, goes."

He looked at Marcus, then stepped aside.

Marcus swallowed the rage and fear. He stared back at faces that surely mirrored his own inner struggle. He took a deep breath. "We don't have a lot of information right now. What we do have is sketchy at best. I need a list of all the residents on Seventh Avenue and the streets that block it in. You know how this works. The clock has started. Saddle up, people. Someone had to have seen something. Let's get our girl back."

SIRENS BLASTING, LIGHTS FLASHING, Marcus pushed the accelerator to the floor, prayed they wouldn't have to bury another one of their own. Panic rushed him. *I can't lose her. Not now.*

Turning onto her street, he slammed on the brakes, tires squealing, and spun the wheel. Hard. His car skidded into the driveway. He threw it into Park and jumped out before Derek could say anything. Sanderson stood on Evelyn's porch, arms folded. Benjamin Findley sat on the stairs. He held a hand to his chest, his face pale.

Marcus tipped his head toward Sanderson and they exchanged a silent acknowledgment. Sanderson headed toward the arriving squad cars. Marcus turned and squatted in front of the young officer. "Fin, you okay?"

"Yes, sir." Fin blinked slowly, patting his chest and wincing. "Thank God for Kevlar. I'll have a hell of a bruise. But no cracked ribs."

"Good to hear." Marcus put his hand on Fin's shoulder and squeezed. Derek joined them and leaned against the porch railing. "This is Agent Derek Moretti. He's a profiler with the behavioral science unit and a brilliant criminal psychologist. He's consulting on this case, as well. Tell us what happened."

Fin shook his head. "I thought we were going to Starbucks, but when Detective Davis blew past the exit, I knew something was up. She refused to tell me why, but insisted on coming here. Even pulled the rank card."

Derek chuckled. Marcus threw him a hot glare. Derek cleared his throat, looking abashed.

"When we got here, I told her that I didn't care if she outranked me, I would clear the house before she entered."

"Good man," Derek said.

"Go on."

"I cleared both floors. She went upstairs and told me to stay downstairs. The front door was still open, but I heard something in the back. I went to check on it, and when I turned, a man stood there."

"Did you get a look at him?"

Fin shook his head. His shoulders sagged. "He had on a baseball cap and glasses. You'd think I'd remember something, but the prick shot me point-blank in the chest and the force knocked me out. I'm sorry, Agent Moretti. I don't remember anything."

THEIR TEAM CANVASSED the neighborhood. Derek and Marcus took the homes sharing property lines with Evelyn's house. Blood thundered in Marcus's ears after leaving the fourth home with nothing. He clenched his fist. *Someone had to have seen something.*

They walked up to the last home. Derek knocked on the front door and stepped back. "How you holding up?"

"I can't lose her, man."

"You won't."

Derek reached over, knocked on the door again, louder. The door swung open. A tall muscular man answered.

"Yeah?"

"I'm Special Agent Derek Moretti, and this is Special Agent Marcus Moretti. Is Craig Meyer available?"

The man frowned. "No, afraid not. He's ill, in bed. Doctor's orders."

He extended his hand and gripped Marcus's in a tight handshake. "I'm Ed Meyer, his grandson. Can I help with something?"

"Did you notice anything next door in the past hour? Any disturbance?"

He looked up and away, as if trying to remember. He squinted his eyes, then shook his head. "I'm afraid I can't help you, Agent Moretti. I was out getting medical supplies. When I got back, I didn't notice anything aside from that kid sitting on Evelyn's porch. Sorry I couldn't be of more assistance."

Marcus swallowed the disappointment that washed over him. He reached into his coat pocket, pulled out his card and handed it to the guy. "If you notice anything or remember anything else, please call me immediately."

"Of course, Officer." Ed closed the door.

Derek clasped Marcus on the shoulder. "We'll find her."

"Can you promise that?"

Derek didn't respond. They both knew he couldn't.

"Yeah, I didn't think so." Marcus headed toward his car. "Let's get back. We're done here."

Back at the precinct, angry, concerned eyes stared at him as he approached the group of officers. "Listen up, folks. Our first sweep didn't yield anything. But we aren't rolling over. The lab is making this top priority. So everything gets copied to headquarters and all divisions. I know the past few weeks have been hell for everyone, but we need to keep it together. The clock is ticking. Canvas everywhere. Talk to everyone. We *will* find her. That's all for now."

The officers dispersed. Marcus ran a hand through his hair and over his face. With each tick of the clock, every cell in his body screamed at him to do something. The same bastard who had killed Ryan and his family without hesitation most likely now had Evelyn. No, he *did*. Marcus knew the bastard had her. He could feel it.

"He's got her, Derek."

"We don't know—"

Fin approached them. "Sir, I shouldn't have let her—"

"There was nothing you could've done. He got the drop on you. It happens to the best of us."

Fin shook his head sadly.

Marcus put a hand on the young rookie's shoulder. "Every officer in the city will be on this until we find her. And we *will* find her."

Fin dipped his head and walked to his desk.

Marcus waved to Derek and motioned toward the conference room. He closed the door behind them. "Something's gotta break."

"Nothing from Alexis?"

Marcus scrubbed his hands across his face, shook his head. "What you know, I know."

"Call her. Maybe we'll get lucky." Derek tossed him his cell. "Use my phone to keep your line free."

Marcus punched in the familiar number, turned and studied the murder board. Urgency inched up his spine, dread wrapped itself around his heart and squeezed. *Where was Evelyn? Was she even alive? And what the hell was that psychopath doing to her? If he lost her...*

His stomach dropped.

"Easy, man," Derek muttered.

Marcus paced, waited for Alexis to pick up. *Easy, his ass.* Lady Luck had played hard-to-get throughout this whole damn case. Somehow he doubted she'd suddenly show up.

Alexis answered on the third ring. "Hey, Derek."

"It's Marcus."

"Why are you calling me on D's phone?"

"Evelyn is missing," Marcus said quietly.

"What? I don't understand," Alexis squeaked, her voice high. "What's going on? When did this happen? Do you think it's the same—"

"Alexis." Marcus cut her off. "I don't have time to explain. I need good news. And I need it now. Tell me you have something for me."

Silence hung in his ear. Marcus's heart sank. *Shit.* Lady Luck had just fucking flipped him off.

"Lex…" He swallowed his frustration.

"I've been working around the clock and I'm close, I can feel it." She hesitated. "But I don't have anything yet."

Marcus punched the table. Derek turned from studying the board, took a step toward him. Marcus shook his head.

"Not good enough, Alexis. I need your A-game. Do whatever you have to. Call in favors. Pull strings. I don't care what you have to do. I need that information. And I need it now."

"Marcus…"

"Damn it, Alexis, do whatever it takes." Marcus hung up and slumped into the chair. "Shit."

"You were a bit rough on her, don't you think?" Derek said, his voice hard.

"We need that information."

"I understand that. But stressing out your baby sister isn't going to make the information fall out of the sky, Marcus."

"We both know she works best under pressure."

"That's total bullshit, and you know it."

"We need that information," Marcus argued.

"Yes, but you didn't need to be an asshole about it," Derek retorted. "If it's out there, she'll find it."

"But will she be too late?"

CHAPTER THIRTY-EIGHT

THREE AGONIZING HOURS slipped past. They'd gone through traffic camera footage, hoping for a hit. Nothing. Kessler sent out another team to canvas Evelyn's neighborhood again. Nothing. CSI combed through Fin's clothing, searching for a fiber, a piece of hair, anything that didn't belong to the rookie. Nothing. Marcus paced the conference room, anxiety chipping away at him. With each passing second, the chance of finding Evelyn alive faded a little more. His chest tightened.

Derek's phone chirped. He looked at it and tossed it to Marcus. "It's Alexis."

"Alexis, it's Marcus. I was an ass. I'm—"

"Yes. You were. A complete ass. But—" her voice softened "—no apology is necessary. I'd be an asshole, too, if the person I loved went missing."

The person he loved. Was it that obvious? He rubbed the back of his neck and swallowed down the emotion that burst into his throat.

"Thanks for the grace, sweetheart." He pushed a button, set the phone on the table. "You're on speaker. Talk to us."

"I've got news. It's not everything. But it's a start. And you owe me big-time. I've done things that we will not discuss. Ever."

Marcus shifted uncomfortably. He didn't even want

to know what things—probably illegal things—Alexis had done to get him the information he'd demanded. He hated to put her in that position. But he'd do it over and over again if it meant it brought Evelyn back.

"And, God forbid, it ever comes back to bit me in the ass," Alexis continued, "I'm calling you *both* to cover for me. You got it?"

"Yes, ma'am," they said in unison.

"Lex, what have you got?" Derek asked.

"I have an address and a name for you—Nick McClain. He currently lives south of Seattle, in Woodmont Beach. I'm sending over photos now."

"Excellent, great work. Thank—"

"That's not all, Marcus."

Marcus and Derek looked at each other.

"Not only is that the current address to your print, that print also has a connection to Evelyn's family."

"Holy shit. How...when—"

"Derek asked me to find any connections to Evelyn's family murder M.O. and other murders in the same time period. Well, I found one. Actually, I found a lot. I've been sorting for—"

"Lex," Derek said softly. "Focus."

"Right. McClain's father was killed two weeks before Evelyn's family. His two daughters were murdered three weeks before that. The connection, aside from the similar time frame of murders? Evelyn and Nick McClain's oldest sister, Angela, were at the same modeling agency together. Apparently the two girls were up for the same contract to Milan. Evelyn got it. Angela didn't. Nor did she get booked again after that. Two months later, Angela, her kid sister, Sandra, and their father were dead. The oldest child, Nickolas McClain, was never found. He just disappeared, at least until now. It's a leap, I know. But…"

"No, it's a good start." Marcus paced. "Are there any other properties listed to him or any close kin?"

"Checking that now. As soon as that I have that info, you'll have it."

Derek pulled up the photos, pushed them to the large screen at the end of the conference room.

A twenty-something man looked back at them, his face hard, stony. A tattoo spread across the left side of his bald head.

"This is our guy?" Derek asked. "He looks like a biker."

"Yes…" She faltered.

"Talk to me, Alexis," Marcus said. "Is this the guy or not?"

He hadn't meant to be sharp with his baby sister. *Again.* Shit, he was being such a prick. But every cell in his body screamed at him to hurry up, to move. Alexis would most likely be the variable that cracked this case wide-open. But her hesitation sent cold fear down his spine.

"The prints match, yes. But I can't be sure if the guy you're currently seeing is our guy."

"Why not?" Derek took another look at the image.

"This photo seems off, Marcus. But I'm not—"

"Alexis!"

"There's an electronic shadow of a footprint that's all wrong. I think this file has been hacked into, the photos swapped. You'd have to have some serious high clearance, know someone who does or just be that good. None of those options are positive. Let me dig into this, but I hope I'm not right."

"Aside from obvious reasons, why do you hope that?" Marcus asked.

She took a deep breath. "Because then whoever did this is smart—like my kind of smart."

The two brothers glanced at each other. Derek whistled.

"Can you get me his real photo?" Marcus asked.

A long pause filled the room.

"Alexis?"

"It might take me a while, depending on how good he is, but yes. I can get his real photo."

"I need this guy's face. Like yesterday."

"Marcus, I know that. You're being an asshole again." Derek chuckled.

"Sorry." Marcus shook his head and stared at the photos illuminating the conference wall.

Her voice rose an octave. "Listen, I don't think you guys are hearing me. If he's the same guy you're dealing with now, you're talking about going up against a psychopathic genius."

"We're hearing you."

"Marcus, don't brush me off. This kind of twisted mind is dangerous. Derek, do you hear me?"

Derek smiled up at Marcus and rolled his eyes. Marcus swallowed the chuckle that rose in his throat. Now was not the time for jokes. With every passing second, he was one step further from Evelyn. His stomach sank. Anxiety clawed his soul.

"I hear you," Derek said. "We both do."

She continued, voice louder. "Marcus, if I'm right and he has Evelyn—"

Marcus interrupted her. "Then let's hope you're wrong."

He hung up and sagged into a chair. His heart beat wildly against his chest.

"She's going to be pissed you hung up on her," Derek said.

Marcus looked up, stared at the photos. He crossed his arms over his chest and a muscle in his jaw jumped. "We both know Alexis is not going to be wrong."

"I know."

She wouldn't be. Which meant, not only were they dealing with a maniac, but they were also dealing with a genius. *Shit.*

CHAPTER THIRTY-NINE

A MILLION TINY razors pricking all at once, all over her skin, woke Evelyn. She stirred, groggy. Her head pounded. Everything hurt. A herd of elephants stomping on her brain would've felt better than the present throbbing in her skull. She blinked against the dull light in the room and squeezed her eyes tight. She shifted and tried to move, but her muscles shrieked. She went from groggy to alert in a microsecond. Her legs were shackled together and her wrists clamped tightly behind her.

Breathe.

She twisted, turned, flipped to her side and came nose-to-nose with her elderly neighbor, Craig. He stared at her with shocked, vacant eyes, a single bullet hole in his wrinkled forehead. Evelyn screamed a noiseless scream. The duct tape across her mouth prevented any sound from escaping her parched throat. She bucked against her restraints, desperate to get away from the corpse touching her. She kicked her feet and tumbled from the bed. The wind left her as she hit the floor.

Collecting her breath, she listened and watched the door. If anyone were here—*and where was here?*—they'd surely come to check on her.

Heavy footsteps sent her heart into her throat. She pulled at her wrist constraints. They didn't budge. The footsteps came closer. With each heavy step, her pulse jumped. She pushed with her bound feet, awkwardly scooting across the floor, eyes never leaving the closed door, until her body pressed against the far wall. Her back covered, she commanded her racing heart to settle. It refused to cooperate.

The door swung open. The man who'd attacked her stood at the entrance. Panic tightened its firm grip around her mind. He was a mountain of a man. His head almost reached the top of the door frame, his wide shoulders straining against the black T-shirt he wore. Vibrant tribal tattoos covered his massive arms. His hands fisted at his sides and his mouth twisted in a cruel smile. His brown eyes were those of a killer—cold, calculated and deadly.

He pinned her with his glare and her skin crawled. She looked away. Dread clawed at her throat.

He approached her.

"Well, well. How'd you get down there?"

He hauled her up and threw her back onto the bed. She bounced, every muscle in her screeching at the sudden movement. Craig rolled onto her legs. She bucked and fought to get the dead man off her.

Her abductor laughed, then ripped off the duct tape.

She gasped. Her skin burned where the tape tore her skin raw. "Who are you? Why are you doing this?"

He pushed Craig off the bed. The body landed with a hard thump. *How long had Craig been dead?*

Her abductor sat next to her. "No need for formal introductions. It's actually quite simple, Evelyn. You took my family from me, so I took yours from you. Twice."

His words felt like a wrecking ball slamming into her gut. She couldn't breathe, couldn't move. She went numb. *This* was the man? Her mind raced to catch up to her waking horror. This was the man who'd stolen her family, who'd taken her precious Olivia from her.

"That's right. *I* took your family. Me." He grabbed her roughly on the chin, jerked her head up and pushed his face close to hers. "Mystery solved. I killed your fucking family."

She fought against her restraints, raw vengeance pushing at her. "I'll kill you, you bastard."

"Somehow I doubt that. You haven't been able to save a single person I've set my sights on."

Guilt crashed into her. She went still. He was right. She'd failed them—all of them. She closed her eyes.

"What? That's it? I figured you'd put up more of a fight. How disappointing."

She felt the bed shift as he got up. She opened her eyes.

"Why those other families?" She pushed the question out through clenched teeth, desperate to know.

"I had to get your attention somehow."

Her stomach heaved. She swallowed back the sob lodged in her throat. "And Ryan's?"

Her abductor's face grew cold, hard. His eyes glinted. "He pissed me off with all that talk about being smarter than me. I had to teach him a lesson. Just as I'll teach you one."

He returned to the bed and picked up the tape. She thrashed her head back and forth. "Hold still."

She fought harder.

"Hold still!" His fist came down, hard. Her cheek exploded in pain. She went limp. He covered her mouth with the duct tape, then smacked her burning cheek. "Can't have you raising hell, now, can we?"

He moved toward the door, stopped and turned.

"On second thought…" He looked at her. The coldness in his eyes chilled her to the bone. He pushed her facedown onto the bed. Her heart raced. He jerked up her bound wrists and cuffed them to the bedpost. "Can't have you escaping out the window, either."

He left her there, slamming the door behind him.

When his footsteps faded, Evelyn fought against her restraints until stars danced behind her eyelids and biting pain stole her breath. She didn't know how, but she eventually dozed off, only to be awakened some time later by the feel of his hands on her.

"Now, it's time to teach you your first lesson."

He tossed a knife from hand to hand. Evelyn watched the blade closely. Her pulse pounded in her ears. He took the knife and drew the edge along her collarbone, pressing it into the soft part of her throat. She felt its bite, but didn't dare swallow, or move. Or even breathe. He traced the knife up her throat. She tilted her chin. He cut at her clothing, then yanked the tattered pieces and dropped them to the floor. Her heart seized in her chest. He slipped the edge of the knife under her bra strap, and every muscle in her body tightened. He looked down at her, laughing as he cut it away. Cold air washed over her exposed breasts, and they responded in kind. Heat rushed her face.

He drew the knife in a figure eight around her breasts, nicking one nipple. She sucked in a breath, swallowed the pain. He trailed the sharp blade down her sternum, past her navel. He pushed it under the edge of her panties, cut through the thin fabric and pulled them from her body.

Evelyn's breath hitched. Her mind tumbled over itself.

He set aside the knife, then reached for her. She twisted her head to look away.

She was powerless against his touch, couldn't defend herself. She wanted to cry, to sob uncontrollably. But that would've only given him satisfaction and fed his twisted need for revenge and power. *He will not rape me.* It was the only thought she could focus on, the only thought she could draw strength from. So she repeated it over and over in her mind...and she fought like hell.

He struggled against her wild thrashing. "Bitch, hold still."

She fought harder, ignored the fire in her muscles. She bucked against the cuffs, her shoulders screaming. If she was going to die, she was going to die fighting this bastard.

He pulled out a gun from his waistband and pistol-whipped her once, twice, three times. Her vision blurred and she slumped over. She willed herself to sit back up, but her muscles refused to act.

Evelyn felt him unlock the cuffs anchoring her to the bed and pull her off it, onto her feet. Her bound legs wobbled beneath her. Her body wouldn't respond to her mental commands. Her legs buckled. Her captor laughed, then yanked her to her feet again. Evelyn wept on the inside as he hauled her out of the room toward the steps. He forced her, naked, battered and defense-less, in front of him. Her legs barely kept her weight up. At the top of the steps, she froze. She stared down the wooden steps, her heart thumping in her chest. *How was she supposed to get down them? Hop?* Her eyes filled again as embarrassment crashed over her.

"Move it." He prodded her with the tip of his knife. Its sharp tip cut into the softness of her back.

She tentatively hopped from one step to the next, down the wooden stairs. Her breasts bounced with each jump. Cruel laughter echoed in her ears. She clenched her teeth, ignored his taunting.

Five steps from the bottom, he pushed.

Evelyn went flying. Her head connected with the wood floor.

Her world went black.

CHAPTER FORTY

MARCUS HADN'T WAITED for backup. Urgency to find Evelyn, to hold her in his arms, drove at him relentlessly bombarding his conscious thoughts. With Derek and Fin, he'd raced to the address in Woodmont Beach. The apartment they found was immaculate and tiny. Marcus had taken the right, Derek the left. Fin covered the front door.

Derek stuck his head out a bedroom door. "Marcus, you need to see this."

Marcus made his way toward his brother. "Fin, call it in. Let the captain know she isn't here. Cancel the backup."

Fin nodded, then reached for his radio.

Derek led Marcus into the smaller bedroom.

Photos—some black-and-white, others vibrant colors—covered two full walls of the cramped bedroom. Every single one of them showcased a different angle of Evelyn: Evelyn glancing over her shoulder while walking down Pike Place Market; Evelyn walking out of the original Starbucks, juggling a latte in one hand; Evelyn sitting on her front porch, rocking in the worn, green rocker; Evelyn coming out of the precinct, exhaustion clearly written over her face; Evelyn running down the beach.

Marcus felt sick. His throat tightened. He stared at the images of the woman with whom he'd completely fallen in love. How was it possible it had only been a few short weeks since he first laid eyes on her? His pulse quickened. It felt like she'd been part of his life for years. The thought of her not being next to him for the rest of his life sent ice into his veins.

He'd never known true heartache before.

He did now.

He couldn't lose her. He had to find her. Would find her. He turned back to the wall of photos, bile rising in his throat.

"Son of a bitch." The last photo had been taken the day of Ryan's funeral. In full parade dress, Evelyn sagged, crumpled in Marcus's arms. His temper flared. He yanked it off the wall.

"This guy has been stalking her for a long time, Marcus." Derek walked up. "I know I don't have to say this—"

"Then don't."

Derek sighed. "The urgency to find her just quadrupled. Now that he has her, that the chase has ended and he's finally proven he's the alpha hunter, he'll tire quickly...."

His heart jumped into his throat, choking him. He swallowed down the fear. "And kill her."

"Yes, and judging by those photos..."

Every one of them had been mutilated. The place where her heart had been was carved out. Red marks were drawn crudely over her arms and legs. The word *bitch* was scrawled across several of them, and there were knife slashes through all of them.

Derek shook his head. "He'll make it as painful as humanly possible."

"There's nothing human about this bastard."

"That's why we have to find her."

"Sir." Fin stuck his head into the room, caught sight of the photos. His eyes grew large. "What the f—"

"What is it?" Marcus asked.

Fin straightened his shoulders. "Just got a call. They found another land parcel that belongs to Nick Mc-Clain's great-aunt. She's dead. The house is supposedly vacant."

"That's where he has her," Derek said.

"Send me the address." Marcus started for the front door.

"Already done, sir."

Marcus turned and glanced back at Fin. The kid was impressive. "Good man. Care to take a ride?"

Fin nodded. "I thought you'd never ask. I owe Detective Davis."

"I already told you, Fin. It could've happened to anyone."

Fin looked Marcus in the eyes. "But it happened to *me*. And I need to make it right."

Marcus couldn't argue with Fin's logic—he shared it. "Then let's go get her. You drive."

"Shouldn't we call for backup?" Fin followed Marcus through the front door and down the steps.

"We will, on our way." He opened the car door.

He got in, then pulled the door shut. Derek sat behind him. He leaned in close. "How many men are here again?"

"Don't be an ass. You know there's three."

"Marcus," Derek spoke quietly. "That's not a lot of manpower."

Marcus glanced over his shoulder and shot him a scorching glare. "Given the circumstances, it's better than nothing. Evelyn needs us there, now. Not in a few hours. Now."

Derek held up his hands, then sat back. "Okay. Let's ride."

They talked through a thin tactical plan, then rode in silence. Marcus's phone rang. He picked up before it had time to ring twice. "Talk to me."

"I was right," Alexis said. "This is one instance when I wish I weren't, but I am. Someone hacked into that file I sent and swapped out the photos."

"Did you find the correct one?"

She hesitated. "Yes."

"Good, send it."

"Sending now. I should have caught it sooner. MK, I'm so sorry." He could hear she was close to tears.

"Alexis?"

"Yeah?"

"No one else would have been able to see that shadow. You did a good job."

"Be safe," she whispered.

"When are we not?"

Silence met him.

He sighed. "We'll be safe. I promise."

"You better be."

Alexis's email came through quickly. Marcus hit the links and waited for them to download. A soft chirp announced they were done. Marcus looked down.

Ed Meyer, Evelyn's neighbor, stared back at him.

Marcus's heart seized.

"Son of a bitch."

Derek glanced up from his notes.

"Fin, turn around," Marcus said.

Fin's eyebrows scrunched together. He glanced over

at Marcus. "Sir, with all due respect, we're only ten minutes from this address. If Evelyn's there, we need to keep going. She needs us."

"Turn around. They won't be there."

Derek set his papers down. "Marcus?"

"Turn the fuck around," Marcus yelled. "Now."

Fin jerked the wheel, spun the car around one hundred and eighty degrees and floored it. "Sir? Where am I going?"

"Head back to Evelyn's place. Step on it." Marcus slammed his fist against the dashboard. "Call the team. Have them proceed to the original location. But it's only a precaution. They won't find her."

"Take a look." He tossed the phone back to Derek and swore again. "The bastard has her next door."

CHAPTER FORTY-ONE

EVELYN'S HEAD THROBBED. Her lips burned. She blinked, the fog in her mind clearing. *Why'd he take the tape off?* She tried to breathe through her nose and quickly understood. She couldn't. *Apparently suffocating her to death wasn't part of his playbook for today.* She huddled in the corner, wrists tied behind her, ankles bound. She'd managed to draw her knees to her chin and twist her body to cover her nakedness. Stripping her had been a psychological play on his part. And it had worked. For about five minutes. Then it had just pissed her off. Now, she waited and watched the door. He had to be former military of some sorts, or just plain screwed in the head.

She trembled, praying it was the former.

The back door swung open. The man walked in, carrying a roll of plastic tucked under one arm and a black satchel in his hand. Evelyn eyed him, but couldn't keep the fear at bay. One only had to watch a few cop shows to figure out why he needed that plastic.

"What do you want from me?"

"I want you to suffer." He set the plastic by the fireplace and tossed the bag next to it. "And then, I want you to die."

"Think that through for a minute. Killing me is a bad ide—"

"Killing you is all I've thought about for the past fifteen years." In three giant strides, he stood in front of her, eyes wild, then his fist connected with her face. Her head bounced against the wall, and her vision blurred. She tasted metal and swallowed blood as the split in her lip grew.

Blinking back tears of pain, she watched him calmly walk back to the gear he'd dropped.

He picked up the plastic, moved to the center of the living room and set it down. Kicking it with his foot, he rolled it out toward the fireplace. Without a word, he marched out of the room and returned moments later with a chair. He set it firmly in the middle of the plastic. Then he went to the fireplace and grabbed the satchel. With his back to her, he opened it.

Evelyn trembled. The guy was obviously smart. He'd outmaneuvered them for weeks now. And clearly unstable—in less than a minute, he'd swung from rage to calm. Her mind tumbled over itself. *Think. How can I stay a step ahead of him? How can I placate him, without offending that tender balancing act between composed and murderous?*

If she'd been studying this case, she'd be fascinated with the complexities he exhibited.

But she wasn't studying it.

She was in it.

And that changed everything.

"All of SPD will be looking for me," she whispered, waiting for his reaction.

He shrugged, cast a cruel look over his shoulder and sneered. "Along with your pretty Fed boyfriend, no doubt."

She'd known he'd been stalking her. Why, then, did shock slice through her?

"Yes, you're probably right," she answered slowly, with a steady voice. "Which brings me back to my point. Killing me is a bad idea."

"No." He walked toward her.

She scooted farther into the corner and pushed back until the exposed brick cut into her. He grabbed a handful of her hair and hauled her up. She cried out, then bit her lip to keep another moan from escaping.

"It's what you deserve, and what you'll get. Later."

He dragged her across the room, then shoved her into the chair. He circled her. She twisted in her seat and mirrored his movement with her own. Naked or not, she didn't want to turn her back on him.

"Did you know I watched my father beat my mother to death?"

His statement threw her off balance. *Where was this coming from?* She quickly regrouped, stared straight into his cruel eyes and took a deep breath.

"I'm so sorry. That must have been painful for you," she said with as much empathy in her voice as she could muster.

Keep him talking.

His left eye twitched, then he backhanded her, sending her tumbling. Her head smashed against the brick mantel. She saw flashes of light spark behind her eyes. Blinking hard, she willed herself to not give in to the darkness that rushed through her. She rolled to a sitting position as blood dripped from a gash in her head.

He gripped her wrists and yanked.

Evelyn swallowed another cry as searing pain shot through her shoulder. She wouldn't give him the satisfaction. But she'd heard a soft pop and, judging by the way her shoulder sagged and the excruciating pain radi-

ating down her right side, she'd guess it was dislocated.
He dragged her to the chair, picked it up and slammed
her down into it again.

"You don't even understand the meaning of painful. I was ten."

His knuckles connected with her face. Again. She
spit out blood, then looked up at him through one eye.
The other had swollen shut.

"He told me if I said anything, he'd kill both my sisters. Make me watch that, too."

She shuddered. *What type of monster had he lived
with? What type of monster had he become?*

He reached for his bag and pulled out a hunting knife.

Recognition, then panic, ripped through her. It
looked exactly like the knife that was used to kill her
father. She should know—she'd been studying it for
fifteen years.

He walked around and stood behind her. She tensed,
waiting for the same fate. Her mind rushed to Liam,
then to Marcus. He shoved his hand onto her injured
shoulder. She cried out, doubled over. He grabbed her
wrists, then sawed through the ropes binding them. He
took her right arm, twisted it and slammed it down
against the chair arm, palm up. She sucked in air. Then
everything started to go black.

"Oh, no, you don't. Stay with me." He slapped her,
jarring her back to reality, to the agonizing pain she
couldn't escape.

"Did you know that my fucking father also had his
way with both my sisters? Of course you didn't, Evelyn." He cinched a zip tie so it bit into her right wrist,
then quickly repeated the motions with her left. "You
were too busy living your perfect little life."

Her head hung down, blood dripping from her chin to her thigh.

"When I got big enough to fight him, he shipped me off to military school. After I graduated, I tried to get my sisters out. He and I got into a fight. He called the police. And you know what they did? Look at me!"

She raised her head, pushed away the fear coiling itself around her heart.

He looked down at her with cold eyes.

She shook her head. No, she didn't know what they did.

"Instead of serving and protecting my sisters, like those pigs had sworn to do, they hauled *my* ass to jail and let my father go back to my sisters. That bastard greased the hands of a local judge, and I got shipped off again, this time to the army."

He knelt in front of her, then took her ankles in his hands. "Do you know I heard my older sister try to protect our baby sister from that shit of a father?"

He sawed at the rope, jerked one ankle to the right, pushed it against the chair leg and tightened a zip tie around her ankle until it slashed into her flesh. "She walked in on him trying to have his way with my little sister. With his child! No one should have to endure that."

He caught her other ankle and tightened the tie, hard. Evelyn sat bound, naked and completely vulnerable. She stared down at him as he spoke, as if in a trance. Her heart broke for his sisters. He was right. No one should have to endure that. He looked up at her. Pain radiated in his eyes. A minuscule tremble pulled at his lower lip. Shock swept through Evelyn. She hadn't expected to see sadness in his face. He shook his head.

"I'd just returned from the sandbox, just landed at JFK. I was on the phone with her when she tried to make sure my father never touched her, or our baby sister, again.

"She was no match for him. I heard it all. Him beating her. Her crying as he killed our baby sister to spite her, then turned to her. I heard it all." He turned stony eyes on her. "And I couldn't do a fucking thing."

The flash of emotion she'd seen was gone, along with any shred of humanity in him. She stared into the face of a psychotic killer. She scrambled to keep him talking, to keep him focused on something other than killing her. "That must have been so horrible for you. But what does that have to do with me or my family?"

He brought another chair over to her and set it down. He straddled the chair, leaned his elbows on its high back and glared at her. "I still can't figure out why the Bureau has such a hard-on for you."

How did he know?

"And what I also can't figure out—" he waved the knife around "—is how someone who's supposed to be so brilliant can't see what's right in front of her face. If Angela had gotten that modeling contract instead of you, we would've had the means to take my baby sister away from my father, away from his perverted mind. But no. You stole it from her, Evelyn, and left us with nothing."

She shook her head. He was out of his mind, completely unstable. "No, I didn't. I never met your sister."

He got up and backhanded her. "Shut up. Just shut the hell up. You did. You bitch, you did. And you stole my family in the process."

As he paced, she debated her next words. She had to keep him talking, to keep him occupied until Marcus and the team found her. *Please let them be on their way.* She took a deep breath.

"So you had to take my family," she said quietly.

He stopped pacing, then pointed the knife at her. "You're finally seeing. Yes. You took my family. So I had to take yours. It's only fair."

"But why the others?" She pushed against the vivid images as they rushed into her mind's eye, focused on the monster in front of her. "They didn't do anything to you."

A bored look swept across his face. "They were merely the snare I used to trap you."

Bile rushed into Evelyn's throat.

He knelt in front of her and shoved his face closer to hers. She fought the urge to shrink back, refused to give him the satisfaction.

"The closer I got to your inner circle, the more it chipped away at your resolve." He stood and laughed.

"I watched it happen. Your slow emotional breakdown. How long did it take you to put the pieces together? I'd have expected more from—" his voice took on a singsong tone "—'Seattle's star detective.' Isn't that what the newspaper article dubbed you?

She clenched her teeth. *That stupid, stupid article.* If only she'd refused the mayor. *No!* She couldn't think about what-ifs. Her mind shifted to Liam.

"Why'd you save him? Why'd you save the little boy?"

"I'm not a monster."

Says the man who brutally murdered all those people just to get my attention! Her mind screamed.

"Tell me about the army." She switched the subject.

She couldn't bear to hear him talk about Liam and see the excitement shine in his eyes.

"There's nothing to tell." He tilted his head, pierced her with his strange, icy glare and smiled. "I did, however, learn how to do some very interesting and useful things with a knife."

He tossed the hunting knife from one hand to the other, toyed with it and marched toward her. A foot in front of her, he stopped and knelt. He removed a velvet bundle from the black bag. He unsnapped its clasp, then unrolled it to reveal a collection of knives and other tools she'd never seen before. Dread consumed her. Marcus was going to be too late.

"Which one shall we start with?" He reached for the scalpel, pulled back and laughed. He grabbed the hunting knife. "Still think you're going to kill me?"

He approached her and held the knife under her chin, slowly lifting it. Her breath came in rapid, shallow gulps. She didn't move, willed her body to freeze. She looked into his face and locked eyes with him.

He leaned close. "My name's Nick."

"Why are you telling me this now?" Her eyes flicked to his collection of instruments. Her heart hammered against her ribs. *Keep him talking. Keep him talking.*

"Because soon you'll be begging, screaming for me to stop." The knife bit into the flesh of her chin and cut through muscle until it hit bone. Pain flashed behind her eyes. He pushed his face close to hers and sneered. "And I want you to scream my name."

Her heart constricted. She was going to die. Marcus was going to be too late, and she was going to die. She squeezed her eyes shut.

He scraped the knife along her jawline until the tip

rested just beneath her ear. Her eyes popped open. With a cruel smile on his face, he pressed hard and drew the knife in a slant across her cheek to her mouth.

Like a tsunami, white-hot agony crashed over her, shook her body with searing pain. She bit back the scream that rushed to her throat. Blood gushed from her face and down her arms. She felt it drip from her fingertips.

He chuckled and slowly moved the knife to the other side of her face.

CHAPTER FORTY-TWO

Marcus spotted Sanderson, hunkered down in his front seat, car idling, as they turned onto Evelyn's street. Marcus didn't have time to deal with this guy's shit. His temper flared. "What the hell is he doing here? Fin, pull up behind that car."

Fin slowly came to a stop behind Sanderson's car.

"Why are we stopping? Who is that?" Derek unbuckled his seat belt and reached for his gun.

"Josh Sanderson." Marcus opened his door and frowned. "Evelyn's nemesis."

Derek scrambled and followed Marcus out of the car. "This should be interesting."

Marcus stalked up to Sanderson and rapped on his window. It slowly came down. Marcus leaned on the window's edge with one hand. "What are you doing here?"

Sanderson pushed open his door, forcing Marcus to step back.

Sanderson shut the door and stood in front of Marcus, feet spread wide.

What is this, the fucking Wild West? Marcus flexed his fists and took a step toward the short man. "Sanderson. Why. Are. You. Here?"

"Heard Fin over the radio request backup for the place down in Woodmont Beach." Sanderson shrugged, then smirked. "I called in a favor and tracked your car. Funny how it was coming here."

"Leave."

Sanderson crossed his arms over his chest. "Hell, no."

He peered around Marcus's shoulder. "From the looks of it, you need me. Where's your backup? You can't go in there, not knowing what to expect, with only three of you. Even the mighty Feds know that. This prick screwed with the wrong people. Evelyn and I may not see eye-to-eye—"

Marcus snorted.

Sanderson glared at him before continuing. "But she's SPD family, which makes her *my* responsibility. I want to find her and get this son of a bitch just as much as you do."

"He's right, Marcus," Derek called from his perch on the hood of their car.

"Fine. You come with me. Fin, you're with Derek."

Fin's eyes grew wide.

"Relax, kid. I'm not just a paper-pushing psychologist. Ever heard of black ops?"

Marcus's head snapped up. *What the...?* He glanced at his brother. "Black ops?"

Marcus turned back to Sanderson. "Better yet, you go with Fin. Take the front. Derek and I will take the back."

Sanderson pushed off his car and reached for his gun. "Whatever you say, boss man."

Fin and Sanderson made their way toward Evelyn's house, careful to hug the tree line. Marcus and Derek skirted Evelyn's backyard.

"Black ops?" Marcus whispered, eyebrows arching.

"Tell me that was some joke to make Fin feel better about clearing the house with a shrink."

"Another day, brother. Another day," Derek said over his shoulder. "Today, we take this prick down and get your lady back."

Marcus gritted his teeth, then cleared his thoughts. Derek was right. The only thing that mattered today was getting Evelyn back—alive. He sprinted toward Craig Meyer's backyard, mindful to stay within the shadows. Derek silently followed. Once they cleared the backyard, they moved to the back porch.

Marcus's heart raced. Every muscle in his body tightened. They climbed the steps slowly, then flanked the entrance. Marcus tested the door. Glanced at Derek, shook his head. Locked. No surprise there. Marcus holstered his weapon, reached into his back pocket and extracted a tiny tool. He knelt, quickly worked the lock until he heard a small *pop*.

"Atta boy," Derek whispered. "That's a record time."

Marcus glared at his brother. In one motion, Marcus pocketed the tool and unholstered his gun. He pushed his spine up against the outer wall, looked at Derek. He nodded. Marcus pulled in a deep breath. With one hand, he turned the doorknob and creaked the door open, then charged in.

Ed Meyers—aka Nick McClain—bent over Evelyn, slowing tracing a blade across her deathly pale skin. A sick, delighted look danced in Nick's face as he caressed her cheek with the knife's edge. Blood flowed freely from the left side of her face, down her arm and onto the floor.

"Get the fuck away from her," Marcus yelled, cocking the trigger of his gun. "Now!"

Nick looked up and rushed Marcus, tackling him and sending them both flying down the steps. Both men scrambled to their feet and circled each other.

Marcus saw his brother creeping toward Nick. "Derek, go. Get her out."

Derek nodded and turned just as the killer reached behind him, grabbed a gun from its hiding spot and fired. Derek went down. Hard.

Marcus let out a roar as righteous fury spread through his veins.

He lunged and tackled Nick to the ground, straddling him, and landed blow after blow into the killer's face. Nick finally managed to block his fists and flipped Marcus over his shoulder. Marcus landed on his back, and the huge man was on him immediately, reaching for his throat. Marcus drove the heel of his hand up into Nick's nose, felt the cartilage crunch. Undeterred, the killer clasped Marcus's throat and squeezed. The killer smiled.

Marcus reached for his ankle gun. His fingers brushed against the metal and he pulled, shoving the muzzle into Nick's belly. He fired, but the man refused to let up on his viselike grip.

Marcus fought him until he heard two soft *pops*. Nick fell forward, landed hard on top of Marcus. He pushed the killer's body aside, scrambled away and searched the yard for his brother. Derek rose from his shooting crouch and nodded.

Marcus leaned over and pushed his fingers into Nick's neck. No pulse.

"Nice shot, *Doctor*," Marcus said, his own pulse racing. "You okay?"

"Yep. Bullet just grazed me." Derek walked over,

extended his hand and helped Marcus up. "Now, let's go get your girl."

Marcus ran into the living room and stumbled over the plastic covering the wood floor. *What the hell?* Evelyn was in the middle of the room, strapped to a chair, naked. Her eyes were closed and her head hung to one side. Cuts covered her legs and her arms. Blood dripped from her elbows and pooled on the plastic sheet under her. It was everywhere. Her face was swollen, and an angry, deep gash crossed her left cheek. His heart pounded. If the bastard who'd done this to Evelyn wasn't already dead, Marcus knew in that instant that he'd hunt the prick down and kill him himself. Slowly.

"Easy," Derek said.

Marcus shook the murderous thoughts from his head. Nick McClain could no longer hurt her. He focused on the woman in front of him. The woman he loved and had almost lost. His chest constricted. *He could still lose her.* She wasn't moving.

"Evelyn, sweetheart," Marcus called, slowly moving toward her. "You're safe. We've got you."

She didn't respond, didn't stir.

Sanderson and Fin burst through the front. Both halted as they saw Evelyn. Fin turned away and vomited. Sanderson's face blanched. "Oh, shit."

Marcus glanced over his shoulder. Both men looked at Marcus. A deep primal need to defend rose in Marcus as he watched the two men gawking at Evelyn's still form. He wanted them out, needed to protect Evelyn's last shred of privacy. Hadn't she been through enough already?

"Sanderson, get medical in here. Fin, go watch the

front. Now," Marcus yelled, then rushed to her side. "And get me something to cover her."

Derek followed closely behind him. Marcus knelt in front of her, shielding her nakedness with his body. His throat tightened. They couldn't help her until they cut her loose. He reached for her neck, gently pressing his fingers to it. *Please be there.* A pulse. His shoulders sagged. *Thank you, God.*

His head dropped. Tears gathered in his eyes. "She's alive. But her pulse is weak. We need to get her to the hospital."

Derek nodded, then slipped his knife between the plastic zip tie and Evelyn's skin. It sliced easily through the tie. A deep wound encircled her ankle. He moved to the next.

Marcus pushed the hair from Evelyn's face and got a better look at the damage. His jaw clenched. His stomach rolled. He gingerly skimmed his thumb over her forehead, the only smooth skin left on her face. She stirred. One eye blinked, and her gaze met his.

"He killed my family," she whispered so faintly that he barely heard.

"I know, sweetheart. But he can't hurt you anymore."

Her brows pulled together, and she winced. "You killed him?"

"We did." Since Derek had cut away the ankle restraints, Marcus shifted to his left, giving Derek room to work on the ties biting into her wrists.

"*I* wanted to kill him."

Amazement rushed him. Even now, even in the midst of this hell, she fought for, wanted justice. *Could this woman be any more incredible?* Marcus smiled, tucked her hair behind the ear that wasn't bleeding. "It's over now, Ev."

Tears streamed down her face. "You came for me."

"Of course I came for—"

Her eyes rolled back. Her head dropped to the side.

Marcus leaped up and pushed his fingers into her neck. Her pulsed jumped, halted, then skipped again. "Shit! We gotta go. Now."

Derek sliced the last tie and freed her wrist. He caught it as it fell limply.

Marcus gathered her into his arms as Derek shrugged out of his jacket. He covered her body with it, careful to avoid as many of her wounds as possible.

"I can't lose her," Marcus said, throat thick, tears pooling in his eyes.

"I know. You won't."

She'd gone lax. Her face was white. Marcus cradled Evelyn to his chest. He got to the front door just as the ambulance arrived.

Marcus leaned his mouth close to her ear. "I love you, Evelyn. Do you hear me? I love you. I need you to fight, just a little bit longer. Fight, damn it. I need you. Liam needs you. Fight for us."

CHAPTER FORTY-THREE

One week later

EVERYTHING IN EVELYN'S body still hurt, including her heart. Liam slept beside her in his car seat. When they pulled up in front of her home, she took a deep breath, then winced. Maybe her insistence on being released from the hospital so soon hadn't been the best idea. Crap. Marcus opened her door and helped her out of the car. She gathered Liam into her arms and followed Marcus up the sidewalk. He'd gone ahead of her to unlock the door.

Derek walked out.

"Derek?" Evelyn frowned. "Why are you still here? I thought you went back East."

"Nope." He leaned against the door frame, hands in his pockets. "Not until you came home, safe and sound. Turns out I'm quite fond of you."

Evelyn laughed, then stopped abruptly when her muscles screamed at her.

Derek took Evelyn's bags from Marcus and stepped aside. Marcus helped her into the house.

"I'm going to put this little guy to bed. I'll be right down."

Marcus and Derek exchanged a quick glance, which Evelyn caught. "Am I missing something?"

Derek threw up his hands. "I'm innocent."

He walked over and kissed Evelyn on her good cheek. "Duty calls. I'm heading to Omaha. Take care of that brother of mine. Got it?"

She nodded, her throat tight. Derek drew Marcus into a massive bear hug, then slapped his back. Then he left, shutting the door behind him.

"What's going on, Marcus?"

"This way."

Evelyn followed Marcus up the stairs. Her head spun and her heart ached. She wanted to keep her word to Derek, but somehow she didn't see her and Marcus living happily ever after in the cards.

Marcus stopped in front of her office. He reached for the handle. "I hope you don't mind."

"Don't mind what?" She peeked over Liam's tousled curls.

Marcus opened the door to her office and flipped on the lights.

The walls that had once housed painful memories of the past were now decorated with colorful jungle animals. She gasped.

It reminded her of Liam's room at Ryan's. Only fresher.

"How?"

"I took a photo. Derek and I tried to recreate it."

"When?"

"While you were in the hospital recovering. I hope you don't mind. All your evidence has been boxed and labeled. It needed to be done, Evelyn."

She nodded, eyes glistening. "You're right. It did."

Liam stirred, reminding Evelyn that her left arm was tired. Her right one was in a sling.

"I need to put him to bed," she whispered.

"Sure." Marcus walked to the side table, tucked against a chocolate-brown leather rocker, and clicked on the light. Then he took Evelyn's face in his hands, bent his head to hers and left her breathless. "I'll be downstairs if you need me."

EVELYN WALKED DOWN the stairs sometime later. Marcus leaned against the post at the bottom of the steps. He lifted his eyes, smiled. Her heart swelled in her chest. She couldn't think of any place she'd rather be than right here, right now, with this man. And yet...

She swallowed hard. "He finally fell asleep. Poor little man."

Marcus handed her a glass of wine and studied her. She felt herself flush.

"You look like hell."

She laughed. "Thanks."

"I'm worried about you."

She took a sip of wine, went to the living room and sank into the overstuffed chair. She moved slowly, still recovering, and tucked her legs beneath her. Marcus sat on the sofa.

"Liam and I will both be okay." She stared at the fire. "It'll take some adjustments—for both of us—but we'll be fine."

Marcus put down his glass and moved toward her. Her heart raced, like it did every time she saw him. He stood over her, took her chin in his hand and lifted her face. She stared at him and got lost in his warm brown eyes. She memorized his features, committing every detail of his strong, handsome face to her memory.

He lowered his head and brought his lips to hers. The

kiss was soft and gentle. That same breathless feeling washed over her. Then his kiss grew, became demanding and heavy.

She wanted to throw herself into the kiss, to think about nothing but the moment. She needed Marcus more than anything.

Her brows furrowed. *Oh, no.* She couldn't handle it if he left her, not after all that had happened. She wasn't strong enough for that yet. As much as she pretended not to care, to just enjoy this time in space, let the cards fall where they may, she couldn't.

Not when she loved him. And she did. Completely and irrevocably.

She knew she couldn't ask him to love her back.

Not now.

Not when she was a package deal. Because she was. She wouldn't abandon her responsibility to Liam. Her heart whimpered. *So much loss.*

She pulled back, shaking her head. "Don't. Please don't. Not unless you've really thought it through."

"Look at me."

She refused to meet his gaze.

"Evelyn, look at me."

When she did, her heart seized in her chest.

She loved him. How could she tell him goodbye?

"I don't know what's gotten into that pretty little head of yours."

She cringed. The muscles in her upper back tightened. "I won't ask you to take this on—"

"Good." He stepped toward her, closing the space between them. "I don't need you to ask me. I don't need you to—"

She went to argue, but his eyes flashed, so she snapped her mouth shut.

He shook his head. "It's already decided. I didn't come here expecting to find a woman I couldn't live without. Heaven knows I didn't come here looking to start a family. But it happened. You happened. You've gotten under my skin and into my bones. I can't live one day without you. So I'm not going anywhere. I love you, Evelyn Davis."

He gently pulled her to him, lowering his face to hers.

She jerked her head back. "You love me?"

"Why is that so hard to believe?"

"It's been such a long time since something good has happened. It's hard to imagine it being so simple."

"I'd hardly call this simple. Complicated? Emotional? Yes. Simple? Hell no." He laughed. "But I wouldn't have it any other way. I don't want to wake up next to anyone else but you."

Her muscles relaxed as relief washed through her. He loved her. Her stomach tickled at the thought.

He cleared his throat. His face softened. "Marry me, Evelyn. Grow old with me."

"What?" Her head spun. She'd steeled herself to say goodbye tonight. To let the man of her dreams go. She hadn't expected a marriage proposal. It was all too much, yet just right.

She looked up at him, her eyes sparkling with tears.

It was as if they'd always been Marcus and Evelyn. They just fit.

"Yes."

EPILOGUE

Three months later

MARCUS WALKED EVELYN and Liam up to his family's home in San Diego. Evelyn commanded her heart to settle down. *Breathe. Just breathe.* She hitched Liam higher on her hip, reached up and gingerly traced the scar on her face. Even with multiple surgeries, an angry line reminded her daily of what she'd almost lost. Liam shifted his weight, his arms wrapped tightly around her neck. Marcus put his hand on the small of her back. Just his slight touch soothed her.

He opened the front door without knocking and walked in. The foyer was silent, deserted. Evelyn took a deep breath, glanced at him and followed.

"Hello?" Marcus called out to the quiet home.

Excited, loud voices broke the silence. An older man and woman came around the corner from the kitchen.

"MK! You're home!" a younger woman yelled as she ran down the steps and threw herself into Marcus's waiting arms.

Evelyn shifted Liam onto her other hip and stepped back. The instant flurry in front of her amazed and overwhelmed her. She hadn't been around such excitement for a very long time. Mesmerized, she watched as hugs and kisses were exchanged, along with a lot of joking. She felt herself begin to shyly pull back, shrink from the human contact in front of her.

Then there was that constant, strong touch. Marcus had managed to untangle himself from Alexis's arms and stood next to Evelyn once more. She smiled up at him, grateful that, once again, he'd sensed her need for his closeness. He beamed at her, then glanced up at his family.

"Everyone, this is Evelyn."

Marcus's father smiled, his face warm and inviting.

Alexis threw her arms around Evelyn. "It's about time we get to meet you."

Instantly, Evelyn felt at ease. Being in Alexis's arms felt familiar, like hugging Kate, or Olivia. Sadness washed over her, followed quickly by an overwhelming sense of gratitude. She'd lost so much. And gained so much in return.

She let her guard down and returned Alexis's embrace. She pulled away when Liam squirmed in her arms, whimpering.

"Yes, dear, it's so good to meet you." Charlotte Moretti's blue eyes sparkled. "We've heard so much about you."

Evelyn glanced at Marcus, arching an eyebrow. "Oh, really?"

"If we had our way, we would have met the woman who stole our son's heart months ago." Charlotte winked, then turned her attention to Liam. "And who is this handsome little guy?"

Liam tightened his death grip on Evelyn's throat, buried his head into her chest and trembled.

"This is Liam," Marcus explained to his family.

Evelyn's chest constricted, watching happily as Marcus gently ruffled Liam's tousled curls. Liam peeked out from his hiding space. Charlotte took a step toward them. Liam's head snapped around. With hawklike attention, he watched her move next to Evelyn. Charlotte smiled at him. He buried his head in the crook of Evelyn's neck.

"Hey, little guy," Charlotte whispered in a soft, buttery voice.

Evelyn looked over his curls and caught Marcus's eye. She held her breath. *You're safe, little man. I promise.*

Slowly, Liam peeked out again, curls bouncing as he nodded. A tiny smile twitched at the corner of his mouth. Marcus's eyes grew warm. Charlotte smiled back at Liam. Evelyn's heart fluttered.

"I have fresh cookies in the kitchen. Do you want one?"

The toddler's eyes widened. He moved slightly in Evelyn's arms. Charlotte opened her arms and waited. He glanced up at Evelyn's face. She smiled, then kissed the tip of his nose. He visibly relaxed.

Then he reached up, took Evelyn's face between his chubby, baby hands and leaned his forehead to hers.

Soft gasps came from the adults gathered in the foyer with them. The tender, intimate moment melted Evelyn's heart. *How was it possible to love this little man so much?* She pulled him close, felt the rapid beating of his tiny heart.

"You're okay, little guy," she whispered. "You're safe now. We're safe now."

Liam dropped his hands, turned slightly in Evelyn's arms and reached for Charlotte. A smile burst across her face as Liam climbed from Evelyn's arms to her own.

Marcus's father whistled softly. "Well, there you go."

He winked at Evelyn, then followed his wife into the kitchen.

Marcus reached over and pulled Evelyn to him. He tucked her to his side and draped his arm across her shoulder.

She felt safe and secure under its weight.

"Welcome home," Charlotte called softly.

Liam's giggle bounced off the wall. Evelyn smiled.

"Yes, my love," Marcus whispered into her ear. "Welcome home."

* * * * *

ACKNOWLEDGMENTS

THEY SAY IT takes a village to raise a child. I think the same can be said about bringing a book to life.

It's a bit overwhelming to think of all the people it took to help me get here, but I'm so grateful for this incredible group of people:

Jill Marsal, agent extraordinaire at Marsal Lyon Literary Agency. I will never forget your call in that busy airport—best eight-hour flight of my life! Thank you for believing in me. Here's to many, many more.

Lauren Smulski, my incredible editor at HQN and fellow lover of wine. You answered my million-and-one questions like a pro—I owe you a bottle of Malbec!

Susan Swinwood, Margo Lipschultz and the amazing team at HQN for making this book the best it can be.

Kate Dresser, for originally bringing me into the HQN family.

Amy B., for reading and re-reading and re-reading each of these drafts.

Lynnette Labelle, developmental editor (and now friend!) who pulled the gold out of me and gave me invaluable advice.

My sister, Lynette Ruiz, who has been cheering me on since childhood and is always there when I need her.

My brother-in-law, Nathan Ruiz, for demonstrating

crazy military moves, answering my million logistical questions and being just plain awesome.

My parents, Tim and Raenell, for always believing in me and teaching me that no dream is too lofty.

To all the sassy, courageous, gorgeous women in my life—you know who you are. Most only have one or two such friends; I've been blessed with several across the world. And for everyone else who has supported this dream in one fashion or another, thank you.

Last, but certainly not least, my champion of a husband, Drew. You are my rock and number one fan and encourager. I couldn't do this without you. Thank you for cheering me on like only you can do. I love you.